ANY WITCH WAY

ANY WITCH WAY

THE WITCH NEXT DOOR™ BOOK THREE

JUDITH BERENS

LMBPN Publishing
PMB 196, 2540 South Maryland Pkwy
Las Vegas, NV 89109

First US edition, September 2019
Version 1.01, December 2020
ebook ISBN: 978-1-64202-443-2
Print ISBN: 978-1-64202-583-5

THE ANY WITCH WAY TEAM

Thanks to the JIT Readers

Dave Hicks
Jeff Eaton
Dorothy Lloyd
Deb Mader
John Ashmore
Peter Manis
Jeff Goode
Larry Omans
Paul Westman

If we've missed anyone, please let us know!

Editor
SkyHunter Editing Team

DEDICATIONS

From Martha

To everyone who still believes in magic
and all the possibilities that holds.
To all the readers who make this
entire ride so much fun.
And to my son, Louie and so many wonderful friends who
remind me all the time of what
really matters and how wonderful
life can be in any given moment.

From Michael

To Family, Friends and
Those Who Love
To Read.
May We All Enjoy Grace
To Live The Life We Are
Called.

ONE

"**M**om!"

Lily Antony bolted upright in her bed with a raw gasp and her chest heaved.

Romeo jolted beside her and kicked and punched reflexively at the comforter. "You...what... Huh?" He finally stopped struggling with the blanket and stared at her with wide eyes from his half-propped position in the bed. "Woah. Are you okay?"

A dark shadow flickered in the corner of her bedroom for a moment before it vanished. She tasted something burnt in her mouth and smelled the same campfire smoke odor with something a little more metallic laced into it. *I smell that every time I see that stupid shadow.* She smoothed the hair back from her sweat-damp forehead when she finally caught her breath and released a deep sigh. "Yeah. Sorry." She sent him an apologetic smile.

"Hey, don't be sorry. Are you sure you're good?"

She slithered under the covers and dropped her head onto the pillow to stare at the ceiling of her bedroom in the 2002 Winnebago Adventurer. "I think so. But I had this... crazy dream."

He tucked her hair gently behind her ear, his head propped on his other hand as he lay sideways to face her and cupped her cheek for moment. "Do you wanna talk about it?" he asked and lowered his hand.

"I probably should, right?" She raised her eyebrows as if looking for encouragement. "If I dreamed about my mom, it might be important."

"That's up to you." He smiled. "But knowing you and knowing your mom, plus the whole reason we're out here in the middle of nowhere, it's probably safe to say we shouldn't ignore anything. Even a dream that makes you wake up screaming like that."

Lily closed her eyes with a tired half-smile. "Again, I'm sorry. That's gotta be the worst way ever to wake up."

Romeo snorted. "Hey, it's not even close to Julian Stephens' 'bang a pot with a metal spoon' salute."

"Oh, my God." She covered her laughter with a hand and stared at his face only inches away from her on the bed. "He woke us up like that almost every morning, didn't he?"

"Leave it to my dad to make camping a good ol' time." He studied her for a few seconds before his pursed lips pulled sideways in consideration. "Admittedly, I changed the subject. But I still wanna hear about your dream."

She took a deep breath. "Well, there was that black

shadow-bird. You know, the one that's been...following us, I guess."

"Not the heron."

"Right. More like a crow or raven or something. It was still shadowy, only it was...huge. And its talons or whatever were wrapped around my mom's arms. I've never seen anything so clearly in a dream, Romeo. She looked exactly like she does in all the pictures I have—like she does when she's right in front of me."

He raised his eyebrows. "Was she... scared?"

"No." She turned her head on the pillow to meet his gaze again. "That's the really weird part. She was carried off by this giant shadow-bird, flying way up over the entire world, and she simply had her eyes closed. Like she was meditating or something. That thing dug its talons into her arms, and she merely looked...peaceful, even though she was all dirty and beat up. Honestly, she looked like she'd been dragged down a dirt road but she was fine."

"Weird."

"I know." She let out a wry chuckle. "Normally, I'd say it's only a dream, right?"

"But that kinda dream about your mom and that bird thing—"

"Yeah. It feels like more than a dream."

"It might be." Romeo scooted toward her on the bed and wound his arm around her to pull her closer. "We'll find her, Lil. Maybe the dream is a sign that we're getting close."

She pressed her forehead against his bare chest and let

him hold her. "I hope so. It'd be kinda nice to still have a storyteller around. I bet Amal knows all kinds of tricks for interpreting dreams. Especially since she...uh, coughed out that same bird thing during the spirit walk."

"And another black cloud." He stiffened against her, then pulled away so he could look at her. "Do you think that's what the rock's for?"

"What?"

"You know." He released her to stretch onto the narrow shelf built into the wall over the head of the bed. His fingers curled around the heavy wooden box Lily's mom had left for her in Melissa Bore's magical vault number four-fifty-two. They sat together and leaned against the headboard, and he handed it to her. The lid's carved engraving of a lily on a long stem was impossible to miss.

Lily undid the little golden clasp and opened it. There were only two things in it now. Melissa Bore—the potions witch hiding in a Mexican werewolf den from the pissed-off vampire who'd burned her house down in Colorado—had told them she recognized the creepy-looking stone head with black holes for eyes and a mouth. "They're everywhere at this...healing temple in Guatemala," the woman had told them. "Ichacál, I think it's called." While she still didn't know what to do with the apparent good-luck charm, it was one more clue her mom had left.

She first withdrew the large lapis lazuli stone the ancient storyteller Amal had given her before they left Santa Rosa Lake Park in New Mexico. Its lumpy shape was worn into a smooth surface that glinted even in the low light of sunrise peeking through the bedroom window. "I don't think that's what she meant." She turned the stone in her fingers and glanced at Romeo. "She said when I see only darkness, this would show me what I was always meant to see."

"That could apply to a dream, right?" Romeo stared at the stone.

"Maybe. But I honestly think she meant it literally. The part about seeing only darkness."

He raised his eyebrows with a snort. "Yeah, she made at least one prediction that was very literal."

"What prediction is that?" She set the lapis lazuli back in the box, frowned at the eerie stone face from Ichacál, and closed the lid.

"I can't stop thinking about it, actually. Remember what she told me before we left? When she grabbed my arm?"

Her eyes widened with the realization of what he meant. "'Do not let them break you.'"

"Yeah."

"That was, what? Two days before you..." She paused and studied his face for signs that he didn't want to keep going.

He smirked. "Before I what? Was kidnapped by a bunch of psycho werewolves in Mexico, drugged, chained to a tree by my neck, and almost forced into a wolf fight so people could bet on whether or not I'd die?"

A laugh of surprise burst from her lips, and she clapped a hand over her mouth. "Sorry. I shouldn't laugh at that."

"Okay, admittedly, it's quite funny now." He chuckled. "And I learned my lesson. There have been a few of those on this trip."

"Oh, yeah?" she pressed her lips together and tilted her head to regard him teasingly. "What else?"

"Well, the biggest lesson so far is that you are one seriously persistent witch."

She laughed again but this time, she didn't try to hide it. "I would've thought that was a lesson you learned when we were kids."

"Well, yeah." He shrugged. "But you're a lot stronger now than when we were kids. I don't think I would've made it out of that potion witch's house if you hadn't…" He frowned and tried to recall the story the way she'd told it to him.

"What, you mean if I hadn't force-fed you poison and relieved your allergy to magic so Melissa could suck a curse out of your chest before your skin oozed green sludge?"

Romeo's nostrils flared although he chuckled. "Yes. That. See? It's funny when you say it like that."

"I guess." Lily laughed. "I would've done anything to not lose you in that woman's house." She studied the scar in the center of his chest—a purple-red imprint of Melissa Barre's hand left there forever after the woman had more or less exorcized the curse her werewolf neighbors had put on the lone wolf who'd innocently sniffed around their territory. Slowly, she settled her hand on the scar.

"Well, you didn't lose me." He covered her hand with his own. "Because you did what you had to do and I'll never forget that."

She snorted. "You don't even remember it."

"You know what I mean."

Smiling, she looked into his green eyes flecked with gold and bit her lip. "I want to find her, Romeo."

"We will."

"I know. But I have a feeling we're not as close as I wanna be if that makes sense."

"But we're getting closer. And hey, after everything we've seen, I'm convinced she's still out there. Screw what everyone else thinks. Whoever faked her will, whoever doesn't want you to find her, has no idea who they're messing with."

She smiled and removed her hand from his chest to lace her fingers through his.

"By the way, I'm totally not talking about myself."

"Oh, really?" She raised an eyebrow.

"Really." He released her hand and slid his arm around her waist again. "I'm talking about the beautiful, kickass witch"—he slid her down on the bed and leaned over her —"who doesn't let anyone stop her from doing what needs to be done."

Her smile widened and she held his gaze and slipped her arms around his neck. "She sounds amazing."

"She really, really is." Propping himself up with one hand on the mattress, tilted his head, and smirked as he inched the other under her tank top. "But that's only my personal opinion, of course."

Lily laughed. "I'm sure she appreciates it." When he eased forward slowly to kiss her, she ran her fingers through the dark curls at the back of his neck. With a quick snap of her fingers, she drew the curtain at the bedroom window completely closed with her magic to block out the rest of the light. Then, she forgot all about dreams and shadow-birds and unknown witches trying to kill her, at least for a little while.

TWO

After a quick breakfast of the tamales they'd bought off a street vendor in Sombrerete—having decided to spend most of the day before in the small town outside the Sierras de Órganos National Park to stock up on food—they cleaned the Winnie, put everything away, and set out on the road again for their incredibly long road trip through Mexico to Guatemala.

"For a city that apparently has considerable historical tourism, at least there was more than enough space to park an RV overnight and not worry about stepping on anybody's toes." Romeo steered them back onto Highway 145D to head south through the brown, dry desert that stretched endlessly past a few mountain ranges.

Lily laughed and grabbed his cell phone from the cupholder in the huge center console between them. "I don't think we've stopped anywhere that had many toes to step on. I'm simply waiting to get out of the desert, though. It gets more...tropical the farther south we go, doesn't it?"

"You're still waiting for that five-star resort, huh?"

"Hey, you asked me if I'd ever been to Mexico before and I told you."

He chuckled. "I know. You can take the girl out of South Carolina..."

"Oh, yeah? You like this better than home?"

"Think about it, if we're talking about a preferred method of being cooked, I'd take a dry oven over suffocating in a steamer any day."

"Well, you and I are gonna have to agree to disagree, my friend." She glanced out the window and made a lazy study of all the red-brown dirt and the short, coarse, yucca plants and cacti that dotted the landscape. "I still don't think I'm into the desert. I couldn't live here all the time."

"You could if you were born here."

She rolled her eyes and frowned playfully at him. "And this conversation would then be pointless. And you wouldn't be here with me. Which, by the way, is the only thing I'm enjoying about this part of Mexico right now."

Romeo clicked his tongue and smirked. "Well, that's sweet."

"You're welcome. Hey, what's the passcode for your phone?"

"What?" He looked quickly at her, then back at the road.

"To unlock your phone. We're on this highway for, what? Fourteen hundred miles? You might not need a navigator, but I can at least put music on."

He squinted at the road and held his hand out. "Let me do it."

"Wow. Hey, if you don't wanna give me the passcode, you only have to say it. I can respect your privacy."

"No, I don't have a problem with it." He turned again slightly to shoot her a frown. She laughed. "I only..." His fingers wiggled in his open hand. "Let me open it."

"Hey, it's okay." She handed his phone over and smiled as he proceeded to look up and down between the screen and the highway while he punched the numbers in. "I promise I'm not trying to dig through your phone or anything. It's only that you already have music on there and it's synced to the Winnie—"

"Lily." With a short laugh, he handed her his unlocked phone and put both hands on the steering wheel. "I don't care about you being in my phone. It's not like I'm hiding anything from you."

She grimaced but in a joking way. "It kinda seemed that way."

"Nope. Five-four-five-nine. See? No big deal." He glanced askance at her, then focused on the road. "That's been the code for so long, I simply forgot the numbers. It's all muscle memory."

"Okay..."

He felt her staring at him from the passenger seat and laughed quietly. "Everything's in the music app, so go ahead and pull it up."

"Sure." *There it is. The first awkward we might be a couple but we're not gonna talk about it shuffle. I don't know if that's a requirement, though.* Smirking, she pulled his music up and scrolled through the artists. "Wow."

"What?"

"You literally have...everything."

Romeo shifted and leaned back comfortably in the seat with a grin, awfully proud of his collection. "I told you my taste in music was eclectic."

"Well, yeah. But this is... Big Bands of the 1930s. Frank Sinatra. Korn. Taylor Swift?"

"Hey, there's literally an artist and a song for everything."

Lily laughed and scrolled through his massive album list. She'd honestly only heard of half of them. "Okay. So what do you wanna listen to?"

"Hmm...today, I'm feeling like some Cake. Put on 'Fashion Nugget.'"

She snorted. "We're not going with your usual 'shuffle all?'"

"Nah. Mix it up. I usually get bored listening to one album all the way through, but those guys switch it up enough anyway."

"Alrighty, then." She pulled the album up and pressed play. The guitar and drums of the first track, "Frank Sinatra," came through the Winnie's recently updated sound system, and he stretched forward to turn the volume up. After a few minutes, Lily turned toward him and raised an eyebrow. "Would it make sense if I said this actually sounds like driving through the desert."

He chuckled. "Totally. Of course, I can't say I hear the same thing, but everyone has their own take."

"What does it sound like to you, then?"

"Beyond the fact that they literally can't be mistaken for anyone else?"

"Come on..." she said and sighed.

"I'm kidding. If I had to pick something, I'd say...they sound like smoking a giant cigar."

Laughing, she frowned at him. "What? Wait, you smoke cigars?"

Romeo stared straight ahead at the highway rushing toward them and couldn't fight back another smirk. "Nope."

They pulled off the highway onto a wide shoulder for lunch—*brujitas* filled with shredded pork, also from Sombrerete. Lily swallowed her last bite and washed it down with bottled water. "It's a little weird that there are way fewer gas stations and rest stops than any state we drove through in the US."

"I kinda like it." He crushed his plastic water bottle after draining it dry. "It feels like we're out here all on our own, pushing through to the next town or city big enough to have what we need." He snatched up both their plates and stuck them in the dishwasher.

She laughed. "Because that's exactly what we're doing."

He flashed her a grin, stepped back toward her at the small two-person table, and leaned down. "Yeah, but here, we could get stranded and have to fend for ourselves in the desert. It's dangerous." He wiggled his eyebrows, then straightened and headed to the driver's seat.

Lily snorted. "You need a danger fix, huh?" She slid out of the booth and joined him in the front. "Honestly, I think it was more dangerous before we crossed the border.

The witch who tried to kill me in Charleston knew exactly where to find me, remember."

"That's my point." He buckled his seatbelt and shifted into drive. "He found you 'cause you'd been in that parking garage for a while, right? When you were—"

"Don't say boondocking again." She smirked at him.

"Okay...when you were independently parking there." He drove them off the shoulder and back onto the mostly empty highway. "You didn't have to keep moving. Everything you needed was right there all the time. And it's still easier to hide in a city with lots of people than out here in the middle of nowhere if you don't spend too long in one place."

"Yeah, but at least out here, we can see whoever's coming from a mile away, at least."

He looked a little scornful. "You mean like those three seriously creepy women outside Camargo?"

She frowned. "Okay, those women were the exception to the rule. It's not a normal thing to cover huge distances in seconds like that. Or levitate. Or whatever they did with their mouths, too."

"It looked like they were wearing *Scream* masks." He glanced at her. "And you still have no idea what they were?"

"Nope. I haven't been able to make sense of that yet. Or why they thought they needed my blood 'to complete the circle,' whatever that means."

Romeo curled his hand into a fist over the steering wheel. "One more point for the shadow-bird showing up at the last second to make sure we never find out."

"Yeah. But I'd really like to know what that is too. And why I dreamed about it carrying my mom around." They fell silent for a few minutes and the ambient, jazz-organ funk played through the speakers. She tapped his phone to check who it was—a band called Medeski, Martin, and Wood. That might have added to the eeriness level of their conversation.

"We totally could've taken those creepy *Scream* ladies," he said after a while and broke the silence.

She chuckled and thumped her head back against the seat. "You and me? Definitely."

THREE

When they'd logged eight hours on the road, they stopped in Córdoba a little after 6:00 p.m. and decided to call it a night. "Okay," Romeo said once he'd studied the town and slowly nodded approval. "It looks like a decent place."

"More than decent. There are actual trees here—palm trees—and flowers. Honestly, this is much better than Mexico City." Lily smiled at the brightly colored buildings and the crowds of people milling along the streets. "We can definitely find a good place to hang out for the night."

"I'm sure we can." He pursed his lips in a mock pout. "Mexico City's supposed to be like New York on steroids but in Mexico."

"Are you upset about missing out on that?"

He leaned forward to peer out his window at the tops of the bright-yellow, square buildings across the street and shrugged. "Kinda."

"This'll still be fun. And I'm sure it's a lot safer here all around."

"Hey, if we pull over for a minute, I can find us the best place to camp."

She pointed toward a hotel coming up on the right. "What about right there?"

"Yeah, okay." He turned into the parking lot, took his phone from her, and worked his special kind of magic with travel planning and somehow always finding them a place for the RV.

"I'm gonna stretch my legs for a minute." She unbuckled her seatbelt and stood, grateful to be out of the passenger seat for the day. "Maybe get some fresh air."

"Sure." His focus remained almost entirely on his phone. "I'll be quick."

Smiling, she watched him for a few seconds longer, then turned and headed down the two steps toward the Winnie's side door. She'd expected to be blasted with another wave of dry, baking heat when she opened it but it was surprisingly pleasant out. The sun was still up and a little breeze blew across the parking lot, bringing with it the smell of sweet cooking spices and what sounded like a mariachi band playing.

Lily let the door shut behind her as she stepped farther into the parking lot. There was a fair number of people out on the street, some of them walking in groups toward the music she estimated was a block or two away. Three kids sprinted toward the sound while they shouted, grinned, and waved brightly colored streamers on sticks behind them. She grinned and stepped around the front of the Winnie toward the driver-side door.

When she opened it, Romeo opened his mouth and paused, still staring at his phone. "I think I found something. Only another minute. Maybe."

"I think that can wait for a sec."

"I'm almost done."

"Hey." Lily stepped into the Winnie, her toes balancing at the edge beside his seat. She caught the steering wheel to steady herself, then leaned over Romeo's lap to block his view of the phone.

He laughed. "What are you doing?"

"There's something going on out there." She nodded across the parking lot. "And I wanna find out what it is."

"What kinda something?"

"Well, I highly doubt the kids here get all excited and run around with streamers when it's the bad kinda something." She stretched across his lap to retrieve her purse from the center console, swung back to the edge of the platform beside the driver's seat, and grinned. "It might not be particularly dangerous. Do you think you can still have fun?"

"That sounds like a challenge."

"It probably is."

"Good." Romeo lurched from the driver seat and snaked his arm around her waist. She shrieked in surprise and laughed when he lifted her away from the seat and jumped down from the vehicle.

Though he set her down gently enough, she thumped

him lightly on the chest and pulled away. "Don't do that again."

He smirked at her and his eyes glittered in the setting sunlight. "You liked it."

"Come on." She motioned again toward the trumpet music and the steadily increasing sound of people cheering and singing. With a chuckle, he snatched the keys from the ignition and his phone from the driver's seat, locked the door, and stuck them both in his back pocket. She already half-skipped and half-danced across the parking lot and he hurried after her.

"So what exactly are we about to see?"

"I have no idea." She grinned at him. "But it sounds like everybody's having fun." They waited for a few cars to pass them on the street before they crossed and moved between the tall buildings in shades of sky-blue and bright yellow. Virtually all of them were built with arches and detailed metalwork around windows and on the surrounding fences. Following the music, they stepped between the last few buildings and found themselves in a wide, open plaza. An incredibly long, two-story building lined with arched windows stretched across the area, lighting up the entire space with small outdoor lights in every archway in front of the door and every full-sized window on the second floor. A pole flying the Mexican flag rose from the raised platform on top of the building's center.

There was definitely a brass band playing across the plaza. Lily only recognized the sound of trumpets and drums. "Okay," she said and clasped Romeo's hand. "This is definitely some kind of celebration."

People wandered about the plaza outside the long building. Children ran in circles around the large, fenced-in area in the center of so much space. Only one of them tried to climb over the small metal fence toward the grass and the tall trees before she was swept into her parent's arms and whisked away for fun somewhere else. A few tents along the walkway sold street food and bottled drinks. Lily caught sight of a lit water fountain on the other side of the well-maintained lawn. A breeze blew across the plaza and rippled into the city from the mountain range in the distance.

"Wow." Romeo gazed at everything with wide eyes.

"See?" She walked backward in front of him and dragged him along by the hand. "This is the Mexico I'm excited about."

He laughed and let her pull him toward the band. A crowd had gathered in front of the musicians and they laughed and cheered when the song finished and brought a lull in the dancing. But the band didn't waste any time in striking up the next song with a quick tempo led by a man with gray hair slapping at his conga drums.

"Oh! You know *merengue*, right?" Lily yanked Romeo toward the group of dancers in front of the band, grinning and swaying to the rhythm.

He laughed. "Just because I speak Spanish doesn't mean I know how to dance."

"It's the easiest one—side to side, like this." She stepped in illustration with the music, swung her hips, and scrunched her face in mock disapproval. "Come on, Romeo. We're in Veracruz. You can let yourself enjoy it for at least one dance."

"I have no idea what I'm doing." He chuckled and shook his head.

She pointed to her feet, which hadn't stopped moving from right to left. "Stop thinking." She tossed her hair back with a grin, and he gave in enough to at least attempt a few measures of the steps with her.

When she spun in a quick, tight circle and threw her arms out before drawing them close to her body again, he stepped back to watch her. "Okay, I'm clearly holding you back." She laughed. "Go on. Dance your heart out. I'll stay right here."

"Are you sure?"

"Yup."

Lily twirled again, gave in to the music, and winked at him before she was swallowed by the rapidly growing crowd on the dancefloor in the plaza. Amongst the dancing couples and a few others enjoying the band on their own, her blonde hair and pale skin made her impossible to miss, even with a Charleston tan. He folded his arms, laughed again, and couldn't take his eyes off her. The song ended and she turned with the other dancers to applaud the band before they moved into the next song.

She met his gaze, held up a finger, and mouthed, "One more."

Romeo merely spread his arms and tilted his head with a wide grin, leaving it up to her. She blew him a kiss and disappeared again among so many dancing strangers. He soaked in the high energy of celebration and glanced at the other people gathered in the plaza—locals and tourists like them—and noticed two men on the other side of the impromptu dancefloor. They didn't look particularly threatening, but they both smirked with hooded eyes. One had his arms folded and the other stood with his hands thrust into the pockets of his shorts. They both stared at Lily.

He bristled. Still, he didn't smell magic in the plaza and he didn't smell another wolf. Ever cautious now that he'd been alerted to something that didn't feel right, he maintained his smile and made a closer scrutiny of the individual faces gathered in front of the band.

A woman in a red dress and a man with sunglasses pushed up onto his head walked slowly between him and the dancers. The man with his arms folded caught the woman's gaze and nodded into the crowd toward Lily. She followed his gaze, then turned fully to watch the dancing and gestured at her own hair. A few nods passed between all four of them and the song ended.

"Nope," Romeo muttered. He moved quickly through the crowd of dancers, all of whom laughed and caught their breaths as they turned to applaud the band. He didn't have to look for his friend. She stood out like a beacon and he rushed to her side. When he grabbed her hand, she laughed.

"Are you hungry?" he asked and stooped a little to say it in her ear. "I'm starving."

"Yes." She leaned back and smiled at him. "Wanna see what they're dishin' out over there?" Her eyebrows raised, she pointed past him toward a white-and-red-striped tent across the plaza beside the fenced-in landscaping.

"Absolutely." He laced their fingers together and maintained a tight hold as they wove through the dancers that had already begun moving again to the band's next song.

"Wow." Lily wiped her forearm across her brow. "I haven't danced like that in a long time."

They emerged onto the much less-crowded walkway through the plaza and he smirked at her. "I didn't know you danced like that at all."

She glanced at him with a playful frown. "What are you trying to say?"

He laughed. "There's no hidden message in there, Lil. I simply didn't know." After a quick glance over his shoulder, he shrugged and squeezed her hand. "I knew about the mixed martial arts."

"Right."

"And all your mom's puzzles and games and stuff. And the fact that you've always been..." He chuckled and shook his head.

"I've always been?" She flashed him a challenging look and fought back a laugh.

"Better than everyone else at virtually everything you do."

"Well, thank you." She grinned and batted her lashes.

"I merely didn't know dancing was in there too."

"Oh, always." They stepped up to the red and white tent behind the two other people in line. "I started with ballet, actually."

Romeo snorted. "For real?"

"See, that's why you didn't know about the dancing."

He shrugged again and leaned away. "You really don't seem like the dancing type."

"I'm not sure what type you're referring to, but it's not like I had a reason to tell you. When we were kids, the taekwondo and the jiu-jitsu was cool. The puzzles were cool. You apparently always thought it was awesome that I was a witch. But seriously, I knew when I was nine that you had absolutely no interest in hearing about ballet and tap."

"Tap dancing too?" His eyes grew incredibly wide.

"My mom had me in a ton of classes. Summer camps. You name it."

"Okay, how did you even have the time for this? The way I remember it, we spent all our time together as kids."

Lily turned away from him, lifted her shoulder, and grinned. "Magic, I guess."

He laughed and pulled her toward him. She draped her arms around him and tilted her head back to look up at him with a smile that made him want to go back to the Winnebago and skip dinner altogether. "Yes, you are."

FOUR

They bought two bowls of *arroz a la tumbada* from the tent—rice with fish and shellfish, tomatoes, onions, and green chili peppers. Lily withdrew the magically converted pesos from her purse to pay the man running the tent, then turned to look at the band and all the people enjoying themselves on a Saturday night in Córdoba. Romeo and the food vendor had a brief conversation in Spanish, which she tuned out in lieu of all the other sounds—the music, the laughter, and the kids screaming in joy and running all over the place. A small group of kids, maybe nine or ten years old, tossed a frisbee. Even now, as the lights lit the plaza and the last of the daylight faded into twilight, the city was incredibly alive.

He turned toward her and offered her a bowl. "I assume it's like paella."

They each took an experimental bite. "Definitely," she agreed around her mouthful. She smiled up at him, but he looked over his shoulder again at the crowd with a tiny frown. "Okay, spill it."

"Huh?" He blinked at her, his spoon of seafood and rice paused halfway to his mouth.

"You've been watching someone since you dragged me away from the band." She shifted her weight and gestured with her spoon toward the now even larger crowd of dancers. "Which, by the way, wasn't as subtle as you thought it was."

Romeo sighed, glanced across the plaza, and leaned toward her. "You were having such a good time. I didn't wanna say anything."

"Well, now I'm asking you to."

"Okay. Do you see the guy in the dark-green polo?"

She swept her gaze across the plaza and masked her hasty glance at the man with a smile and a continuous search of the celebration around them. "The one staring at us with his friend?"

"Yep."

"Witches?"

"No, I'm reasonably sure they're only regular humans. But they still give me a bad feeling. They were..."

Lily returned her attention to him, still smiling but way more than merely a little curious now. "They were what?"

He held his breath for a moment before he released it sharply. "Watching you and not in a very friendly way. Or maybe a little too friendly. I dunno." He stuck the spoon in his bowl and settled his arm over her shoulders again. "Let's keep walking for a minute. I think they're trying to follow you."

"Us," she corrected.

"Right." He smirked. "I don't think they're all that worried about me."

"Yeah, well, they should be."

"There's a woman in a red dress and a man with her. They're part of it too, whatever it is. I honestly don't like it."

She moved her rice bowl to her other hand and put her arm around his waist. "I don't either. And to be clear, you telling me this doesn't in any way ruin how much fun I'm having. For future reference, of course."

"Got it." He chuckled. "I won't try to spare you any discomfort in the future."

Her sideways glance was both serious and playful. "That's very much appreciated, Romeo."

A red-crowned parrot swooped from the fenced-in trees on their right and fluttered past them and over the milling crowd in the plaza. She pointed at it and used the opportunity to turn and search the faces behind them again. "Yes, I'm pointing at a bird. And yes, those guys are following us."

"Awesome."

The couple passed the group of kids tossing a frisbee and slowed a little as they turned once again to apparently watch the parrot. She let her gaze settle on the two men who were definitely following them, and the guy in the dark-green polo saw her looking at him. His lips parted in a crude smile, and he ran his tongue over the edge of his teeth and actually winked at her.

"Oh, gross." Lily looked away when one of the kids

beside them flung the frisbee across his circle of friends. She pointed casually at the frisbee and flicked her wrist toward man. The plastic disk rose over the kids' outstretched hands and sliced in a perfect sweep to crack against the creepy man's nose. He cried out in pain and doubled over, his hand on his face. A collective groan of sympathy sounded from all the people who'd witnessed the obvious misfortune of a bad throw, and a few kids laughed.

"*Lo siento!*" one of them shouted, darted toward the man to retrieve the frisbee, and fled, his friends calling out behind him as they sprinted across the plaza.

Their pursuer removed his hands from his face and stared at the blood that poured from his nose and splattered the cobbled stones. A low, smoky laugh spilled from the woman in the red dress who stood only a few yards away as the man's companion leaned forward, probably to ask if his friend was okay.

"I'm never gonna stop telling you how much I love that." Romeo smirked, rested his hand against the small of her back, and led her away down the path beside the fenced-in greenery toward the lit fountain.

"Did you see the way he looked at me?"

"Yep. I'd say he deserved it."

"He'll deserve much more than that if he keeps following us." She brandished her spoon as if to emphasize her point and took another warm, delicious mouthful of rice, shellfish, and spices. He laughed and removed his hand to continue his meal. "Hey, what were you talking about with the vendor?"

"Oh. I asked what was going on here tonight. That's the municipal palace." He jerked his head at the long two-story building with all the lit windows and arches. "And apparently, this happens almost every weekend. At least, when it's not raining, so it's a good night for it now." He glanced at the clear night sky and the stars mostly drowned by the plaza's bright lights. "I guess it's the rainy season down here right now."

"Huh." She looked at the sky. "That explains why it's so nice out right now."

"I think it's gonna get colder."

"Well, we gotta take advantage of no rain in the rainy season, don't we?" She made a face at him and took another bite.

By the time they finished walking the long loop around the fenced-in park in front of the municipal palace, the temperature had dropped dramatically. "Man." She rubbed her bare arms, free now of the paper bowls and plastic spoons they'd dumped in a trash can on their stroll. "You know, in a lotta ways, this feels like Charleston—humidity, nightlife, and amazing food. It does not get this cold back home, though."

He chuckled. "I think maybe by 'rainy season,' what they really mean is winter. Maybe."

"It's almost July." She rolled her eyes dramatically. "Please don't start talking about winter when it's almost July."

"Fair enough. Do you feel like staying out or should we head back?"

"I feel like being warm." She slipped her arm through his and curled both hands around his bicep. "And I think the best way to do that is to get to the Winnie. With you." She grinned disarmingly and he laughed.

"Are you sure you can't read minds too?"

"Admittedly, that's a different kind of magic I don't have."

They completed the circle and found the alley through which they'd entered the plaza less than two hours before. For most people in Córdoba, the night was still young. The couple slipped through the alleyway between the brightly colored buildings that had now faded to shades of gray in the darkness.

Before they reached the other end, a loud metallic click echoed behind them, followed by a scrape of metal against stone. "*Oye!*"

They both turned swiftly. The man in the green polo stood in the entrance to the alley, his face illuminated by the outer reach of the plaza lighting. His nose was clearly broken and had swelled alarmingly, and he clutched a switchblade in his hand.

"Seriously?" Lily muttered. Their pursuer's friend turned into the alley behind him, his hands still thrust into his pockets.

"Come on." Romeo put a hand on her back again and guided her down the alley. In a moment, the man who still thought it necessary to wear his sunglasses on his head blocked their path. The woman in the red dress leaned against the wall and appeared to study her manicured nails despite the lack of light.

"Okay..." The couple stepped back again to center themselves between their would-be attackers. "*No queremos problemas*," he said and raised his hands in surrender.

"Do you think they're gonna let us talk our way out of this?" Lily muttered.

"You mean bribe our way out of this." He turned sideways in the alley so he could easily see each duo hovering at either end. "I would've said maybe if he hadn't already pulled a knife."

"Okay," the wounded man shouted. "*Ningunas problemas si me das un...regalo.*" His friend sniggered.

Romeo leaned toward Lily and whispered, "He says he wants a present."

She glared at the man and pressed her lips together. "I don't think he'll like what we give him."

The woman in the red dress pushed off the wall and took a few slow, carefree steps toward them, her heels echoing on the stone. "*Si no tienes dinero*"—she shrugged —"*está bien. Apuesto a que ella vale mucho más.*" She stopped and pursed her lips to scrutinize Lily from top to toe.

The witch scowled at her. "Okay, I'm a little rusty," she said to her friend, "but did she start talking about how much I'm worth?"

"Yeah, that's what gave me a bad feeling about these guys." His knuckles cracked and he balled his hands into fists.

The men on the plaza side of the alley chuckled. "*Que*

bonita," the first added, clicked his tongue, and waved the switchblade from side to side.

"Well, that I understood." Lily raised her hands a little from her sides and wiggled her fingers. "I'm officially done trying to be nice."

"I'm right there with you."

The woman in the red dress uttered a mocking little sigh and tilted her head in a gesture toward the tourists she was so certain would give in to her rather demanding offer. "*Eliges.*"

Romeo met her gaze and leaned forward a little to be sure she heard him clearly. "No."

Her lips twitched into a bitter smile and she nodded at the armed man and his friend. They both chuckled and the sound echoed through the alley and was quickly swallowed by the music and the noise of so many people behind them in the brightly lit plaza. "*Ven acá.*"

Lily tilted her head. "I'd rather not."

The man with the blade leapt toward her, and Romeo stepped into his path to catch the wrist of the hand that swiped viciously with the knife. She focused on his partner, who half-crouched in a shifting fighting stance, his arms raised at the ready and his fingers wiggling as if they itched to snatch her out of the alley. The sound of her friend's head when it pounded into his partner's already broken nose startled him out of his focus on her.

She stepped forward and struck him in the jaw with a swift right hook. He reeled under the blow and his eyes narrowed furiously, while she shook her hand out with a grimace of pain. The wounded man shrieked in agony, followed by the sound of his opponent's fist connecting somewhere on his body—and that body thumping against the alley wall—and she spun and brought her heel into the side of the other man's head with a resounding crack. His eyes rolled back before he dropped.

"*Hazlo tu.*" The woman in the red dress nodded at the man with the sunglasses. He drew a knife from his pocket and stalked down the alley with a sneer.

"This is ridiculous," Lily muttered. Before he even moved close enough to pose a real threat, she swiped her finger through the air and her quick spell jerked his feet out from under him. He thumped onto his back with a gasp of surprise. The couple moved down the alley, and Romeo paused only long enough to stand beside the man who would've attacked them and deliver a punch that was both fast and powerful enough to bring the unconscious-idiot count to three. He stood, wiped his hands on his shorts, and followed his friend.

Her chin tilted defiantly, the woman in the red dress scowled at their approach. "*Mala decisión, gringos. Te encontraremos y—*"

The witch flicked her hand at the woman's face to expel a burst of glittering blue fumes that made the target's eyelids flutter rapidly. By the time she crumpled, they had already exited the alley.

He turned slightly to assess the slumped forms of four bodies in the darkness. "Is that gonna wipe twelve hours of her memory too?"

She shrugged waited for the next car to pass before she stepped into the street to cross it. "Maybe. I simply wanted her to stop talking."

"I guess that works." He snorted. "That last guy's gonna remember your spell taking him out, though."

"For all he knows, he slipped on something in an alley. We didn't need my magic or your wolf for two of those idiots. Red Dress Lady won't remember us, but she'll have more than enough proof that it's a bad idea to try anything else."

They stepped onto the sidewalk and made their way back toward the Winnie in the hotel parking lot. "Not that I can take it very seriously now, but she did say she'd find us." He stopped to retrieve the keys from his pocket and unlock the RV's side door before he opened it for her.

"Well, we'll be long gone by the time any of them can even try." She looked at him and smirked as she stepped into the Winnie, but he grabbed her hand and spun her back toward him.

"This is still the best trip to Mexico I've ever had."

She shifted all her weigh on one foot and cocked her head. "Even with non-magicals trying to rob us or...what, kidnap me?"

"Especially with non-magicals trying to rob us or kidnap you."

A wry laugh escaped her. "Why's that?"

He set his hands firmly on her hips and pulled her closer. "Because you don't need anyone to save you. And we make the best freakin' team." Whatever else she might have said was cut off by his fierce kiss. She laughed again when he lifted her up the two steps into the vehicle and let the side door slam shut behind them.

FIVE

While they didn't anticipate further trouble, they decided to move the Winnie somewhere else for the night anyway. Romeo found a huge shopping center in the Dos Caminos barrio—northwest of central Córdoba—and they slept with the cool air from the Sierra Madre mountain range blowing through the open windows and the warmth of sharing Lily's queen-sized bed in the tiny RV bedroom.

They woke early the next morning and made a few brief stops in the city before heading out—first to refill the giant RV water tank and to buy more bottled water to keep in the vehicle, which was far more expensive down there but offset by the relatively cheap food. With a small bag of produce and a few local staples safely stored, he drove them toward the Playa del 21 Mayo park. "We need breakfast," he said. "And coffee."

Lily laughed. "Don't we still have coffee?"

"Not like this, we don't." He raised his eyebrows and

blinked at her. "Wait, are you telling me you haven't even heard of *café Veracruzana?*"

"Well, I didn't actually tell you anything, but judging by that look..." She couldn't hold back another giggle. "Is it really that good?"

"This place literally has a coffee tour."

"Well, now we have to go."

He smirked at her and caught her hand. "That was already the plan."

They stopped at a little shop on Calle 2 called Hêrmann Thômas Coffee Masters and bought themselves the largest sizes available of *café con leche* and a few donut-like *conchas* to go. "This is really the biggest one they have?" She lifted the cup that maybe held sixteen ounces.

Romeo took his first sip and closed his eyes. "It's all you need."

The *conchas* weren't half bad, either. "You know, if this was any other trip for any other reason..." Lily sipped her coffee and gazed lovingly at her cup. "Mm."

"You mean if we weren't following your mom's clues?" They walked down Calle 2 and simply enjoyed the morning and the cool, damp air.

"Yeah. If this was a vacation with only you and me, I don't think I'd ever wanna leave."

"Well, maybe we'll get the chance." He smiled at her over the lid of his cup and slurped. She rolled her eyes and grinned. "Wait, that includes the adventuremobile, right?"

"Oh, are you developing an attachment to my Winnie 2.0?"

"Actually, yeah. We've had a lotta good times in that

thing." He winked. "But it's more like 1.5. As soon as I can take a shower without rushing to finish under four and a half minutes, we can call her new and improved."

She rolled her eyes. "Okay, that mechanic in Sombrerete said there was absolutely nothing wrong with the water tank or the shower pipes."

"Yeah, but you didn't tell him your hard-water spell backfired."

"I'm not gonna tell a non-magical mechanic that my magic screwed the shower up." Smirking, she shook her head and gave a half-hearted shrug. "Fine. The next magical RV expert we find, I'll bare my soul and beg them to fix it."

"Woah. You don't have to go *that* far." He nudged her with his elbow and grinned. "Don't try to pretend you wouldn't be a little happier with a nice, long, steaming-hot shower—"

"Okay! Yes. I'll get someone to fix it." She tilted her head and turned to shoot him an exasperated glance. "Happy now?"

Romeo laughed. "Very happy." When he held his hand out, she slapped the paper bag from her *conchas* into his open palm and he tossed it with his as they passed a trashcan on the street. He opened his hand again, stared straight ahead, and shook it in front of her.

Lily snorted, sipped her *café con leche*, and held his hand all the way back to the Winnie.

By the time they navigated the RV out of downtown Córdoba and onto Mexico Highway 150, the morning sun had disappeared behind a thick blanket of dark-gray storm clouds. "That was fast." She leaned forward in the driver's seat to peer into the blackening sky.

"Rainy season," he muttered.

"Yeah, no kidding."

"If you want me to drive when it starts raining, I have no problem with it."

She glanced at him and smiled. "Thanks, but I think I can handle a little rain."

He tipped his head and pressed his lips together. "Cool."

"THIS IS SO NOT COOL." Lily gripped the steering wheel so tightly her fingers hurt and squinted to see through the windshield and beyond the deluge that poured onto the 150.

Romeo leaned toward his window but it wasn't like that gave him a better view of the thick sheet of rain in every direction. "Yep."

"Okay, it was perfectly clear last night. The weather was perfect last night. We had almost four hours on the highway without any rain at all, and now...what, I get to drive right into a hurricane?"

"It's the rainy season."

She scoffed and wanted to stare at him but the real possibility that it would cause them to hydroplane all over the highway stopped her. "Will you stop saying that?"

He chuckled. "Sorry. Do you want me to drive?"

"Look, I appreciate you trying to help. But no. I don't

want you to—oh, my God." Apparently, the storm had held back until that moment. Rain pelted down onto the vehicle with renewed force and she could barely hear herself think. "Okay. Okay, yeah. Can you drive?"

"I told you I would."

"Yeah, I can't see anything in this—what's that?" The Winnie took a bend in the road and beyond the tall Amazonian hardwood trees lining the narrow, one-lane highway was a large white rectangle. Lily squinted and slowed in case it moved.

"It looks like a van."

Lily rolled to a stop beside the other vehicle apparently stranded somewhere between Nanchital and Villahermosa. Steam puffed from the white van's open hood into the heavy rain. A man and a woman both had their heads bent under the hood. The woman gestured wildly at him, clearly furious, and opened her mouth for a huge, lung-shocking breath when she stepped back into the ridiculous amount of rain. Both of them looked up at the huge RV at least twice the size of their plain white van with tinted windows in the back. It was a little dented in a few places but mostly looked well-maintained, except for the engine trouble.

Romeo rolled down his window enough to shout at them. "*Necesitan ayuda?*"

"*Cómo?*" The man turned to the woman and rivers of rainwater streaked down their faces and trailed clumps of hair into their eyes. His companion's long black hair clung to her neck and shoulders beneath her tank top. They held a short inaudible conversation in the rain before the man stepped toward the Winnie's open window. "You're American."

"Yep." He smiled and nodded at the van. "It looks like there's something wrong with your engine. Maybe the radiator. If you want, I can take a look."

"No, *gracias*." The man shook his head and lifted his hand for a terse, anxious-looking wave at Lily. She returned the gesture and leaned toward the window to hear better. "I'm sure we have it covered." As soon as he said it, another huge burst of steam or smoke spewed from the open hood. The woman leapt back and flung out a string of curses in Spanish. Her companion at the window looked briefly at her, then offered Romeo an apologetic smile and shrugged. "This happens all the time. We'll be fine."

He tilted his head and studied both the broken-down van and the woman in front of it, who now couldn't decide if she wanted to pace in frustration or kick the front bumper. Instead, she slapped one hand on her hip and the other against her forehead in an effort to shield her eyes from the rain.

"Are you sure? I think we passed maybe two other people today coming from Córdoba. There was no one behind us or in front of us that I could see. You guys might be here for a while if you don't get that thing up and runnin' on your own." He stuck his thumb over his shoulder. "I have my tools in the back, though. I can take a look. I'm usually good with engines, but if I can't fix anything for you, we're happy to drive you both as far as Villahermosa. That would at least get you out of the rain instead of being stuck in the middle of nowhere." He shrugged and raised an eyebrow to emphasize his win-win offer.

The man frowned and glanced at the woman, who scoffed and jerked her arms out as if she waited for him to do something. He took a deep breath and sighed while the rainwater streamed down his face and over his lips. "Okay."

"Okay?"

"Yeah. *Muchas gracias*." The man nodded and lowered his arms to his sides, giving up his fight to not accept help from passing strangers in a huge American RV.

"*De nada*. We'll pull up ahead of you, okay? Then, I'll grab my stuff and see what I can do."

"Yeah. Okay." He raised his hand in another half-hearted wave before he turned and joined the woman in front of the van again.

Romeo nodded at Lily. "Go ahead. Park as close as you can in front of them." He rolled his window up and pointed ahead.

Lily turned the wheel and eased the huge RV onto the shoulder. "I didn't know we have tools in the back."

"We don't." He took a deep breath and turned to look at her. "I smelled magic, Lil."

She paused. "I definitely wouldn't have pegged them as witches."

"I don't think they are. Which is why I lied about the tools and why I think we should check it out."

"Do you think some magical's messing with them? Hexed their car to...what, leave them stranded out here?"

He shook his head and unbuckled his seatbelt.

"Maybe. I don't know. I understand being frustrated that their van broke down, but she seemed a little overly pissed. And he looked scared of something. Most people would've said something about not wanting to trouble us or that we should stay out of the rain and head on anyway." He shifted in his seat, started to stand, and sat again to frown at her. "I can't shake the feeling that they're hiding something."

"Well, I'll be the first person to tell you to go with your gut." She turned the engine off and took the keys from the ignition to be safe before she unbuckled her seatbelt and shoved the keys in the back pocket of her jeans. "You've trusted mine enough times."

"Okay." They stood together and he headed through the RV's living area. "Can I use that duffel bag under the bed?"

"The one that's full of books?"

He raised his eyebrows and nodded.

"Why—oh...tools. Yeah, but make sure it's zipped all the way."

"Thanks." When he'd hauled the bag out from under the bed and slung the strap over his shoulder, he nodded at her again and opened the Winnie's side door into the rain.

The minute she stepped out behind him, she was soaked all the way through. The rain wasn't exactly cold but there was so much of it that the sheer volume of it was overwhelming. She opened her mouth wide to catch a breath. *It's like breathing in the shower.*

They walked along the shoulder flooded with rainwater that streamed down the shallow hill behind them.

The rain was so loud, they didn't hear the couple arguing in front of the van until they'd passed the RV's rear fender and stopped between the vehicles. The woman yelled so quickly in Spanish that even Romeo couldn't catch what she said over the rain. She cut off mid-sentence when she saw the strangers standing there, drenched and smiling, and snorted in disgust before she glared at her companion. "*Si pasa algo, te culpo.*"

Romeo cleared his throat. "All right. Let's take a look." He dropped the duffel bag with a thud and stood over it to lean over the exposed engine.

For all Lily knew, he was actually trying to fix their car, too. The man turned to give her another apologetic smile. When the woman saw it, she slapped his shoulder with the back of a hand and started in on him again in rapid Spanish.

"Okay, okay." He raised his hands in surrender, backed away, and folded his arms. The woman sent Lily another scathing glare and gestured toward the werewolf bent over the hood.

She merely shrugged in the face of the animosity. *Yeah, there's definitely something weird going on.*

Her friend ducked his head to avoid hitting it on the lifted hood, straightened, and scratched his head. "Hey, Lily. Come here for a sec."

"Yep." Her one word was stolen away by the fierce rush of the storm around them and she stepped forward quickly.

He leaned toward her and pointed at the engine but said only loud enough for her to hear over the rain, "I have no idea what's going on with their car. But the magic I smell is definitely not from either of them."

"Well, we didn't ask if there was anyone with them."

"I have a feeling they wouldn't tell us even if we did ask. Follow my lead, okay?"

"Yeah."

"Hey." He nodded at the stranded couple, who'd started walking toward them the minute he lowered his voice. "It looks like what you really need is...oh, maybe four quarts of 15W-40 and probably some extra coolant to be on the safe side." He didn't miss a beat with rambling quickly in English as he stepped around the side of the van and headed toward the back. She moved with him, close to his side. "I always like to go with Delo with an oil tank that's giving me the runaround at the last minute. Do you guys have any on you in the back?"

The couple exchanged a confused glance. "*Que hace?*" the woman asked.

"Yeah, of course you do. I'll take a quick look—"

"Carlos!" The woman glared at her companion and gestured fiercely at the back of the van with an anxious grimace.

"*Oye!*" The man jogged a few steps toward them. "I didn't hear everything you said. Why you gotta be back here to fix the engine, huh?"

The woman glanced nervously from one man to the other, and Lily prepared to cast whatever spell she had to at this point.

"I'm only lookin' for oil, man." Romeo smiled. "Come on. Nobody drives around down here without supplies."

He stretched his hand toward the black handle on the van's back double doors.

"*Ni a putas.*" The woman lurched toward them, shook her head, and waved both hands. "No. No! *No abras esas puertas!*"

"What's going on?" He gazed at each of them in turn while both babbled incoherently at him under the pelting rain. "Wait, what? I can't...I can't hear you—"

"*Basta!*" the woman shouted and shoved him hard in the chest.

He stumbled back. "Woah, hey. I'm only trying to help."

"You better go," the man named Carlos shouted.

A bright flash erupted inside the van—bright enough to be seen through the darkly tinted windows—and the vehicle rocked wildly on its tires. Everyone froze to stare at what the couple definitely didn't want anyone else to see. Romeo met his friend's gaze, nodded, and reached for the door again. The woman shrieked and attacked him with her fists this time, but Lily clenched her fist around thin air and jerked her arm back. Her spell caught the woman and yanked her back across the asphalt. Her sneakers slid across the flooded surface and her arms flailed in front of her as she tried to break free and keep the couple away from the back doors. Carlos didn't really do anything but stare at his companion in complete shock, and that gave the werewolf the opportunity to grasp the handle of the double doors and haul them both wide open.

Lily almost lost her grip on the spell when she saw what was inside. "Oh, my God."

SIX

Two kids—maybe ten years old, if that—barefoot and in dirty clothes, huddled together inside the van. The little girl threw her arm around the boy, who rocked constantly with his knees drawn to his chest and his hands clamped over his ears. Although she breathed heavily, the girl glared fiercely at Romeo from the van's dark interior. She blinked when she realized she was staring at a completely different face she didn't recognize at all.

"*Ayúdanos.*" Her voice was small and terrified, but the force of her plea broke through the heavy rain, fueled by desperate courage to ask for help in the first place.

"*Están heridos?*" he asked. She shook her head and wrapped her other skinny arm around the front of the boy.

"Romeo?" Lily stared at his clenched fists. *He's about to lose it.* The woman she held fixed in place with her spell stopped struggling and now stared in horror at the interlopers.

"Okay," Carlos said and stepped toward the open doors. "Let me tell you—"

Romeo moved with a speed only werewolves could manage. He snatched the front of the man's shirt in his fist, growled, and pounded him against the inside of the open door. Carlos' mouth fell open in pain and he clenched his eyes shut. "Tell me what? Why you have two kids in the back of your van, scared out of their minds and asking me to help them? Yeah, go ahead and tell me. And I swear, if it's not the truth, slamming you against the door is gonna feel like a massage."

"*Sí. Sí.*" Carlos nodded vigorously, his hands raised almost to his face in surrender. "Okay. We are only supposed to bring them to Oaxaca."

The woman struggled again within Lily's spell and shouted something else in rapid Spanish.

"Why?" he growled.

"I-I don't know. We only grab the kids and drive them, okay?"

"Carlos!"

"Raquél, *cállate!*" For the first time, he looked angry when he told his partner to shut it.

He shoved the guy against the door again to redirect his attention. "What happens in Oaxaca?"

"I don't know. We hand them over, and that's it, *hombre*. I swear."

"If I have to ask you another question, Carlos, you'll have to spit a few teeth out first to answer."

"Yeah, okay. I get it. *Oye*, we get a call. *Llamada por*

teléfono, okay? I don't know who. They say, 'Go to this town.' We go. We grab *los niños*. We drive them to Oaxaca. Then whoever meets us there takes them, and that's it."

"And you get paid."

"Well, yeah."

Romeo growled again and shoved the man so hard against the door that he uttered a strangled cry.

"All right." Lily divided her focus between holding the snarling Raquél in the snare of her magic and stepping toward the van. "Romeo, I don't think you'll squeeze anything else out of him."

"*P-por favor*," Carlos stammered. "Don't squeeze."

The werewolf glared at him for a few seconds and his jaw muscles rippled as he clenched his teeth and held himself back. "Don't talk."

She slipped between Romeo and the other open door and smiled gently at the kids in the van despite an almost overwhelming desire to annihilate these people first. "Hey. Everything's okay."

The boy hadn't stopped rocking with his hands on his ears and his head tucked between his knees. The girl, though, was clearly aware and alert, but her wide eyes flickered toward Romeo in confusion.

With a sigh, he held Carlos pinned to the door with both hands now and turned to look at the kids. He asked a series of questions in Spanish, and the girl replied quickly in very few words. At his last question, she nodded vigorously and looked from him to Lily and hope flared in her eyes. "*Por favor*."

"They were kidnapped, Lily." His voice trembled with restraint. "By these assholes." He knocked Carlos against the door again and released a spray of rainwater onto everything that was already soaked through. "Yesterday or the day before, she thinks, because they haven't been out of this van once."

I should tell him to rip this guy apart. She took a deep breath, released it slowly, and wiped the rain out of her eyes with the hand she didn't currently use to hold her spell on the woman behind them.

"We have to take them with us," he added. "The kids. They wanna come with us."

"Okay." She nodded her head toward the little girl and stretched her hand out. "Come on. It's okay."

The child nodded, then rubbed the boy's arms and turned to him in an attempt to coax him out of his ceaseless rocking. Lily didn't think the boy could manage it, but he finally lifted his head, sniffed, and crawled after his companion toward the open doors. He didn't look at Lily when the girl took her hand and accepted help out of the van. His friend had to grab his hand to lead him out, and Romeo said something to the kids in Spanish. With their hands clasped tightly, they both stepped off of the shoulder until they were almost hidden in the huge, tall leaves of the plants beside the highway, the fronds bent low beneath the endless rain.

"I think we're done," Romeo growled at Carlos.

"W-what are you—"

"Shut up." He hauled the man completely off his feet with both hands and launched him into the back of the van like a suitcase before he jabbed a finger at him in a gesture to stay where he was.

Lily looked at Raquél, who seethed at them and obviously waited for the opportunity to lash out. She wouldn't get it. "You too." She jerked her closed fist down to her thigh and the prisoner lurched toward the van under the pull of the young witch's spell.

As she whisked past her captor, she raised a clawed hand for what would have been a vicious slap to whatever she could reach. Lily whipped her fist in a circle, and the woman spun with a shriek before she toppled onto her miserable partner. She scrambled off him and turned her ire on Carlos, spitting and cursing in Spanish until Lily had enough and swept them both with her memory-wipe spell. The sparkling blue mist cut Raquél's words off, Carlos coughed, and they both slumped in a heap.

"If I knew how to make that spell go farther than the last twelve hours, I would've." She glanced at Romeo, her lips pressed so tightly together, they began to tremble.

"I know." He glared at the slumped bodies. "Should we call somebody?"

"Like the cops?" They exchanged a hesitant glance. "Well, yeah, these people need to be locked up. But... honestly, I think getting involved in a criminal case or whatever in Mexico, especially with non-magicals..."

"Yeah, I know." He sighed. "That's time on the road we can't really afford to lose right now."

She nodded but it felt wrong to smile right now. "Okay. So we leave them— Hey—"

The little girl walked boldly between them and

stepped up into the van. The couple exchanged glances, then looked at the little boy still partially hidden behind the huge leaves. He watched his friend and the van with his fists clenched tightly at his sides.

"What's she—"

The child stepped over the unconscious bodies of her kidnappers and paused long enough to spit. Lily jerked her head back in surprise, and the corner of Romeo's mouth twitched. She walked all the way to the front and opened the center console. When she retrieved whatever she wanted from that, she closed it again and snatched something else from the depression in the dash between the cupholders. She returned quickly to the open back doors, leapt out, and tossed a cluster of zip-ties held together with a twisted piece of wire onto the rough carpet. She tipped her head back to shoot Romeo a pointed glance and stepped back.

"Yes, ma'am," he muttered, pulled two strips of plastic from the bundle, and held one out to Lily. When she looked at the little girl, she found only a dauntless persistence in the child's eyes. Without comment, she took the zip-tie and hopped into the van with Romeo.

They had Carlos' and Raquél's wrists bound behind their backs in less than a minute, and she had almost forgotten about the constantly pouring rain until she stepped back out into it. The little girl hadn't moved an inch and now, she slowly raised both hands to show her rescuers exactly what else she'd pulled from the van—two cheap cell phones.

"Smart kid." Lily raised an eyebrow. "Do you think she—"

The child threw one device onto the ground and stamped on it with her bare heel, over and over. She grunted with the effort but making little other noise. They let her take out the rest of her anger on the phone, and when she lifted the other one to hurl onto the highway, Romeo stepped toward her. *"Espere."* She froze and looked at him. He held his open hand out and nodded slowly, and the girl looked a little disappointed but gave him the cell phone anyway. He held her gaze as he took the phone in both hands, broke it in half, and scattered plastic and tiny metal shards over the road.

The girl stared at the destruction and a slow smile spread across her lips. *"Vámanos."* She spun on her heel and stepped across the soggy, overgrown earth to take the boy by the hand and walk with him toward the Winnebago. The couple stared after them until the girl opened the side door and ushered the boy inside without another word.

"Well." Romeo tilted his head, his expression a little bemused. "That seems good enough to me."

"Yeah, I think she nailed it."

"Almost." He grasped both doors and slammed them shut. Then, he walked to the driver-side door, yanked the keys from the ignition, and moved around the front of the van. Lily heard the jangle of keys before she saw them careen over the bushes and ferns and narrow, twisted trunks of the tall trees. They disappeared without a sound over the rain, and he walked back toward her with her duffle bag of books in tow. "I think they're dry." He shrugged. "If not, I'm sorry and I'll buy you new ones."

She shook her head firmly. "If sacrificing a few books is what it took to get those kids back home, I'm totally okay with it.

SEVEN

They returned to the Winnie to find the kids seated on the couch. The boy had curled into a sopping-wet ball, his knees pulled to his chin and his skinny arms wound around them. The girl sat cross-legged beside him and she straightened when they entered through the side door. The rain still poured as ferociously as before, but it was much quieter in the RV and Lily shivered in the cold air left from running the AC while they drove.

"We should go," Romeo said.

"I know. We have time for one more thing, though. I'll be right back." She smiled at the kids, dropped her purse on the center console, and hurried toward her bedroom and slid the door shut behind her. That was simply so she could change quickly in private, but she also found two oversized t-shirts in the built-in wardrobe—the gray one with the Phish logo and a white one with the Charleston River Dogs' yellow mascot biting a wooden baseball bat in half. She held them out for a second and shook her head. "Like they're gonna care."

When she stepped out, her friend sat in the swiveling armchair across from the couch and smiled at the little girl. "*Y ella se llama* Lily." He gestured toward Lily and met her gaze. "This is Rosalía and Filipe."

"*Mucho gusto*," the girl said.

"Yeah. *Mucho gusto*, Rosalía. Um..." She held the t-shirts up. "*Quieres...otra camiseta?*"

The child smiled, nodded fiercely, and considered her options before she selected the RiverDogs shirt.

"I thought you might choose that one. Oh." She stepped aside and slid the bathroom door open. "Here's the bathroom." Rosalía leapt off the couch and went in to strip out of her sopping clothes and into a shirt that was way too big even for Lily. It looked like a sack on a kid Rosalía's size. Despite that, the kid smiled and returned to the couch, took the other shirt on the way, and climbed next to Filipe to explain to him in a hushed voice what the gray t-shirt was for. The boy didn't say a thing or move at all. He merely stared at the floor. With a shrug, she pulled the Phish shirt over his head and his bare torso, ruffled his damp black hair, and whispered something else.

"Okay, that's good enough." Romeo stood from the armchair and headed toward the front. "Do you still want me to drive?"

"In the rain? Yes, please." She had to return to her room to rescue the keys from her wet jean shorts and hurried back to hand them over. When she sat in the passenger seat as Romeo started the Winnie, she strapped her seatbelt on and paused. "They don't have seatbelts back there."

He smirked and opened his mouth, then closed it again, saving himself from the mistake of a poorly timed joke about tying the kids down for safety. "I think they'll be okay," he said instead. "And I'll be careful."

"Okay." She turned in her seat and smiled at Rosalía. The girl nodded and returned the smile like this was all simply a normal day for her—a witch, a werewolf, and two kidnapped-and-rescued kids heading off on another adventure. With a sigh, she shifted into a comfortable position and watched the continuous rain as he pulled them back onto the highway.

THE FIRST HALF-HOUR passed in silence beyond the ambient music playing through the Winnie's speakers, punctuated once and a while by a jazz trumpet. Lily must have looked back at the kids on the couch every couple of minutes. "Did she tell you where they live?"

"Um...a little village, maybe. I think it's outside Plan de Ayutla, but I'll have to check."

"How far is it?"

"In the Winnie? Nine hours. Maybe ten."

She glanced at the clock—2:07 p.m. "Okay, so we have a couple of kids overnight." She stopped herself from looking at them again. *They're still there, Lily. And they're still okay.* "Did she say...anything else? About what happened?"

"Not really. I mean, we only talked while you were changing, but at least I got their names and where they're from." He glanced at her and smiled. "We'll get them home."

"I know." She leaned her head against the seat for only a few seconds before she bolted upright again. "Romeo, they're witches."

He shot her a playful frown and chuckled. "Well, yeah. That's how we found them."

"Right. No, I know. I only..." With a sigh, she stared through the windshield and tried to think past her surprise. "I didn't even put two and two together until right now. Which is weird for me, because I always—"

"Woah. Hey." He stretched his open hand over the center console and she took it. "It's totally normal to feel a little scattered after seeing some sh—" He jerked his head like he meant to glance at the kids but chose to keep his eyes on the road instead. "Something awful like that. Trust me, I was too."

"But you didn't forget about the magic part. One of them cast a spell in that van. I'm sure it was only light and a little force, but still. That shouldn't have *slipped my mind.* That's what I do, Romeo. I look at all the pieces and I fit them together—"

"Lil?"

She puffed out a breath. "Yeah."

"Please stop beating yourself up about it, okay? We got them outta there. That's what matters."

"I know, but—"

"You fit all the pieces together. I know." He squeezed her hand. "And you're ridiculously good at it."

"Yeah, but you—"

"Hey." When he squeezed her hand a little harder this time, she looked at him. He glanced sideways at her and smiled. "You remembered the important stuff. You did what you had to do. We both did. And I didn't forget about that flash of light or the magic because I literally can't when it's right in front of me." He sniffed and wrinkled his nose with an airy chuckle. "I can smell it."

Lily blinked. "Right."

"Right. Which is something you can't do. That's not me bragging, Lil. That's me reminding you to let yourself off the hook. Okay? It's not like you forgot how to use your magic or anything." He chuckled. "You're always right on the money with that."

"Well, not always." He looked quickly at her before turning back to the road, but she knew they had both thought the same thing. *The black cloud is still an exception.* And she hadn't quite discovered how to control it completely.

"Okay, ninety-nine-percent is still amazing. And we're moving forward, okay?"

"Okay."

The Winnebago fell silent again as Romeo took them carefully around the occasional winding curves in the highway. The drive now definitely started to look more and more like the tropical-rainforest Mexico Lily remembered, even through the thick rain.

"Lily?"

She jumped a little, surprised out of her silence, and turned around to see Rosalía staring at her with a smile. Filipe, apparently, had fallen asleep sitting up, nestled in the corner of the couch's back cushion and the armrest. "Yeah?" The girl asked her something, but her voice was too soft and her Spanish a little too rapid. "I'm sorry, I didn't... What did she say?" She turned to Romeo, who glanced into the rear-view mirror that only showed the inside of the RV.

He smiled and said something to Rosalía. The girl grinned and moved out of her cross-legged position to kneel on the couch and sit back on her heels. They continued the conversation in Spanish, speaking rapidly between, and the child uttered a long, pealing giggle.

"Okay, so I didn't catch any of that." She smiled at the girl and glanced at her. "What are you guys talking about?"

"You."

"What?" A surprised chuckle escaped her. "You're talking about me and it made her laugh?"

"Not exactly." He smiled and shook his head. "She wants to talk to you about magic."

She raised her eyebrows. "Oh, really?"

"Yes. She wants you to teach her new spells." He smirked. "Because you're the most powerful witch she's ever seen."

She froze for a second under the weight of that surprisingly poignant compliment and looked at Rosalía again. The girl grinned at her, studying her face. "So why did she laugh?"

" 'Cause I said you're the most powerful witch I've ever seen."

It made her laugh too. "Way to build me up like that. Okay, I appreciate the sentiment, but..." She glanced at the child once more. "I have a feeling that kid's smart enough to see through even white lies."

"Oh, absolutely." He sent her an appraising look for as long as he could before turning back to the highway. "It's not a lie, though."

"What?"

"Not even a little."

Lily studied his profile and the smile that tugged at the corner of his mouth, although he tried to hold it back. "You simply haven't seen very many witches, then."

"Lily, I've run into more witches in the last couple of weeks on this trip with you than I've probably seen in my entire life before this. That's enough."

She thumped her head against the headrest and smiled. "Well, the most powerful witch I've ever seen is still out there." *I'm coming, Mom.*

EIGHT

About an hour later, Rosalía stood from the couch and crept carefully toward the front seats. Lily didn't see her until the girl's hand settled around the armrest and startled the older witch out of her wandering thoughts.

"Oh, man." She caught her breath and had to laugh at herself. "You really snuck up on me."

Chuckling, Romeo translated. The child grinned and fired off a rapid string of Spanish in response. "She wants you to teach her."

"What?" She looked at the girl again, who nodded and clapped her hands as if in prayer. "I... Romeo, I don't know how to teach magic."

He translated again and this time, he and Rosalía held a much longer conversation that she couldn't even begin to follow. *The total irony that Spanish is the one romance language I never had the chance to pin down.* She caught a few words—*bruja, estudiante, mágico, família*—but other than that, she was clueless.

He became as animated through their conversation as Rosalía did and his eyes widened with whatever story she told him next. They continued the discussion for what felt like forever until he finally said, "She wants to learn your kind of magic, Lily. I think her family and her village might be in a little bubble out where they are. Most of what they do is..." He chuckled. "Agricultural?"

"Farming witches." she smiled at Rosalía, who'd squatted behind the center console for at least an hour and grasped the armrests of the driver and passenger seats while she'd been totally consumed by her and Romeo's conversation. "They use their magic to grow crops, then?"

"Something like that. She said something about rain and death that I don't exactly understand, but yeah. They could be farmers."

"It makes sense if they don't have much access to magical texts and histories. Or even new teachers, I guess—oh..."

Romeo laughed. "Yeah, I think that's her point. It looks like you found yourself an apprentice."

"Wow." Lily took a deep breath. "It's literally never crossed my mind that I'd end up teaching anyone anything."

"Well, there's a ton she could learn from you. That's even better, right?"

"I guess..." She gazed at the girl, unable to keep herself from mirroring the fearless, determined smirk on the little face. "Okay."

Rosalía squeaked. Her hands balled into fists and her eyes clenched so tightly when she grinned that her whole body trembled in excitement. Then, the girl sighed heavily. "*Gracias,* Lily! *Muchas gracias.*"

"*De nada.*" She laughed and shook her head. "I guess I need a lesson plan. When we stop for the night, I'll...find something to start with."

Romeo repeated what she'd said in Spanish, and Rosalía bounced behind the center console. Her eagerness started to infect Lily too.

"First, though, I gotta figure out a way for us to understand each other."

"Oh, a translator simply doesn't cut it, huh?" He chuckled.

"You translating is fine. But we can get much more done in less time if we don't have to do it with you in the middle." She smirked and folded her arms. "And I have this feeling that you're translating way more for her than you are for me."

He stared directly ahead for a moment, then snorted. "Okay. You caught me. We've had a few conversations between the actual translating parts."

"See, that kinda side talk is only gonna get distracting. And magic doesn't need an interpreter, anyway. It's universal."

"Universal," Rosalía repeated.

Lily eyed her with a skeptical smile. "Is she copying me now?"

Her friend chucked. "Nope. It's the same word in Spanish."

THE RAIN EASED ONLY a little before they stopped for the night outside Chancalá, but it still pounded onto the Winnie's roof with a steady, unending rush. "It's a good thing we bought a supply of food this morning," Lily said and opened the fridge to survey what little they kept in there. "It's probably not a great idea to step into a restaurant with missing kids, even though we're taking them home."

"Yeah, I had the same thought." Romeo stepped up behind her, put his hands on her hips, and muttered in her ear. "It's a good thing we hadn't planned on going anywhere."

She grinned.

"Oh," Rosalía called behind them. "*Están enamorados?*"

He stepped away and turned toward the girl with a surprised laugh. "*Eso no es asunto tuyo. Ve a despertarlo.*" He nodded toward Filipe still sleeping on the couch.

The child pursed her lips, mocking him with a little wiggle of her head, then turned and leapt onto the couch before she spoke softly to the boy curled in the corner of it.

"What was that about?" Lily turned toward Romeo and tilted her chin with a raised eyebrow.

"I told her to wake him up." He smiled but didn't quite meet her gaze.

"Uh-huh." She waited and he took a deep breath before he finally looked at her.

"Do you want help making dinner?"

"Sure." *He definitely doesn't translate everything.*

THE SMELL of the frozen meals reheated on the stove did more to rouse Filipe from his deep sleep on the couch than any combination of Rosalía's shaking, prodding, poking, and even uttering his name in a range of volumes from whispers to near-shouts. Lily had just finished stirring the now steaming mix of rice, beans, green peppers, onions, and chicken in the pot when the boy's head jerked up. Rosalía leapt away from him with a giggle and spoke to him in a low voice. Together, the kids slid off the couch and headed to the table Romeo had set for them five minutes before.

"Someone's hungry," the werewolf said from the armchair beside the Winnie's side door. When the youngsters had settled themselves in the booths at the table— which definitely wasn't big enough for all four of them, Rosalía and Filipe's scrawniness notwithstanding—the boy stared silently at Lily's hand and the food she was almost ready to set down in front of them.

Rosalía asked him a question but he didn't answer. He pressed his lips together and watched the pot cross the narrow kitchen. His gaze followed the serving spoon's every movement as she piled two heaped spoonfuls on his plate. The minute she moved the pot toward Rosalía's plate, the boy snatched a handful of the hot food and crammed it into his mouth. Rice fell down the front of the oversized Phish t-shirt and across the table. Rosalía hissed, slapped his arm, and pointed at the spoon beside his plate. He stared at her and swallowed.

"*Água?*" the girl asked.

"Oh. Yeah." Lily quickly scooped food onto the girl's plate.

"*Gracias.*"

"*De nada.*" She set the pot down and brought the kids two bottles of water. Filipe almost ripped the lid off and chugged half of it before he thumped it on the table and shoveled more food into his mouth.

Lily turned slowly toward Romeo with wide eyes. "He's really hungry."

For the first time, Rosalía looked nervous. She looked from one adult to the other and said something that prompted another conversation between her and Romeo. Fortunately, it was much shorter than the others. He chuckled at the end and the girl frowned at Filipe and shook her head. He didn't seem to notice anything but the food.

"What's wrong?" Lily asked.

"Nothing." He stood to serve her a plate first, then one for himself. "I think she was worried you'd change your mind."

"Change my mind?"

He nodded. "About being her teacher. That you wouldn't want a student with, and I quote, 'a pig for a brother.'"

She snorted and clapped a hand hastily over her mouth. "I totally shouldn't laugh at that."

"I did," he said with a shrug, stood at the end of the short kitchen counter, and started eating.

"He's her brother?"

"They are twins."

When she turned to look at the kids again, Rosalía's gaze darted away from her as the girl turned back to her food with a hidden smirk. "I can't blame either of them for being hungry. And I'm reasonably sure manners are the last thing on the list after being—" She hunched forward and whispered, "Kidnapped."

"I'm totally with you on that one." He swallowed and coughed a little. "Hey, could you hand me a—"

"Yep. Got it." She retrieved two more bottles of water.

"Thanks." When he'd washed his food down, he held her gaze for a few seconds longer than normal. "I think he's having a harder time with what they went through over the last few days. At least he's eating, so it could be worse. Honestly"—he chuckled and leaned over the counter toward her—"I think she was more upset that being kidnapped didn't make him more polite."

Her eyes widened. "Did she say that?" She wanted to laugh but that would have felt so completely wrong.

"More or less. She said he always eats like this, and I... had to remind her it's because he's a boy." He held her gaze as he scooped a heaped spoonful of rice into his mouth, and they both had to fight their laughter.

"If eating habits were a deciding factor in who I spend

my time with, I'm sure I would've kicked you out of the Winnie when we were on our way to Canada."

"Fair enough." They turned their attention to the food for a while, and the Winnie was completely silent beyond the sounds of chewing, swallowing, and silverware on plates amidst the background melody of the constant rain.

NINE

Rosalía could hardly reach the faucet at the sink, but she'd cleared both her and Filipe's plates and made an admirable effort to wash them. Romeo stopped her gently and showed her how to load the dishwasher. That was all it took to get them talking again.

Lily glanced at Filipe and thought she'd maybe sit with him at the table and try her halting Spanish with him. His silence was a lot more her speed. But the boy slid out from the booth and walked on the tips of his toes back to the couch. His damp shorts had soaked through the bottom of her oversized gray shirt but he apparently didn't care. Without even a glance at her, he curled in the corner of the couch again and went back to sleep.

"Okay." She turned toward Romeo and Rosalía. "I'm gonna go and try to think of a way to make sure we can all understand each other. I'll be right back."

"That sounds good." He gave her a thumbs-up. "We got it."

Rosalía spun away from him and mirrored his gesture with a huge grin.

Laughing, Lily moved down the short hall into her bedroom but she didn't close the door. It was a little after 7:30 p.m. which would hopefully give them enough time to satisfy Rosalía's excitement and curiosity. *Hopefully, it's not anything like mine was when I was her age.*

Romeo had left the duffel bag of books in front of the bed, the waterproof canvas still covered in beaded drops of water. She tried to shake most of it off, wiped a spray from her face, and unzipped it. "Okay, it's admittedly not the best place to store books," she muttered. "It's not like I have room to stack boxes, though."

The contents were scattered inside the bag and a few pages had bent under others, but at least they were all still dry. She found her mom's old book of spells at the bottom —the one she hadn't been allowed to touch until she graduated high school. "Not that her literal electric-shock wards ever stopped me from trying." Even three years after she managed to open it for the first time, her ingrained reaction was to hesitate before she touched this particular grimoire.

She snorted at herself and pulled the large dark-purple hardcover from the bag, climbed onto the bed, crossed her legs, and got to work. *Boy, I really haven't had to look spells up in a long time.*

Margaret Antony had always specialized in revelatory magic—unlocking secret doors, discovering hidden secrets, clearing illusions and wards and whatever stood between her and what the woman wanted to see or know or understand. *Like mother, like daughter. Or maybe it's one of those nature-versus-nurture things.* She skimmed through the pages of the spellbook. Most of the spells, wards, and charms she already knew, but seeing them laid out like this in her mom's handwriting—feeling like she was studying again with the goal of uncovering one more unknown—helped her put the pieces together.

Twenty minutes later, she thought she'd found three spells she could use together to achieve what she wanted. She closed the book, set it on top of the bag, and leapt off the bed to rejoin the others.

Romeo and Rosalía now sat cross-legged in the center of the living area, facing each other and talking. Of course, Filipe hadn't moved from his position on the couch, and the sound of his sister's excited chatter and the man's deep voice obviously didn't bother him.

"We're almost ready." The girl spun on the floor and they both looked at her as she stepped into the kitchen to fill a bowl with a little water from the sink.

"*Verdád?*" the girl squeaked in excitement.

"Yep." Lily brought the bowl with her and wondered where she would sit.

Romeo pushed himself off the floor with a sigh. "Yeah, I want a good seat for this."

"Well, don't get too excited." She flashed him a sideways glance and smirked before she replaced him on the floor in front of Rosalía. "I gotta make sure it actually works, first."

"It always does." He stretched his legs out in the swiveling armchair and folded his arms.

"Eventually, yeah. Sometimes, though, it's not on the

first attempt." She set the bowl down between her and the girl, who squirmed over her own crossed legs and pressed both fists into her lap and grinned at the bowl. "Can you tell her not to do anything until I'm finished?"

Romeo frowned. "Like what?"

"Like try to copy me or work her own spells. I'm already not a hundred percent sure how this is gonna go, and the last thing I need is a kid witch too eager and too headstrong for her own good."

"Did you really say those words?" He laughed. "Because you know who you actually described, right?"

Lily stuck her tongue out at him. "I said kid witch. So obviously, I'm not talking about myself." *But yeah. That did sound exactly like me.* She shook the thought out of her head and smiled at the girl.

Romeo translated and Rosalía's eyes widened before she said something hastily in response. "She wants to know if it's dangerous."

Trying to look serious, Lily bit the inside of her cheek to keep from laughing. "Not what I'm doing, no, even if it doesn't work. But if she starts tossing around her own unstable spell or doesn't know how to manage something, then yeah. It could become fairly dangerous."

When he relayed all that, Rosalía blinked at her and shrugged before she responded again.

Fighting back a snort, he gave Lily an exaggeratedly somber expression so he wouldn't crack up. "She said she's not afraid of a little danger."

She took a deep breath and nodded. "Well, tell her that if she tries anything before this spell works, whether or not it's dangerous, I'll change my mind and won't be able to teach her anything."

He cleared his throat to interpret but Rosalía instantly stopped fidgeting and a thin-lipped, grim determination replaced her smile. She nodded. "*Listo.*"

"Ready." He nodded, still playing the part of the formal, humorless interpreter.

If I look at him right now, I'm gonna lose it. Instead, she glanced at the bowl of water. "Thank you." She took a deep breath and prepared to start. She dipped two fingers into the liquid, raised her other hand in a fist, and twisted it like turning a key in a lock before she opened her hand quickly. With her water-dipped fingers, she tapped the center of her forehead. A sharp, cold tingle spread outward along her face and almost instantly disappeared. She moved her fingers immediately to Rosalía's brow and repeated the motion, and although the girl made no sound, her eyes widened at the sensation.

The next spell was as close as she could get to the desired effect without any potions of her own, but she gestured again for this one and touched her own lips before lightly tapping Rosalía's. This time, the girl's only reaction was to study every tiny motion of her hands, her eyes flickering up to search the older witch's as she filed everything she saw away in her memory. *Because that's exactly what I used to do.*

Smiling, Lily readied the final spell and clapped her hands. When she pulled them apart again, a thin, transparent pink film stretched between her palms. She raised her arms above her head and drew her hands farther apart.

The pink film now glowed and stretched wider before she let her arms fall at her sides. The pink light burst all around them, filled the entire RV, and shimmered and faded.

"Hey, that looked like that purple-dome thing in Colorado that made us invisible." Romeo stared at the last of the pastel light before it disappeared.

"It didn't make us invisible," she muttered and looked around the RV for any sign of having missed or part of her spells backfiring. So far, so good, she decided and wiped her fingers off on her leggings to sever the thread that connected everything she'd done. "But yeah, it's almost the same thing but in reverse."

He smirked. "So if an invisible person was standing here right now, we'd see them?"

She looked at him slowly and pushed her tongue against her cheek, fighting the urge to laugh again. "More like if someone had cast an illusion in here, it would now be broken."

"Huh."

They both looked at Rosalía, who hadn't moved an inch and stared unblinkingly at her.

"Did it work?" he asked.

"I have no clue. I've never woven three spells together for a magical DIY translator before, so I guess we'll have to see." After a few awkward seconds of waiting, she was about to have him ask the girl if she'd noticed anything different but Rosalía beat them to it.

"I thought you only knew a few words in Spanish."

Lily barked out a laugh.

"Okay, that doesn't make sense." Romeo frowned. "She said—"

"Oh, I know what she said." Lily grinned at him. "It totally worked."

"Hey, cool."

Turning back to the child, she raised an eyebrow. "And I didn't know you could speak English at all."

The girl glanced at Romeo. "I can't. Where's the magic?"

Chuckling, he started to reply in Spanish and Lily cut him off. "Okay, I probably should've included you in this spell too because you're the only person I can't understand right now. So cut it out. Please." He laughed again when she batted her lashes at him and leaned back in the armchair.

"Oh, wow." Rosalía glanced from one to the other. "What kind of magic was that?"

She smiled and focused on the child. "Three spells, actually. The first one drew the focus to our thoughts and kind of...revealed what we're thinking."

"Like we can read each other's minds?"

"Uh...no." She frowned and searched for a way to explain the way stacking spells worked. "That could've happened if it was the only spell I cast, but this was only taking certain pieces from each and mixing them into something completely different. It's a bad idea to start reading each other's minds. Neither of us wants that."

Rosalía laughed. "What were the others?"

"Well, the second was basically a weak version of a truth potion. But put with the other, it's actually much better than a truth potion. It's the same thing with mind-reading, I guess. We're not thinking or speaking any differently than we normally would. We simply got rid of the language barrier, which was what that last spell did."

"Your illusion-busting spell?" Romeo asked.

"Well, yeah. If you think about it, that's basically all language is, right? An illusion. Okay, certain words have more power than others, but most of that power comes from the intention behind them. And you don't become a different person or want different things depending on what language you speak."

Rosalía's mouth dropped open in awe.

Romeo sank farther into the armchair and puffed out a breath. "That is some deeply philosophical spellwork, Lil."

"What?" She laughed and gestured at the bowl of water. "Okay, if my magic's philosophical, so is cooking 'cause I basically put ingredients together."

He shrugged. "And it turned out delicious."

She snorted and rolled her eyes. "Whatever." Then, she looked at Rosalía. "So. What do you wanna learn first?"

The girl's open-mouthed gape morphed into a grin almost bigger than she was. "Everything!"

TEN

L ily couldn't start teaching the girl everything, of course, so they began with the basics. "Show me something you already know."

Rosalía's shoulders slumped. "That's boring."

"Everyone has to start somewhere, even Romeo. I guarantee you he wasn't born knowing everything he knows now."

He straightened a little in the armchair and smirked. "That kinda sounds like an insult, you know."

"You know what I meant."

"Yeah, but I'm not sure what you two are doing and what I do are really the same thing."

"The point is"—she turned back toward Rosalía—"that no matter who you are, what you are, or what you can do, everyone starts at the beginning. Or you wouldn't have asked me to teach you anything, right?"

The girl narrowed her eyes. "I guess."

"The beginning's super-important. It sets up what the

rest of your magic's gonna look like, and it's the safest place to discover what your strengths are." Finally, the girl nodded. "Okay. So...Romeo told me your family—your village—are farmers. Is that right?"

"Sort of." Rosalía wrinkled her nose. "We do some farming, but it's only for us."

"Okay."

"My people grow things. I can't remember what my mom calls it but that's basically what we do."

"Like keeping plants healthy during bad weather or... are you only really good at gardening?"

The child threw her head back and laughed. "You ask funny questions."

"I'm only trying to understand a little better." She smiled at her pupil's open sense of humor. "Can you show me?"

"Um..." She bit her lip and glanced at Romeo. He simply shrugged and gestured to Lily on the floor.

"It's okay if it's something small," Lily said. "Only to show me what you can already do."

"Okay. Something small..." The girl licked her lips and stared at the floor for a second, then leapt to her feet and went into the kitchen. She opened the pantry and scanned the shelves, stood all the way on her tiptoes, and stretched with a grunt to retrieve a bag of piñon nuts. The adults exchanged a glance as she opened the bag, grabbed a small handful, tied the bag closed again, and returned everything to its rightful place. She tossed a few of them in her mouth as she walked through the RV and munched away like their previous conversation had never happened. Then she sat, crossed her legs again, and glanced at them. "Oh, sorry. Do you want some?"

"Um...no thanks."

Romeo shook his head and smiled.

Rosalía shrugged, took one piñon nut out of her hand, and dropped the rest of them into her mouth. When she finally stopped chewing, she held the single white seed in her palm and looked at Lily. "Something small."

"Okay."

Smiling, the girl focused on the seed, covered it with her other hand, and closed her eyes. A small, green glow illuminated between her palms. Lily's skin prickled with goosebumps and the light grew brighter. Rosalía spread her hands apart a little at a time and a tiny green shoot poked from between her fingers. It grew in seconds into a crooked, curving sapling before three small branches split away and sprouted a handful of soft green pine needles. It stopped but only because Rosalía cut her magic and opened her eyes. She grinned at the sapling piñon tree and removed her top hand from the base of its trunk to reveal the intricate pattern of tiny roots that had wound themselves around her other palm, pushed between her fingers, and clung to the underside of her hand.

Lily stifled her surprise and cleared her throat. "That's what you meant by 'grow things.'"

"Yes. I could've made it bigger, but..." She glanced at the RV's interior and shrugged.

"No, I..." Romeo's eyes rolled back in his head and his nostrils flared. "I think that was...a good..." He sneezed violently, swallowed, and blinked heavy eyelids.

The girl burst out laughing, but she soon stopped herself when she realized he wasn't laughing too. "Are you okay?"

"Oh, yeah." He raised a finger and turned his head away to lean forward and fight the dizziness. Thankfully, he managed not to sneeze again.

"Yeah, I felt it too, actually." Lily gave him a sympathetic smile. "Do you want me to go get—"

"No, I got it." He pushed himself out of the armchair, stumbled a little, and swayed to the bedroom to open the drawer of the built-in nightstand on what was now his side of the bed. When he returned, he'd already popped one of the little purple flowers into his mouth and chewed it vigorously. "I only need to give it a minute." With a sigh, he sagged into the armchair and tossed a little plastic bag onto the center console. Inside was what remained of the blossoms Melissa Bore had given him before they left her house in the werewolf neighborhood in Chihuahua.

After a sniff, he took another deep breath and continued to chew. "If you guys are gonna throw spells around all night, I think I'll keep these with me."

"Wait. Do you eat those?" Rosalía pointed at the plastic bag.

"Yeah." He chuckled. "They're actually—"

"What are you doing? Are you crazy?" The girl leapt to her feet and hurried toward him. "Spit it out! That'll kill you." She swiped frantically at his mouth, but he caught her tiny wrist in his hand and leaned away.

"Woah, woah, woah. Hold on. It's okay. I know they're poisonous." The girl froze, stared at him, and took a sharp breath. Then he remembered having been left out of Lily's translation spell and repeated everything for her in Spanish while he nodded to reassure her and held her gaze. She continued to look at him like he was crazy.

"Come sit down." Lily nodded at the floor, and Rosalía lowered her arm slowly and scowled first at Romeo, then at the bag of purple flowers on the center console. But she turned and went back to where she'd sat across from Lily. "It's wolfsbane. The flowers. You obviously know that."

Rosalía nodded, leaned toward the woman, and whispered, "So why is he eating it?"

"Well, ironically, wolfsbane isn't actually poisonous to werewolves. It's more like a—"

"He's a werewolf?"

Romeo laughed again, his eyes much clearer now. "Yup."

The girl squinted at him. "He doesn't look like a werewolf."

"Hey—"

"Aren't you supposed to be...hairier?"

Lily snorted and he said something flippant in Spanish before she raised an eyebrow at him. He shrugged. "Sorry. I only said I'm really hairy as a wolf." He flashed her a goofy grin and she shook her head.

"He's also allergic to magic, basically. Especially if there's too much of it or it's really strong."

Rosalía frowned. "What I did was really easy."

"Well, there are many witches who would find that difficult to do. You clearly have a...special skill."

"Not like what you did to those...people." The girl

might as well have spat again given the way she mentioned them. "That's real magic."

"It's all real magic, Rosalía."

"I know. Mine is only making things grow. Yours is about strength."

Lily shrugged. "Not all of it. Only a few things."

"That's what I want to learn." The girl's dark eyes glittered as she spoke and her face lit up at the possibility of learning how to do things that had taken her teacher years of training with her mom.

And I still don't know everything. "Why?"

The child simply stared as if unable to understand why anyone would ask the question. "To make my people strong."

"Oh." She nodded slowly and tried to hide her surprise. "Yeah, that's...that's a good reason." She glanced at Romeo, who looked a little confounded and scratched the back of his neck. "So you and I can start with something small too, okay?"

The girl smiled. "Okay."

"Something like what you tried to do inside the...van."

Rosalía sat up straighter and nodded. "I almost did it. Well, I know it wasn't exactly right. But you saw it, so it worked. Mostly."

"Yeah, I assumed that wasn't an accident." Lily took a deep breath. "Let's start with the light, then. This was one of my first spells too. And you can't hurt anyone with it, so—"

"That's why I tried to do some—" Rosalía thrust her hands out, then quickly retracted them and offered a sheepish smile. "Something that pushes, right? I want to do both of those, so I..." Her mouth hung open when she noticed the woman's eyebrow raised in warning. "Sorry."

"We'll start with the light. Close your eyes. Now, imagine a tiny, tiny spark in the center of your palm." Romeo shifted in his chair and she turned to look at him.

He retrieved the plastic bag of wolfsbane flowers, opened it, and leaned forward to whisper, "I'm only trying to stay ahead of the game, here. Is it weird that this kinda feels like eating popcorn at a movie?"

Their faces were so close together, she only had to lean toward him less than an inch to press her nose against his. "Yep. Very weird." She smirked, then focused on her newly acquired apprentice. "Only a spark, Rosalía."

ELEVEN

Two hours later, the girl had reached the point of summoning an orb of light the size of an apple and raising it out of her hand, but that was as far as she got. Every time the light left her palm, it hovered in the air for three seconds at the most before it winked out. The last time it happened, Rosalía growled in frustration and blinked heavy eyelids.

"You know, I think that's enough for tonight."

"No!" She straightened again where she sat and shook her head. "No, I want to do more. I can."

"I know you can." Lily tilted her head and fixed her with a firm look. "But it's late and you're not gonna be able to focus the way you need to if you're this tired."

"I'm not. I can stay up."

Romeo forced a cough and she knew it was because he tried not to laugh.

"But you won't," she said. "We're done for now. You can practice again in the morning."

Rosalía clenched her eyes shut with a fierce frown but she didn't say anything else.

Yeah, I know exactly what you feel right now, kid. And I suddenly have a whole new appreciation for the way Mom trained me. She leaned forward and rubbed the girl's arm gently. "You did a great job."

"I didn't do anything."

"Well, you can choose to believe that if you want to. Or you can choose to believe that I won't lie to you." That caught her apprentice witch's attention and the girl stared at her through bleary eyes and looked ten times more exhausted than she had thirty seconds before. "I can make you that promise, at least. If you're really not getting something, I won't tell you 'good job' simply so it doesn't hurt your feelings."

"You promise?"

"Absolutely."

Rosalía gave her a tired smile and heaved a massive sigh from her tiny chest. "Okay. Maybe I am a little tired."

Romeo laughed softly and stood from the armchair. "It's probably time for everyone to go to bed, right?"

Lily nodded. "Hey, I found those blankets."

He frowned at her. "What blankets."

"The ones I was looking for the first night you...stayed in the Winnie. When you slept on the couch." She tried not to look at Rosalía, because now it seemed a little awkward talking about where everyone was sleeping in front of a kid.

"Oh...right. First night on the road. When we stopped to camp in Pennsylvania, right?"

"I think so." She pushed from the floor and tucked her hair behind her ears. "I'm gonna go get those." Nodding, she glanced at the girl and stepped down the hall toward the tiny box of a room barely wide enough to fit a stacked washer and dryer. Even on her tiptoes and propped against the dryer, she couldn't quite reach the extra folded sheets and blankets on the top shelf. With a sigh, she flicked her fingers toward herself and the blankets tumbled into her arms. "Okay, we can probably—oh."

Out of all the things that hadn't woken him—Romeo sneezing, Rosalía screaming in panic about him eating the wolfsbane, the laughter and constant conversation right in front of him—the kid had apparently chosen now as the best time to stir from his heavy sleep on the couch and head to the bathroom. She narrowly avoided bowling him over as he slipped into the bathroom, his eyes still mostly closed, and slid the door shut behind him.

"Well, I was gonna say we can simply put some blankets on the couch as it is, but now might be a good time to pull out the bed. Right?"

Romeo shrugged. "Sure."

Rosalía helped them haul all the cushions off the couch and stack them neatly on the floor behind the driver's seat. Lily pulled out the mattress on its retractable frame, and Romeo covered it with sheets and a thin blanket. The minute the pull-out bed was made, Filipe stepped out of the bathroom.

"Oh. I...don't think I have any extra pillows. But there's a—"

The boy walked past her, his skinny arms dangling by

his sides and almost swallowed by the huge gray t-shirt. He climbed onto the bed, wiggled under the covers, turned away from them, and fell asleep.

"We don't need any pillow." Rosalía smiled and shook her head. "That bed looks really comfortable." She bit her lip and glanced from one adult to the other. "Thank you."

"Absolutely."

"Yeah, no problem." Romeo scratched his head. "I'm... gonna open the windows." He moved through the RV to do that and squeezed past Lily in what little room was left between the end of the pull-out bed and the spinning armchair.

"I guess, if you need anything..." She glanced around. *It's not like I need to give them a tour.* "Help yourself, okay? Bathroom. Water. Food, even. Whatever."

"Okay." The girl had slipped her legs under the sheets beside her twin brother and sat there, smiling at the witch and the werewolf who'd saved them from being delivered to Oaxaca and who knew what else. "Goodnight."

"'Night, kid." Romeo winked at her and shuffled past Lily again, putting his hands briefly on her shoulders.

"Goodnight." Lily smiled and followed him into the bedroom.

"Oh, wait."

"Yeah?"

Rosalía leaned forward over the blankets in her lap and took a deep breath. "I only wanted to say...I'm glad you found us." She nodded curtly at them, which was an oddly adult thing to do in that moment.

Lily's stomach tied itself into a small, hard knot. "So

are we." She flipped off the lights in the short hallway and stepped into the back. Romeo waited for her inside the bedroom door, propped with both arms against the door-frame. He stepped aside to let her in, then quietly slid the door closed. With a huge sigh, she turned beside the bed and let herself fall back onto the mattress. "Oh, man," she whispered.

"I know." He stepped out of his sneakers and walked around the bed before he fell backward onto it in the same way.

She giggled when it bounced beneath his weight and turned her head to see his face upside down next to hers. Then, her smile faded. "You know, out of all the things we've gone through on this trip, I think today was the hardest."

"Yeah." His gaze roamed over her face. "But we got them out of there. And tomorrow, they'll be back home with their family again."

"I can't even imagine." She closed her eyes briefly. "Is there anyone we can call?"

"Rosalía said it's like an hour-and-a-half walk from her village to the nearest phone. And she hasn't been there and doesn't know a number to call anyway. I don't think she's actually used a phone before."

"Well, she knows enough about them to destroy one." She sighed again and dragged her hands down the sides of her face. "And she obviously doesn't want anyone to feel sorry for her, which I totally understand. That's the hardest part, I think. Trying to act like everything's okay when it clearly isn't. They were kidnapped. To be sold."

"I know."

"Like where's the middle ground between making sure those kids know that what happened to them wasn't their fault and wasn't okay and not traumatizing them any more than they already are?" She frowned and turned her head again to look at him.

"Well, I'm very sure we made it perfectly clear that it wasn't their fault or okay. Two strangers found them in a van, roughed up their kidnappers, and left those assholes zip-tied and unconscious without phones or keys. Who knows how long it would've taken the cops to get there, ask all their questions, and take the kids in. That aside, they could be sleeping in a holding cell right now and probably without anyone willing to head out with them first thing tomorrow morning to take them home. And most likely without the most powerful witch they've ever seen sticking around to teach them a few extra spells."

Lily's laugh felt bitter. "I totally agree with you on all those points. Minus me being the most powerful witch." He smiled and ran his fingers through her hair. "I was talking about how we handled it after that, though. For the most part, everything felt so...normal, I guess. Giving them dry clothes and making dinner and sitting around—even laughing at random things." She sighed. "It feels... I dunno. Are we doing this wrong?"

Romeo chuckled softly and shook his head. "I think the only wrong way to rescue someone is to not rescue them at all, Lil. And kids are tough. If anyone knows that, we do, right?" She rolled her eyes but nodded. "What they need is food, a place to sleep, someone who can keep them safe, and to get home to their parents. We're checking all the boxes."

"It doesn't feel like enough."

"Yeah. It probably won't."

She studied his green eyes, which still seemed to glow under the two small lights in the alcove behind the bed. "That's what I mean. What makes it so hard, though, is there's no...way to fix it."

He looked a little thoughtful, then sucked in a breath and sat up on the bed, straightened his legs, and patted them. "Come here."

"What?"

"Come on."

Lily sat slowly with a skeptical smile, and with an exaggerated swoop of his hands, he gestured to his lap again. She rolled over, pushed herself up, and crawled into his lap to loop her legs around his waist.

He laced his fingers at the small of her back and met her gaze. "You can find solutions and fix almost anything. And if it doesn't work the first time, you keep one-upping yourself to be better. To be the best, right? Do it the best way." She simply stared at him, wondering where this was going, and draped her arms over his shoulders. "With some things, though—like what happened to those kids—the best anyone can ever do is to make it better. When someone's not actually broken, there's nothing to fix so better is all we have."

She wrinkled her nose. "Yeah, I have a really hard time with good enough."

"I know you do."

"I thought about making them forget the whole thing with a mind-wipe. Then they wouldn't have to live the rest of their lives with trying to block out the last...however many days."

At that, he shook his head firmly. "And they'd live the rest of their lives not remembering anything about the people who cared enough about them to do something about it." He smirked. "Honestly, they'd probably be terrified of us if they woke up in this RV with the two of us, hours away from their village, wondering why the heck their parents were smiling and totally cool with us when we take them back."

Lily grimaced a little sheepishly. "I guess I didn't think that one through all the way."

"Yeah." His fingers slipped under the bottom of her tank top.

"It's a good thing I was too busy with a new apprentice to think about it."

"Yeah." He slid his hands up her back and unhooked her bra.

"You probably would've stopped me, anyway."

He nodded, pulled her closer, and pressed his lips to her neck. She sighed and ran her fingers through his curls.

"You know, she's actually incredibly talented. It took me at least a month to learn how to summon that light and command it the way I wanted to. I bet she'll get it in—" He pressed his forehead into her shoulder and began to laugh. "What?"

When he looked at her, he grinned and raised his

eyebrows. "Can we stop talking about the kids on the couch? And magic? For at least a little while."

"Sorry." She grinned and bit her lip. "Yeah. No more talking."

"Thank you." He started another line of kisses under her collarbone, and she pulled his face toward her to kiss him. She gasped when he tightened his arm around her and rolled over with her still in his lap. In the next moment, she was on her back and his lips trailed down her neck to the collar of her tank top. He jerked the hem of her shirt up and slid down the bed to continue the kisses down her ribs, past her belly button and lower.

The bedroom door slid open with a rumble and banged against the end of the sliding track. Romeo leapt off her with a sharp breath, and Lily lurched onto one hand while the other summoned a burst of flames—literally the only thing that came to mind. The flare of light revealed a very small form in the doorway.

"Filipe?"

The boy stood there and stared at them with half-closed eyes. "*La cama es demasiado mullida.*" He shuffled forward into the bedroom, lowered himself onto his knees, and curled in a ball on the floor at the foot of the bed.

Romeo uttered a surprised chuckle. "He speaks."

"What's going on?" she whispered.

He propped himself up with both hands on the bed behind him and turned to look at her. "Apparently, the pull-out bed's too soft."

"Too—" She snorted and managed to choke down

anything louder than that. "So we're gonna let him sleep on the floor?"

"Well, we're making it better, right?" He sniggered and pulled his shirt over his head before he dropped it gently on the other side of the bed. "I don't know how many times I'll actually get to say this..." He scooted back until he could lift the covers and slide under them. "But now it's kind of a good thing you were talking so much."

Her mouth dropped open and he flinched away when she slapped playfully at his feet beneath the blankets. He hissed out a laugh, and she crawled up toward the head of the bed before she snapped her bra quickly back in place. She straightened her tank top and crawled under the covers with him. "And I don't know how many times that'll actually be funny."

"Oh, I'm kidding." He raised his arm over the pillows so she could snuggle into him and lay her head on his chest. With his lips pressed against the top of her head, he chuckled again. "I guess if anything's gonna sway someone's decision about having kids, it would be this."

"Yeah, it's a very effective deterrent." She poked him in the ribs and he jerked away with a muffled laugh before he drew her against him again. "As long as he doesn't crawl up onto the bed in the middle of the night. I don't handle surprise wakeups very well."

"Oh, I know."

TWELVE

Lily woke to the sound of two people snoring in her bedroom and it took her a minute to remember Filipe's late-night sleepwalking appearance. Now that the heavy shush of the rain had faded with the storm, the snoring might have been what woke her up. She tossed the covers aside and crawled to the edge of the bed to see the boy still curled on the floor. *Yep. Definitely snoring.*

Quietly, she inched off the side of the bed and walked out into the short hall. Before she reached the bathroom, she noticed Rosalía seated on the pull-out mattress and reading a book balanced on her lap. "Oh." She stopped. "Morning."

"Hi." The girl didn't look up from the open pages in front of her.

"What are you reading?" It was a normal, simple question and it didn't even occur to her that of course, the girl wouldn't have brought her own book with her.

"Your magic book."

"My—" She, spun frantically and stared at the open duffel bag on the floor beside the bed. Her mom's grimoire no longer sat on top of the pile. "Rosalía!" She whirled and ran toward the girl on the pull-out mattress. "Stop. You should not be reading—" Finally, the girl looked up at her with wide eyes. Lily dropped onto the mattress in front of her and took the grimoire as quickly as she could without snatching it out of the girl's hands. She closed the book and pressed her hand on the cover—as if that would draw all the information out of Rosalía's head and back into the pages—and studied the girl's confused frown. "This book is way too dangerous. Especially for witches who haven't covered the basics of this kind of magic."

Rosalía blinked. "I was only reading. I didn't even try any of the spells."

Lily lowered her chin and held the girl's gaze. "Can you honestly tell me, without bending the truth at all, that you won't remember a single thing you've seen in here?" The child pressed her lips together but didn't say a word. *Yeah, I used to plead the fifth all the time too. And I bet her memory's as good as mine.* She sighed and tried another tactic. "You know, until I was eighteen, I couldn't even touch this book."

The disappointment in the girl's eyes wasn't aimed at herself but at Lily. "Because someone else told you not to."

She snorted and shook her head. "No. Because every time I tried, it literally shocked me." Rosalía frowned and cocked her head. "Like a lightning bolt. This book hurled me across my mom's room more times than I can count. She even tried to hide it in the kitchen cabinets once to keep me from hurting myself." She lifted the back of her tank top and pulled down the top of her leggings on the right side to reveal a small, roundish scar. After five years, it was almost the same color as the rest of her lower back but still had the telltale sheen of burned and healed flesh. "I landed on the stove and almost covered myself in boiling water."

"Hmm." Rosalía glanced at the book in the older witch's protective hands, then shrugged. "Maybe you weren't ready."

"I wasn't—" Her eyes widened and she shook her head. *I'm clearly not getting through to her.* "No, I was as ready as you are right now. Which is why my mom kept a ward on this book to make sure I couldn't open it because nothing was going to stop me from trying to read it. Even if I hurt myself." She studied the girl and hoped at least some of this would sink in. "Look, I couldn't open this book until my mom knew I was actually ready for the stuff in here. She was my teacher. I'm yours, at least for a little while, and I'm telling you that you're not ready for it right now."

The girl swallowed, then met Lily's gaze again. "I know how to make it better."

"Make what better?"

"The magic you did yesterday." Rosalía pressed a finger to the center of her forehead, then her lips. "So you can hear everyone and everyone can hear you."

"Oh." She tried to still her racing thoughts and glanced at mom's grimoire in her lap. *The student teaches. And now, I feel like an idiot.* "What did you find?"

"The..." The child closed her eyes and frowned,

searching through the information she now proved was stored away in her head. "*Patefacio.* Put it with the spells you did yesterday. Then you won't have to touch everyone." She grinned and poked her finger in a line through the air. "Everyone in my village always wants to talk."

"Right." Lily slid her hand over the hard, worn darkpurple cover of the book and nodded. *She means when we take them home. I'll have to check that.* "Rosalía, I need you to promise me that you won't try any of the spells you read —wait. You understood the spells in here?"

The girl shrugged and nodded. "I think your magic works for books."

"I guess so."

They sat on the bed for a while longer and she felt oneupped by a tiny, skinny witch with a powerful command over the cycle of life—or at least of plants. Her student, however, felt sufficiently scolded by her new teacher yet still wholly unsatisfied.

"Can we practice more?" the girl asked.

"Um…" She glanced down the hall and into her bedroom. "Yeah. While they're still asleep. But when they wake up, we're gonna stop, eat something, and probably get back on the road again."

"Okay." A tiny smile crept across Rosalía's lips.

"Okay." Lily stood with the book and set it far back on the counter against the wall. *Not that she can't reach it but at least she'll know I'm not being careless with it. I might actually have to hide this thing later.*

When she returned to the bed, Rosalía sat straight, her

open palm resting in her lap as she waited. "Ready," she said without being prompted.

She flashed her a quick smile, then nodded. "Okay. Let's see what you got."

When the girl managed to conjure the ball of light in her hand, raise it half a foot above her hand, and intentionally snuff it out again three times in a row, she decided her student had a good enough handle on it. "Good. You can practice that on your own. That light will do whatever you want it to, eventually, so keep playing with it to learn what that is."

"Will it hurt someone?"

She frowned. "Not unless you make it really bright and throw it in someone's face."

Rosalía shook her head. "That's not what I want. I want to hurt people."

Swallowing thickly, Lily took a deep breath. *This is gonna be a tricky one to navigate.* "Why do you want to hurt people?"

The girl raised her eyebrows and leaned forward. "So people doing bad things will stop."

"You're talking about protecting yourself, right? And your brother? Your family?"

"Everyone."

"Right." The older witch paused. "Well, not all defensive magic hurts people. That should always be a last resort. Do you understand?"

"But what if you already know that nothing else will work?"

"That doesn't matter. If you're gonna learn any offensive magic at all—"

"What's that?"

"Attacks. Magic that hurts people."

Rosalía nodded.

"If you're gonna learn any of that, you have to learn how to defend yourself first. You must learn how to use every other option before you hurt people to make them stop."

"Like when you made it so that woman couldn't move."

She smiled. *Finally.* "Yep. Exactly like that. I didn't hurt her first. I didn't hurt her at all, right? It's so, so important to know how to handle a dangerous situation without hurting anyone first."

The child's eyes darkened beneath a frown and she stared at the bed between them. "You should've hurt her."

I'm not even gonna touch that one. "So I'm gonna teach you how to cast an illusion charm, okay? It's one of my favorites."

The girl closed her eyes in disappointment before she raised her shoulders and lowered them with a sigh. "Okay."

THEY HAD a little under an hour of practice time for a tiny version of the illusion charm Lily had cast around Melissa Bore's burned-down house in Colorado. Then Romeo rolled out of bed and stumbled into the bathroom the same way Filipe had stumbled into the bedroom. The minute he closed the door, Lily and Rosalía exchanged a glance and the girl rolled her eyes. "Take a break."

"Yep." She patted the girl's knee and stood. "Time for breakfast." She stepped across the few feet into the kitchen to look through what they had to feed four people again instead of only two.

The werewolf stepped out of the bathroom, wearing only his shorts from the day before, and stopped. "*Buenos días,*" he muttered. Rosalía merely laughed. Lily turned to watch them as he said something else in quick Spanish and waved across the room. The girl slid off the bed, giggling, and they got to work stripping the sheets and putting the couch back together.

She glanced at her mom's grimoire on the counter. *Patefacio, huh? I kinda hate that I think she's right.*

With limited choices, she selected the half-dozen eggs, small four tortillas, and salsa they'd purchased at the store in Córdoba and decided those would make as good a breakfast as any. The minute she finished scrambling the eggs, Filipe rose from the bedroom floor like a bear stirring from hibernation before he shuffled into the kitchen. He stopped in the bathroom first, slipped into the booth at the tiny kitchen table, and sat there with his hand in his lap and stared at the table.

"Perfect timing." Lily smiled at him but he didn't seem to hear anything.

"Filipe, stop being so rude!" Rosalía leaned forward where she sat with Romeo on the couch—he'd been showing her the GPS map on his phone and the route they'd be driving to get the kids home—and gestured toward Lily. "You should at least look at her when she talks to you."

His head barely moved side to side in a poor attempt at shaking his head. "*No mames, guey*," he muttered.

"Woah." Romeo glanced at Lily with wide eyes.

Rosalía's mouth dropped open. "What? You're crazy!" The boy shrugged.

"Um..." Lily glanced from the boy to his furious sister. "Okay, breakfast is ready. You guys can help yourselves. I'll be right back." She turned off the burner beneath the egg pan and retrieved her mom's spellbook before she hurried into the bedroom and closed the door behind her.

It took her thirty seconds to find the *Patefacio* spell and less than half that time to realize that Rosalía had been completely right about how much it would improve her magical translator. With a sigh, she closed the grimoire again and gazed around her room for somewhere to hide it. "Maybe I should put a bookshelf in here. With locking cabinets." Without any better ideas, she dropped to the floor and shoved the spellbook as far under the bed and she could. She zipped the duffel bag and slid that in place too. "If these kids are gonna be with us for more than a few hours, yeah, I'd probably spend some time on wards." She stood and shook her head. "I don't know how my mom put up with me like that."

With a deep breath, she shook her hands out and repeated the series of mixed spells she'd used with Rosalía the night before and slipped the *Patefacio* in there before the illusion-reversal. This time, casting the spells only on herself, she didn't need the water to help focus the target.

The pink light spread between her hands, grew, and flashed brightly to fill the bedroom in a wave that seeped through the door and out into the rest of the Winnie.

"Uh, is everything okay in there?" Romeo called from the kitchen.

"Yep!"

"Oh, I know what she's doing," Rosalía added.

Lily took the opportunity to change into a fresh tank top and navy Chinos shorts before she opened the door into the hall. "All good." From where he stood in front of the stove, he stared at her and her student flashed her a wide grin. She pointed at the girl. "Don't say anything."

"Okay..." Romeo glanced at Rosalía beside him. "What was she up to in there?" The girl merely shot him a sideways glance and smiled at Lily. "All right. I know she can understand you, so I'll ask you questions, yeah? You can answer yes or no."

"That's probably not a good idea."

Lily folded her arms and leaned against the narrow strip of wall between the laundry closet and the bathroom.

"Nah, it's fine." Romeo turned to the pan of eggs like the conversation wasn't even happening. "Obviously, it was a spell. Pink. Another illusion-thingy?" Rosalía didn't say a word, and Lily raised an eyebrow at her before she stared at the back of Romeo's head as he served the small amount of scrambled eggs into four tortillas. "I'll take your silence as a no." He shrugged. "Okay. Some kind of protection spell, then? No? Yeah, she would've told me if we needed one of those. Wait, did it have anything to do with me?"

"Well, it does now."

He startled a little at Lily's statement and eggs plopped out of the hovering serving spoon in his hand. "What?" He looked at her with a goofy smile.

She pursed her lips and gestured toward the girl. "At least when I ask Rosalía not to do something, she listens."

The spoon clinked into the pan and he turned to lean back against the edge of the stove. He looked at Rosalía, then Lily. "I was speaking Spanish, right?"

"Yep."

"Which you don't understand unless it's Rosalía."

Her grin was wide. "Until about two minutes ago, yeah."

"You... I only..." He sucked in a sharp breath. "Oh..." He turned a mock frown onto the small witch beside him. "Thanks for the heads-up."

Rosalía burst into laughter and took two plates of eggs in tortillas from the counter. With a shrug, she turned toward the kitchen table. "My teacher told me not to say anything."

Romeo narrowed his eyes at her as she set the plates on the table and moved across the kitchen again for the plastic container of fresh salsa—diced tomatoes, green chili peppers, onions, garlic, and cilantro stirred together without any of the sauce. "Yeah," he muttered as she crossed in front of him one more time. "I bet that's the only time in your life you've ever done what someone else told you to." The girl grinned but didn't look at him again.

"You're all crazy," Filipe murmured, his hand already stretching for the salsa.

His sister smacked his hand away, which was the only thing that made him look at her. "I'll eat all your food if you can't be nice." They glared at each other before he grasped the container and tipped a huge pile of it onto his eggs.

"Okay." Romeo turned to Lily again with a sheepish smile and spread his arms. "You got me, Lil. Sorry."

"You know I would've told you what the spell was if you'd asked, right?"

"Yeah, I know that."

"I always tell you."

He sighed, gave her a smaller, more serious smile, and stepped toward her. His expression a little sheepish, he put both hands gently on her shoulders and nodded. "You do."

"And if I don't tell you something right away, there's a reason for it." She maintained her slightly challenging look.

"Yeah. I know, Lily. I was only messin' around. And honestly"—he glanced over his shoulder at the kids and lowered his voice, even though they didn't speak a word of English—"I was only trying to make things seem normal. Like what we talked about last night, you know? Making it all...a little better. I guess talking to them in Spanish feels like part of that." She opened her mouth to speak but he beat her to it. "I know. I didn't exactly choose the best topic of conversation."

Lily snorted. "Not exactly, no."

"I'm sorry." He studied her eyes until she finally caved in with a smirk.

"Lucky for you, I'm better at casting spells than I am at holding a grudge."

He grinned. "And that's why I—" His mouth hung open for a second too long before he finished. "Am constantly impressed by your magic and...your ability to put up with me."

She laughed and looked away. *He was definitely about to say something else.* "Well, good."

With a gentle hand, he cupped her cheek and turned her face toward him. "Is everything okay?"

"Yeah. I'll explain it to you later, okay?" She gestured toward the table and held his gaze, hoping he picked up on the fact that she didn't want Rosalía to hear. *I can't talk about her when she can hear everything.*

Romeo nodded and mouthed, 'Rosalía?'

She merely smiled.

"Okay." He pulled her toward him and wrapped his arms around her shoulders. "Thanks for makin' eggs. Are you hungry?"

Lily hugged him around the waist and leaned back to look at him. "Yeah, I could eat."

They cleaned up after breakfast and prepared to travel again. According to Rosalía—and as much as Romeo could confirm of it—the kids' village was about half an hour away from Plan de Ayutla, though it didn't show up on his GPS. "Five-hour drive, here we come." He slid into the driver's seat and started the engine.

Lily gave Rosalía a big smile as she walked toward the passenger seat. Filipe had returned to the corner of the couch, where he'd curled up again and apparently fell back to sleep after eating. His sister leaned against the other corner, her thin legs stretching almost far enough to touch Filipe, and practiced the illusion-reversal she had been taught. The girl glanced quickly from the faint pink glow that appeared less than an inch between her palms and smiled in return, but her attention went quickly back to her spell.

"Do you want me to drive?" she asked.

"No, I got this. I think it takes considerable brainpower

and even more patience with that one to spend hours on teaching simple spells. They are simple, right?"

She smirked. "Yeah. I wouldn't allow anything else." *Jeeze, I have to talk in riddles simply to keep her from knowing what I'm talking about.*

"You think she's still listening, don't you?"

"You know, I do like it when you can almost read my mind."

He laughed and steered them back onto the narrow dirt road leading to Highway 307. "So do I. You know, it's been a while since I've played a good guessing game."

Lily stared at him. "Are you talking about the same game you didn't think I could understand?"

"The one that got me in trouble?" He looked at her and wiggled his eyebrows. "Yep. We know she can't understand me."

"That might change soon." She resisted the urge to turn and watch Rosalía again.

"Woah. Do you think she's that good?"

She nodded. "Yeah. And it keeps getting proven."

He sniggered. "This is fun. I dunno if it's harder for me to think of the right questions or for you to come up with super-vague, completely useless answers out of context."

"Hurray." She said it so flatly, it made them both laugh.

"Okay. So you came up with a new part of the translator spell."

"Which needs a much better name."

"True. How'd you work that out?"

She stared at him. "Take a wild guess."

"Wow, really? She did?"

"Yep."

Romeo's mouth turned down out the corners and he tilted his head in admiration. "I'm surprised and not surprised at the same time. How'd she even come up with the idea?"

If I just say book or reading, that kid's gonna know exactly what kind of conversation this is. She wrinkled her nose and stared out the passenger window. "From one of your tools."

"Huh?" He glanced quickly at her, then back at the road. "I don't have any—oh." A chuckle escaped him. "Look at us. Solving a puzzle together. That we made."

"It's great that you're so easily entertained."

"Ha! Okay. She found a book in your duffel bag. A magical book?"

"Ding, ding, ding."

"Hmm. I assume she wasn't supposed to."

Lily smoothed the hair back from her forehead and pursed her lips. "And neither was I. For a long time."

"Did you, though?"

"Not until legal adulthood."

"How come?"

She frowned as she tried to come up with a vague answer for that one. "It had very specific...deterrents at the time."

"Oh, it was one of your mom's books."

She turned to stare at him. "How'd you get that out of what I said?"

"Lily, I'm very sure Greta was the only person in your life who's been able to keep you from doing whatever you wanted." He laughed at her darkening frown. "I mean that in a good way. No one can stop you when you really want something. Except for your mom."

"Wow." She smirked. "It's a good thing this game isn't about trying to stump each other. Apparently, you know me too well."

"No." He sent her a glance laced with something she couldn't put her finger on. "There's no such thing." A short silence followed while he drummed his fingers on the steering wheel. "So this little witch sittin' back there on the couch got through the wards or whatever that you weren't able to crack until you were eighteen. And she read the book."

"Uh...it didn't—"

"Oh, wait. Is that what's bothering you? You think she's smarter now than you were at that age?"

"No. You didn't let me finish."

Romeo laughed. "Right. Sorry. Please continue."

She smirked at him. "Those deterrents fell away three years ago, right? They weren't in place for this...most recent instance." The odd way she had to say that made her laugh at herself. "Yeah, I know. That sounded really weird. But you know what I mean."

"Right. Got it. So it was already much easier for her."

"Yep." Lily nodded and looked out the window. *Did he actually nail that on the head? She might be smarter than me, but am I really bothered by that?*

"So what was goin' on with you earlier?" His brows flickered together when he looked quickly at her again. "I know something was bothering you. I could see it. If you were worried about her being a better witch than you or something, I'd simply tell you that was almost impossible. Even if she got through your mom's wards, which didn't happen. So..." He shrugged. "I think I'm stumped now."

"Yeah, this one's harder." She took a deep breath and really had to think about exactly why another knot currently tightened in the pit of her stomach. "I heard something."

"From her?"

"Yeah."

"That's what's bothering you?"

"I think so."

Romeo pressed his lips together. "Did she try to get you to teach her powerful spells again this morning?"

"Bingo."

"And you don't like it that she keeps pushing."

Lily dropped her head back against the headrest and puffed out a sigh. "Nope. This is the most ridiculous conversation we've ever had. We should simply put this on hold until things have cleared a little." She nodded toward the back of the RV again, then glanced in the rearview mirror above the passenger seat. The reflection there showed Rosalía sitting cross-legged with closed eyes on the couch, her head against the back cushion and her hands resting limply at her sides. *She's either really concentrating on some magic, or she fell asleep. I'm still not gonna take the chance.*

"Yeah, okay." Romeo flexed his fingers on the steering wheel and adjusted his grip.

They moved down the slightly winding highway, over

hills studded with trees much taller this far south and entirely tropical plants. After a while, they began to climb significantly in elevation and the trees around them looked more like a jungle as the Winnie struggled up and down on the bumpy roads.

"Do you want any music?" he asked.

She leaned her head against the seat and shrugged. "Sure. Play whatever you want." *I should be talking to him right now 'cause I think I'm starting to worry about what we're driving into.*

"Lily?"

"Yeah."

He fumbled in her purse on the center console without taking his attention off the road and finally found her phone and held it out to her. "Whatever's going on in your head, it's obviously messing with you. We don't have to talk about it. But you can at least write it down so I don't have to sit here wondering what I can do to help."

Lily scowled at the device but took it reluctantly. "I don't know what you can do to help."

"Well, usually, all it takes is me saying a few encouraging things to remind you of whatever you've forgotten, and it ends up working itself out."

She laughed. "Maybe you should be a psychologist."

"What? No way. You gotta go to college for that. Right now, I wanna be...well, I simply wanna help you."

"Which is also something you're really good at." They smiled at each other, but it was a little awkward without actually being able to discuss what was going on. She unlocked her phone and typed a text message out with no receiving number because she wasn't going to send it to anyone.

'*She told me she wanted to learn spells that hurt people to make people stop doing bad things. Now, I can't help wondering how many spells she read in that book and how much she will remember. She won't have anyone to teach her how to use them the right way once we take these kids home. If she tries to use seriously powerful offensive magic on her own, so many things could go wrong and we don't have the time to stick around so I can teach her. We have to keep looking for my mom.*'

She read through the message again and considered it carefully. It would've made a really long text. *I didn't know I could dump that all out in so few words.* She held her phone out again for him, and he took it slowly from her. His gaze flickered up and down between the screen and the road. "Do you wanna pull over for that?"

"Nope. I'm good."

While his driving didn't seem to be affected, she watched the road with him just in case. After a few minutes, he set her phone in her purse and sighed. Lily watched his profile and waited for the encouraging reminder of whatever she'd forgotten.

"Thanks for doing that," he said finally.

"Yeah, well, I'll ignore the fact that it feels exactly like passing notes in fourth grade."

Romeo laughed. "Your writing's definitely improved."

She rolled her eyes and looked out across the sprawling green landscape of hills and blue sky and lush, green forests. "Okay..."

"So, this might be a first for me, Lil, but I don't think I have anything to say that's gonna make you feel any better right now."

"Honestly, that's fine. I didn't expect you to." She nodded slowly. "I should've paid more attention to where I put my stuff and how to...keep everything safe." When she looked into the rearview mirror again, Rosalía hadn't moved from her position. *Maybe she did fall asleep.* "If anything happens and someone gets hurt, at least we'll both know who to blame."

"What?" He startled like he'd woken abruptly and shook his head. "That's not what I was gonna say. Like, at all."

"It's not?"

"No. Lily, this isn't..." He licked his lips and frowned at the highway. "This isn't about blaming someone or failing or guilt-tripping yourself. I wouldn't ever say anything like that to you anyway."

"No, I know that." Her cheeks flared with heat. "I know you wouldn't say that. But if you did, I'd totally get it 'cause that's what I'm already thinking."

"Well, stop it." His playful chuckle died when he looked at her again and saw her tightly pressed lips and the slight flush in her cheeks. "Oh, man. Hey, when I said I couldn't tell you anything to make you feel better, I didn't mean I literally had nothing to say. Or that I think you should punish yourself for...I dunno. Feeling like you failed to keep other people from endangering themselves?" He set the back of his hand on the center console and wiggled his fingers.

"Okay, I admit that I'm totally confused right now."

"Lily." He looked at her and held her gaze. "I won't look at the road until you take my hand."

"Don't do that." She darted a pointed glance at the road. "Focus on driving, please."

"I'm serious."

"Romeo."

He widened his eyes.

"Oh, my God." She slapped her hand into his, and he turned his focus to the highway to correct his blind driving, thankfully before another bend ahead. "Talk about failing to keep people out of danger."

"That's not what I said." He laced their fingers together and squeezed her hand. "I said failing to keep other people from endangering themselves. That's the part of this I know you won't like, okay? 'Cause it's one more thing you can't fix."

She took a deep breath. "Yeah, that doesn't make me feel any better."

He smirked and it slid into a sigh. "Okay, but hear me out. It might take a while, but eventually, it could make you feel better. Are you ready?"

"Oh, come on." She uttered a wry huff of a laugh. "Yeah, I'm ready."

"You aren't responsible for what anyone else does or doesn't do."

"Yeah, but I—"

"Wait. Hold on a sec." He squeezed her hand again. "I know you. And now I know about the conversation you guys had this morning. I can't imagine any other scenario where you didn't stop her right there and explain to her why it's a really bad idea to barge in, guns blazing, without even knowing how to hold or load or shoot a gun. Right?"

"Essentially. Without all the firearms."

"Right. And I know you explained it in a way that she understands because I watched you explain everything else when you guys were doing that ball-of-light thing last night." She snorted, which made him smile. "But seriously. Yeah, it's not ideal that she snagged one of your mom's magical books and started filing away all the stuff in there that even I don't think a kid her age should know."

"Which is why I feel so horrible."

"No, I meant that only as in I trust your mom's judgment."

Lily leaned her head back against the seat again. "Yeah, she knows what she's doing. I understand that much more now, too."

"I'm sure that's how it's supposed to work. It'd be creepy if we appreciated our parents like that from the beginning." She had to laugh at that and he merely shook his head. "Back to my point. You told her what she needs to know and in exactly the way she needed to hear it. Obviously, she's smart enough to put two and two together when the most powerful witch she's ever seen tells her she's not ready to use the things she wasn't supposed to see. Lily, whatever she does after that is on her. It's one thing if you chose not to warn her, but you didn't. Now, it's up to her. Whatever choice she makes on her own and whatever happens because of it is only on her. Ever. Not you. You can't fix other people's choices."

"Romeo—"

"I dunno. Maybe you think that sounds lazy or like you're dumping your responsibility and washing your hands clean. But it doesn't mean you don't have a conscience."

"Okay—"

"I only wanna make sure you know that you're not responsible for everyone around you who makes bad choices. That's way too much—"

"Hey."

He turned to look at her with wide eyes. "Yeah?"

This time, she squeezed his hand and smiled. "You're rambling and I only wanted to say thank you."

Romeo opened his mouth to reply, then closed it again.

"You're totally right. No, it doesn't really make me feel better, and yeah, I have issues with sending the ball off into someone else's court. But I know you're right so that was exactly what I needed to hear."

"Good." Another few minutes passed in silence before he snorted. "I was rambling?"

"A little, yeah." She wiggled their joined hands. "But it was cute so you get points for that."

FOURTEEN

"Hey, Rosalía." Romeo glanced into the rearview mirror as the girl opened her eyes and straightened on the couch to look at him. "We're about five minutes from Plan de Ayutla."

She grinned. "Really?"

"Yeah. I'm gonna need your help to get the rest of the way after that. Do you think you can give me directions?"

"Definitely."

He patted the center console. "Awesome. But be careful coming up here, all right?"

The girl glanced at her still-sleeping brother and slipped off the couch. Lily laughed when she ducked into a low crouch and waddled toward the front seats. She squatted behind the center console and looked with wide eyes through the windshield at the buildings rising up ahead. "It's really easy."

"I like easy."

Needless to say, it wasn't easy at all. The truth was that

they wouldn't have been able to navigate the route to the village if someone had given them written instructions. Most of the roads in Plan de Ayutla didn't have street signs and they couldn't exactly be considered real streets, either.

The girl was a diligent navigator, however. "Oh, there! Turn left there."

"Where?"

"Right after that building."

"Kid, they all look the same."

"After the...one, two, three, fourth building on the left."

This was the way they made their way through Plan de Ayutla and out of it again toward her village. "This doesn't even look like a road," Lily said and clutched the armrests as the Winnie bumped and rocked over the exact opposite of a well-paved road.

"Okay, that bush with the orange flowers..." Rosalía jabbed her finger at the windshield. "You have to go around it and cut back to find the other road. There was a huge sinkhole here last year."

"Oh." The couple exchanged a glance. "That's fun."

The entire half-hour passed in this fashion while he followed impossible directions from a kid who knew exactly what she was talking about. Finally, the undergrowth and the thick vegetation began to thin a little and the Winnie rolled onto hard-packed dirt in front of dozens of buildings literally in the middle of the jungle. Most of them were not much more than boxes with only one room, or two at most, built with plain wooden slats and raised on stilts. Almost all had a platform on one side to act as a porch. Clotheslines held brightly colored belongings out to dry in the sun. A few doorways were covered with woven curtains in the same bright colors, which also matched the brilliant hues in the baskets of fruit on almost every porch, some resting higher on added shelving but most of them on the ground outside the door.

Rosalía squeaked and leapt out of her crouch. "We're home!" She ran to her twin on the couch and almost jumped on top of him. "Wake up. Hey, we're home. Filipe!"

The boy sucked in a breath and jerked awake. He shoved his sister off him with surprising force and she bounced across the couch. Rosalía laughed and pounced on him again. They shoved and kicked and jostled each other onto the floor before they scrambled to their feet and rushed to the Winnie's side door.

The girl thumped against the door so hard, Lily thought it would split. She fumbled with the latch and managed to open it, Filipe pushed her off the last step, and they raced across the packed dirt toward the buildings. By the time they both thought to shout—and alert everyone to the fact that they'd returned—neither Lily nor Romeo could hear who it was who actually yelled at the tops of their lungs.

"Oh, boy." She blew out a long, slow breath.

"Yeah, that feels good." He smiled at her and nodded. "We should at least go say hello, right?"

"We kinda have to." She unbuckled her seatbelt and, for the first time since they'd left Charleston weeks before, left her purse and everything else inside the RV. *Somehow, it feels wrong to take anything with me.* He followed and they stepped slowly out of the Winnebago that looked so strange parked outside a village in the middle of the jungle.

Birds squawked all around them, mixed with the buzz and hum of what sounded like incredibly large insects. A woman's wail rang out from the center of the village, followed by laughter and numerous voices shouting, calling to each other, and spreading the news. The couple didn't have to worry about what to do next. Rosalía and Filipe appeared from between the buildings. Each of them held a woman's hand and dragged her along with them. She laughed and let them pull her, although they clearly would rather have been running although they moved at her more sedate speed. Tears fell from her eyes, and the trio was quickly followed by a tall, thin man who wore only shorts and jogged along behind them. The rest of the village poured out onto the packed earth toward the Winnebago, still lifting laughter and excited conversations into the air.

Lily smiled to see so much joy in so many faces as the twins stopped in front of her and Romeo. The woman pulled her hands free and opened her arms wide. "You!" She leapt toward Lily and wrapped her in a crushing hug. "Thank you. Thank you more than I could ever say." She pulled her closer by her shoulders and left a wet, smacking kiss on her cheek. Without missing a beat, she released her and turned to Romeo. "Thank you both. This is—" She barked out a laugh and wiped at the constant stream of tears on her reddened cheeks. The tall man joined them and extended his hand toward the werewolf. When he took it, he jerked him closer and wrapped both arms around him, although he didn't say anything. There were tears in his eyes too, and they finally started to fall when he reached for Lily's hand and pressed the back of it to his lips.

"Lily and Romeo," Rosalía said and raised her voice so everyone gathered around the newcomers could hear her.

"Call me Chalina," the woman said, clasped her hands in front of her chest, and beamed at the couple who stood before her. She gathered the twins closer and pressed them against her.

"Aluino." The man put his hand over his heart and nodded, his gaze intense as he looked at both of them. "You have no idea what it means to have our children home and safe."

"They're strong kids," Romeo said.

"With strong friends, eh?" Chalina uttered another loud, hearty laugh and rocked her children vigorously by the shoulders. Rosalía and Filipe exchanged perfectly mirrored grins.

"Come with us," Aluino said and waved the two strangers toward the village. "Please."

"Yes! Come eat. Let us celebrate what you've done for us." Weeping and laughing, Chalina turned and herded her children toward the cluster of houses.

The man smiled after her. "My wife and I want to thank you this way. Please." A few other villagers echoed the same sentiments and shouted and beckoned the newcomers with waving hands, uncontained grins, and ceaseless nods. Lily saw tears in almost every pair of eyes.

She looked at Romeo and they both nodded at the same time. "We'd love to."

"That's really generous of you."

Aluino waved them forward, then stepped aside and pressed a firm hand on Romeo's back. "It will never be enough to show how grateful we are. But it is something." The villagers crowded in around them now. All of them spoke at once and reached out to clap one or the other of them on the back or briefly touch their hands. When Romeo reached for Lily's hand, she grabbed his tightly and let the villagers usher them between the buildings and into their home.

FIFTEEN

They were led in what felt almost like a parade toward a large building in the center of the village. It rose much higher on stilts than any of the surrounding houses, complete with a series of wooden steps leading to the entrance. The villagers separated into three different groups. One gathered the baskets of fruit on almost every porch, one had a large cookfire blazing to life with remarkable speed, and the third ushered their honored guests up the wide wooden steps.

"It's cooler in here during the day," one man said with a nod and gestured toward the large entrance at the top of the stairs. "You'll be comfortable. And tonight, we can celebrate outside."

Lily smiled at him and glanced at Romeo. "Something tells me we're gonna be here for a while."

"Well, maybe all this is part of making it better too, right? It'd be pretty rude to leave early, right?"

"Yeah. I think it would."

Inside the giant building, they were led toward a large ring of woven mats around an empty metal dish. "Come. Sit with us." Aluino gestured to the mats, and they chose theirs next to each other. It was much cooler in the building than outside in the sun, where the treetops had been cleared away to allow sufficient space for the homes. The structure also didn't have a back wall, which allowed a pleasant breeze from the surrounding mountains into the large singular room but unfortunately didn't make it any less humid.

Lily wiped the sweat from her forehead and hoped this was as much of a royal treatment as they'd receive there. *I don't know if I could handle anything else.*

Chalina stood at the entrance, still wiping her eyes. "Go sit with your father," she told the twins and hugged them again. "I'll help Mali—"

"Stay." Her husband stretched out his hand from where he sat on the mats. The woman's small smile didn't conceal her hesitation. "Chalina, our children have been returned to us. If it were anyone else's children instead, you wouldn't resent that family for wanting to stay together. They understand. Come and sit."

With a little sigh, she released Rosalía and Filipe to sit on their own mats. The kids scrambled toward their father and their mother stepped gracefully forward to join them, lifting her bright-purple skirts, and lowered herself to the ground.

Aluino smiled at her, ran a hand down the back of her straight black hair, and turned toward their guests. "Any return of a child is cause for celebration. I would be as glad to see others come home again. We've had so many children taken from us, but this...this is the first time anyone has brought them back." The man beamed at his children and slid his long arm around Filipe's shoulders.

"I'm sorry?" Lily leaned forward over her crossed legs, shocked by what she'd heard.

"Rosalía and Filipe are not the first people to be taken from our village," he repeated.

"They were kidnapped," Romeo said.

"Yes." Chalina nodded gravely. "And eleven others in the last three months. We haven't found any of them. And we—" She stopped to lay a hand on Rosalía's knee beside her. "We assumed the same would happen with our children."

"Not only from our village." Her husband frowned. "Our neighbors on this mountain have also lost people. No one knows who is doing this or why. We cannot stop them. They come in the night. Or they find who they want in Plan de Ayutla and take them without anyone seeing their faces. Villages like ours have been safe for as long as any of us can remember but something is changing this."

"I'm so sorry," Lily said. "Rosalía told us a little of what your people can do. The type of witches you are. Are these kidnappings by—"

"Other witches?" Chalina raised her eyebrows. "Magicals? Humans? If we knew the answer, we would tell you everything. But we simply do not know."

"And we are not...equipped to stop it." Aluino's gaze fell to the floor in the center of the mat circle. "Our village and those around us are peaceful. Our magic relies on the earth and the earth needs us." Those words made her look at Rosalía, who stared at her father with heartbreaking admiration. "But we cannot defend ourselves."

"We don't know how." Rosalía's voice was soft and subdued but she looked directly at Lily when she said it.

"We do know how to create what we need from the land," Chalina said and smiled at her family. "And we know of a place that has protected people in need since it was created."

Her husband nodded. "Before our children were taken from us, those of us here with families decided to make this journey. I had hoped..." He swallowed and blinked quickly. "I believed that leaving would protect us. You came to our village at a good time. Now, I can go with the others to Ichacál with my entire family like we planned."

Lily and Romeo shared another surprised glance. "You're going to Ichacál? In Guatemala?"

"Have you seen it?" Chalina's eyes lit up at the thought.

She shook her head. "Not yet. But we're going there too."

"You are Americans?" the woman asked.

Romeo nodded. "That's right."

"And you came all this way into Chiapas to find your way to Ichacál." Aluino chewed on the inside of his lower lip.

"With a few stops along the way," Lily added. "But yes."

"We do not always know the reasons for why we choose a certain path. Or why it is chosen for us." Chalina glanced at her husband. "I believe you came to Mexico to bring our children home. I believe this was your path to Ichacál."

"I do not think you make this journey seeking protection." Her husband narrowed his eyes at his guests. "What waits for you there instead?"

"Oh." She looked at Romeo, who shrugged very unhelpfully. "We heard it's a...powerful place for finding answers."

"Ah." He nodded sagely. "Knowledge is another form of protection. Yes."

Once again, she found herself exchanging a pointed stare with Rosalía. "If it's used the right way."

"This is so." The girl's father looked at her too with a loving smile. "Today, our children come home. Tonight, we will rejoice. We will thank you, Lily and Romeo, with everything our village has to offer. Tomorrow"—he rested his hand on his wife's knee and she settled her fingers over his—"most of us will leave for Ichacál. We would be honored if you joined us for all of it."

"You mean to drive there with you?" Romeo's eyes widened. "I didn't see any cars."

"No. We don't have cars." Aluino chuckled. "Although yours is very nice."

"Then..." The werewolf's expression remained confused. "Well, how will you get there?"

"I will show you." The man pushed himself to his feet and beckoned them to follow.

Romeo stood, gave Lily a hand up, and leaned toward her. "Do you have any idea what we're about to see?"

"I can't even begin to take a guess."

"Yeah, I thought so."

Together, they walked across the wide room of this village's central building and joined Aluino at the far end. The rest of his family followed until all six of them stood at the edge. The hillside descended sharply into a sprawling valley below them, hidden from the rest of the village by the jungle and this elevated building. Six wooden wagons were lined up on the first gentle slope into the valley, all of them in various stages of being filled with clothes, tools, and brightly colored cloth in intricate patterns. Four oxen grazed within an enclosure farther below in the valley—huge white-gray beasts with massive curving horns.

"There aren't even enough animals to pull everything," Romeo muttered.

"You're taking wagons." Lily tried not to sound too skeptical but it was ridiculously hard.

"Yes." Aluino smiled at them and nodded toward the valley again. "And one or two of the animals for the larger ones."

"The rest of us will pull the others," Chalina added.

Romeo simply stared and his mouth opened and closed before he finally settled on, "That's a really long way to walk."

Their host chuckled. "It would take many days, yes. If we were only walking to Ichacál. We will walk some, of course. But the earth will do the rest."

"How's that, exactly?"

Their host and his wife exchanged a knowing glance,

and Chalina offered them a warm smile. "If you decide to travel with us tomorrow, you will see."

"For now, our people turn their hearts to the feast and the celebration tonight." Aluino put his arm around his wife and stepped away from the edge of the building. Filipe leaned a little farther over the edge and peered down until Rosalía caught the back of the oversized t-shirt he still wore and jerked him back.

The girl stepped quickly toward Romeo and Lily and forced them to stop when she leapt in front of them. "I want to show you our village. Before we leave."

"Rosalía." The girl's name from her mother's lips couldn't be mistaken for anything but a warning. "Offer."

Her daughter nodded and turned so her mother couldn't see her roll her eyes. "Would you like me to show you our village before we leave?" It sounded genuine enough but she fought hard to keep a straight face as she made the required offer.

"That sounds great," Lily said.

Romeo smirked. "Yeah, I'll take a tour."

"Okay." She darted toward her parents with a huge grin and hugged each of them fiercely. "Filipe, come on." Her brother merely stared at her, then spread his arms. With a quick sigh, she stomped her bare feet across the wooden floor toward her twin and poked him repeatedly in the ribs until he finally squirmed, fought back a laugh, and headed to the wide stairs.

"Join us at the fire when you're ready." Aluino smiled and leaned toward his guests. "My daughter will show you everything. She will say she is not finished, but Rosalía is never finished. If you let her decide when to return for the celebration, you may never come back. Hm?"

Lily smirked at him and nodded. "Actually, that doesn't surprise me at all."

The man threw his head back, his laugh louder and deeper than she expected from someone so tall and thin. He shook his head and waved them toward the stairs. "Go. Enjoy the views." Still chuckling, he turned back inside and rejoined Chalina.

The twins raced down the stairs, pushing each other and shouting until Romeo and Lily reached the bottom. The girl grinned at them and widened her eyes. "Come see our house first. Then you can see the others." She hurried through the village and turned back a few times to make sure they were following.

"It's one of those tours." Romeo grabbed Lily's hand. "This is probably gonna take a while."

"Well, we can afford to hang around for a day, right? We might be past the point of turning it down now, anyway."

"Yeah." He frowned and glanced at the wooden homes on stilts. "I'm not sure I wanna go to Guatemala with oxen-drawn carts, though. That's gonna take a few weeks."

"I'm right there with you. We can tell them that in the morning before we head out, then. Maybe we should simply roll with everything else tonight?"

"That'll work. A party in the jungle doesn't sound too bad."

SIXTEEN

Rosalía did, in fact, try to show them inside every single house in the village.

"What about the wagons?" Lily asked, and the girl abandoned the houses that all looked the same to sprint across the village and showcase something else. They found that if they asked about a certain location or item, she would instantly switch her startlingly unfailing enthusiasm toward exactly that. Felipe moved slowly on the perimeter of their little tour. He sometimes lagged behind to stare off at nothing and sometimes shoved his sister around and tried to distract her.

"Okay." Romeo scratched his head after two hours in which they'd seen the village houses, the river, the wagons, the oxen pen, the gardens, and another massive sinkhole pit at the bottom of the valley. "I'm actually hungry now."

"Oh!" The girl darted past him and scrambled up the first hill toward the village at the very top. "We have so much food. Sometimes, we can smell it down here but usually, the wind blows toward the village. Come on!"

He groaned at the thought of having to walk up the steep hill again, and Lily laughed. "At least there's more shade now," she said. "A little."

"I'm glad we don't have to cook anything. I don't know if I'd make it that far."

Sweating and breathing a little heavier than usual, they took the worn path all the way to the center of the village and so many huts. When they reached the top, the smell of something cooking was almost overpowering—the sweetness of corn, something mildly sour, and a combination of spices neither of them recognized.

"It's ready!" Rosalía waved them on and they followed her through the few homes beside the larger, taller meeting hut. Behind them, Filipe whacked a large stick against every hard surface he passed.

The massive cookfire that had been lit had also been stoked and put to use in the center of the village only a few yards in front of the wide staircase to the largest hut. Most of the villagers were already gathered here and at least five of them peeked under the huge, broad leaves with which they'd covered the food over blazing coals. A thick pillar of steam and a little smoke spun into the sky, and everyone grinned at Rosalía, Lily, and Romeo. They bombarded their guests again with pats on the back, wooden plates of steaming food were passed around, and a few apparent jokes were shared that Lily missed entirely in the chaos.

"You'll like all this."

"Best of the harvest."

"Water! Go get them some water."

"You might not leave after you eat that, eh?"

The other villagers served themselves plates of the massive meal cooking in the huge pit, and everyone sat on the packed dirt, talking and laughing while they dug into the piping-hot meal with their hands and never once reacted to the heat.

"Ow." Lily flicked her fingers away from the giant helping of food on her plate. "How do they do that?"

"It can't be that hot." Romeo tried to scoop a few chunks between his fingers and gave up. "Yeah, they gotta be born without nerve endings in their fingers." He looked at one woman in a bright-yellow dress who'd stopped to offer them wooden cups of water. "Thanks."

"Thank you." She beamed at them, her dark eyes shining within a round, sun-browned face.

"Can you tell me what's in this?" He gestured to his plate.

"The best of this season's crops. Corn, beans, squash and our own spices from the gardens. Tiko brought some coffee back from—" She turned and shouted, "Tiko! The coffee came from Veracruz?"

"Yeah. The uncle in Plan de Ayutla brought it through."

She smiled at the visitors again. "Coffee from Veracruz for a little better flavor. We've made it last a long time."

"*That's* what I smelled." Lily sniffed her plate again and tried once more to snag a few pieces of chopped vegetables. She could only touch the pieces around the edge but at least she could taste what she'd be able to enjoy when it all finally cooled down. "This is amazing."

"Good." The woman nodded vigorously.

"So it's all...vegetables?" Romeo asked. "No meat?"

"No, no. We don't eat animal flesh. Sometimes, we find eggs, but it's past the season for those now. Eat. You won't even taste the difference." She flicked her hand toward his plate, turned at someone else's shout, and left to tend to someone else's request.

"They don't eat meat." He stared at his plate with a small frown. "This is a vegetarian jungle party."

Lily laughed. "It's actually really good. Try it."

"Yeah, okay." He lifted the cup of water for a sip first.

"Oh, wait." She leaned toward him and tapped the rim of his cup. A yellow light flared on the surface of the water and she did the same to her own. "Just...you know. Drinking water in Mexico, right?"

He smirked. "I bet these people already know how to clean their water, Lil. They're witches too."

"Right." She shrugged. "But they can also eat straight from a cookfire with their bare hands. I'm only saying what they're used to might actually hurt us."

"Okay." He held her gaze over the rim of his cup as he took a long sip. "Well, at least it tastes pain-free."

More villagers came to serve themselves plates. All of them came to personally greet their guests—again—and a few even sat beside the foreigners for quick conversations. Lily caught sight of Rosalía skipping around through her people with a small plate of her own. When Filipe appeared behind her to snatch a handful from her plate, the girl spun and smacked him. They both laughed and sat together and shared it.

"You know, I think it's harder for these people to leave than Aluino let on," Lily said and leaned toward Romeo so hopefully, no one would overhear.

"Yeah, I probably wouldn't wanna leave a place like this either if kids weren't being kidnapped. I've only seen maybe three or four besides the twins."

"I know. Do you think it's all the same kinda thing? People snatching them to take them to Oaxaca?"

"I have no idea. There isn't really a way to know that, though, is there?" He frowned and chewed his expression reflected his distaste at the whole situation.

"Not unless we happen to catch the assholes in the act."

"Part of me hopes we do before we leave." He gazed at all the villagers and the celebration officially intended for the two children out of so many who'd actually come home. "The other part of me does not want to crash this party."

"I know." She scooped up a handful of the vegetable dish and stuck it in her mouth. "Oh, wow," she said around her food. "I think I could eat this every day."

"Without meat?"

"Try it."

He didn't say anything when he finally tasted the meal but his eyes widened and he didn't stop eating.

WHEN THE FOOD WAS FINISHED—WHICH took long enough with everyone milling around, taking more helpings, and trying to get the visitors to eat more even after they were stuffed—there was a brief lull in the conversation.

Romeo squinted and looked around. "I have a feeling there's something else coming."

"Really?"

A loud cheer rang out from the far side of the village. A man with a large drum under his arm stepped through the crowd. Behind him came another man who thrust a wooden flute into the air, and a laughing woman pushed him jokingly from behind. The trio stopped a few paces away from those eating around the fire and sat together in the dirt.

The man with the drum pointed at Romeo and Lily. "For good fortune, eh?" He struck his drum and the sound seemed to echo back at them from everywhere in the mountainous jungle.

The beat reminded her of the storyteller and her clan in New Mexico. This man's beat wasn't nearly as demanding as Amal's five apprentices who played to the blind woman's magical stories, but it carried the same liveliness. The other man added his flute and the woman broke out in wordless song. There was far more celebration in the performance and almost the same level of mystery Amal the storyteller had woven with her presence.

One by one, the villagers seated everywhere on the packed dirt stood to dance. Women laughed and spun with their partners. Spectators hooted and clapped. Anyone who felt like moving to the drums and the flute and the singer's clear voice did exactly that. By the time Lily felt like her stomach could handle moving at all, almost everyone was up and dancing and the sun barely peeked over the closest mountain, cutting off direct sunlight fairly early in the evening there.

"Okay." She turned to Romeo. "I wanna dance."

He laughed. "No one's stopping you."

"With you."

"No. I ate way too much vegetarian stew."

"That's not an excuse." She pushed to her feet and offered him her hand. "Come on. Dance with me."

"Lily..."

A man appeared out of nowhere and hooked his elbows under Romeo's arms from behind. "You do not tell a woman no when she wants to dance." He tried to lift the werewolf, which presented some difficulty until two more villagers joined him to hoist him to his feet. "You see?" The first man laughed and the others echoed the sound as all of them thumped him on the back. "There is nothing to stop you." He grinned and wiggled to the music. His feet shuffled across the dirt until he ended his demonstration with a quick spin and an exaggerated toss of his arms in the air. Everyone around them laughed again and the man clapped briskly. "Dance!"

The others joined in around them, and Romeo looked at Lily with wide eyes and laughed. "I can't dance."

"Neither can he," she muttered, her attention on the man who'd tried to lift a six-foot-two werewolf on his own. "It doesn't matter." She grasped his hands and pulled him through the dancers, watching their bare feet on the dirt and the way they stomped instead of stepping lightly. "You'll regret it if you don't."

He rolled his eyes but squeezed her hands and stamped to the drums and the flute and the singing with the rest of them. When she threw her head back and laughed, she didn't know if it was from the sight of him trying to copy everyone else or from the fact that she hadn't had this much fun in a long time.

SEVENTEEN

The dancing seemed almost endless. Eventually, even Lily had to call it quits for a while, sweaty and out of breath and feeling incredible anyway. "We can sit this song out if you want." She smoothed the hair away from her head and looked at Romeo.

His face was flushed, even in the flames coming from the cookfire that now boasted tall flames in the center of the village. Smaller torches had been lit atop stakes in the ground in front of every home once the light faded entirely from the hillside. He laughed and leaned toward her. "So you do have a limit."

"It's only a little break." She scrunched her nose in mock defiance. "If you wanna keep going, go right ahead."

"Nope." He retreated toward a low wooden bench that had been moved from someone's front porch with a number of others, sat with a grunt, and sighed. "I only wanna sit for a minute to watch."

"That sounds really nice, actually." She sat beside him, and the rest of the village danced and laughed and talked and passed some kind of pipe around that hadn't yet made its way toward their guests.

"Do you have any idea what they're smoking?"

"Nope." She rubbed her palms down her shorts. "Whatever it is, I'm good." She glanced at a man in shorts and a shirt with much less color than the rest of his people. He sat on the bottom step of the staircase up to the largest building, his forearms on his thighs, and didn't smile at anyone. "Have you talked to that guy sitting on the stairs?"

Romeo took a minute to locate him. "Nope. He doesn't look very happy, though, does he?"

"That's probably why everyone's leaving him alone, I guess." She smiled at a woman who passed and offered them more food. "Oh. No, thank you." He placed a hand on his stomach and shook his head. The woman continued with a laugh. "He's been there for a while, simply sitting there and glaring at everybody."

"It's a little weird that anyone would be grumpy at a party like this with kidnapped kids being brought back home and everything."

"I know." The man on the steps swept his gaze across the celebration and the bonfire and the dancing. Lily smiled when their eyes met and simply continued to scrutinize everyone and everything without any reaction at all to her friendliness. "I don't think he's upset about the kids. Or us, honestly." The minute she said it, he stood, moved away from the stairs, and stalked off through the village huts, his hands clasped behind his back as he watched and moved through the flickering shadows.

"Seriously, there's always a Debby Downer." Romeo shrugged. "And if he does have a problem with us, we'll handle that when he brings it up, won't we?"

"Yeah." Lily forced herself to stop watching the man so she didn't miss out on enjoying herself here as much as she could. "But I can't help feeling he knows something that would make things much easier for us if we knew it too."

He laughed and bumped her shoulder with his own. "You could say that about almost anybody, Lil."

She smirked at him. "Well, excuse me for appreciating the things that make people tick."

"No, I like it."

AFTER ANOTHER ROUND of dancing and a second villager who decided to join in the music with his own flute, the people passed around a plate of something like sweet corn pancakes coated in crystalized sugar. "I'm about to eat way too many of these and quickly regret it." Lily snagged one more off the plate before she passed it to the next villager who came to move the plate along.

"You know, somehow, I feel much safer eating as many of these as I want."

"As opposed to what?"

Romeo's nostrils flared at the memory despite how amazing the cakes tasted. "Those bran muffins."

That brought a laugh from them both before a small, cool shiver triggered goosebumps to rise along Lily's arms and legs. "I never expected it to get so cold here at night."

"Well, mountains plus rainy season plus stuffing our faces..." He shrugged. "Do you want me to grab you something?"

"No, I got it." She stood from the wooden bench and gestured at the cakes in his hand. "You hang out and enjoy those." He laughed when she winked and she made her way through the dancing, laughing, high-spirited villagers toward the end of the huts around the large meeting hall and the bonfire.

It was so much darker when she finally emerged from the between the wooden homes and she had to stop for a minute in the packed dirt between the last hut and the Winnebago to stare at the stars. "Wow. We don't get stars like *this* at home."

"You wouldn't see the same stars right now in America, anyway."

Lily jerked her head toward the drably garbed man who'd sat on the stairs and made no effort to enjoy the celebration. Now, he stood in front of her RV, his hands still clasped behind his back, although he stared at the sky. *What's this guy doing out here with my Winnie?* She smiled at him despite the odd circumstances and tried not to jump to any conclusions. "Have you been to the US?"

"No." He turned his head to survey even more of the massive blanket of bright stars that spilled across the night sky. "But I have heard many stories." Finally, he looked away from the sky and met her gaze again, which was easy enough to do beneath all the surprisingly bright starlight. "Not so many about witches and werewolves traveling together, though. Or doing anything together."

Please don't let this turn into another bigoted attempt to kick us out. I held it together in New Mexico but I probably won't be able to here. She took a deep breath. "I guess Romeo and I are a little different than everyone else."

"Yes." The man nodded slowly, still expressionless. "Different enough to find two of our children and return them. Different enough to be headed to Ichacál already, no?"

"I know everyone's talked about it, but we haven't made our decision yet about traveling with your people." *I'm starting to lean toward going on by ourselves, though.*

"If I had more say in it, we would not make the journey to Ichacál."

No matter how long she studied him while they spoke, she couldn't think of any reason why the man seemed so concerned. "I thought the temple was a safe place for anyone seeking protection."

He folded his arms and frowned. "That is what we have heard. But hearing does not always make a thing so."

He sounds like my mom's riddles. "What's your name?"

"Neron." He brought a hand to his chest and inclined his head.

If she'd had any concern about Neron's bad mood having anything to do with her and Romeo in his village, it would have been wiped away by the incredibly genuine gesture and the way he spoke to her. *He really means it.* "Well, it's nice to meet you, Neron. I'm Lily."

He nodded. "Everyone knows your name now. My pleasure to speak with you, Lily."

"You too." She smiled at him and felt a little better about not having upset him personally. *But if he doesn't feel right about the healing temple in Guatemala, that's definitely something I should know.* He didn't return her smile in any way but merely studied her, his hands clasped behind his back again. "So I have to ask what you were doing out here with my RV." *Not like I wouldn't find out on my own if there's magic involved. He still deserves a chance to answer honestly.*

"Oh, yes." Neron turned briefly to eye the Winnie again. "I hear so many stories of…other places beyond these mountains. In my mind, these are completely different worlds. But I have never actually seen a piece of them before now."

"Really?" She moved toward the side door as nonchalantly as she could. "I came back to grab a sweater. It's a lot colder out than I thought it would be."

He tilted his head and watched her approach the door. "That is the time of year. At other times, the heat makes you want to sleep in the river."

She chuckled at that. "I believe you. And you're welcome to come in and take a look if you want." When she held the door open for him, Neron took it and held it open to peer inside with wide, discerning eyes. She walked up the steps and turned to gesture for him to enter. "It's actually pretty cool in here."

"No, thank you." His gaze moved slowly over the living area and what little of the front seats could be seen from the doorway. "I see enough."

Lily studied him a little longer but she only saw genuine curiosity in his eyes. "Okay. I'll be right back." She moved swiftly into the bedroom and found a bulky, seldom-worn sweatshirt at the bottom of one drawer inside the wardrobe. *I never thought I'd need more layers in Mexico than in South Carolina.* But she pulled it over her head, slipped her ponytail out from under the collar, and stopped on her way toward the door.

The carved wooden box her mom had left her in vault four-fifty-two caught her attention. *I don't think Neron's done talking. I might as well take this if we're gonna end up talking about Ichacál.* She leaned over the bed to pull the heavy box from the shelf in the recessed niche, nodded, and took it with her.

When she returned to the Winnie's living area, the side door was closed again and Neron definitely hadn't changed his mind about coming inside. "Huh." she opened the door and peered outside. The man had taken a seat in the packed dirt outside the RV, his legs crossed and his hands resting in his lap. "You didn't have to wait outside." It felt right to stop a few feet away and sit near him on the ground.

"I understand." He took a deep breath, his eyes closed. "It is two different things to admire something from without and to step inside another's home. For now, I feel more useful observing. But thank you."

"You're welcome." *This guy speaks in double meanings*

too, doesn't he? "You said you've heard stories about places like where I'm from. I have a feeling not many people come through your village with stories to tell." He grunted and it sounded like an attempt at laughter. "Do you go looking for the stories, then?"

Neron opened his eyes and turned slowly to look at her. "I have never been more than maybe twenty miles from my village. The stories come looking for me." His gaze fell to the carved wooden box in her hand, but he merely looked away again toward the black silhouettes of the village huts and the orange glow of the bonfire flickering between them.

"Really?" *He might've been a storyteller if he had the white hair. So, this is new.* "What do you mean by that?"

He tilted his head in a gesture that might have been defensive and spoke as if he knew what he said wasn't the best news but that he'd come to terms with it a long time before. "I am a death witch."

Lily paused. "A necromancer?"

A subdued smirk lifted the corner of his mouth. "Your magic that lets us understand two different languages...I do not think it captures full translations."

"The spell's that obvious, huh?"

He flashed her a sidelong glance. "It could be improved."

She laughed. "Fair enough. I'll keep that in mind." They were silent for a moment. "So if necromancer isn't the right word, what's a death witch?"

The man uttered a low hum. "I find my magic in the

death of living things. A type of...exchange. There has only been one of us at a time in this village. For balance, yes?"

"Can you speak to the dead?" Her hands tightened on the wooden box in her lap as she thought of Amal the storyteller and the woman's inability to connect to any spirits wanting to pass a message through to Lily.

"I can."

"I assume that's where all your stories came from, then."

Neron met her gaze fully with wide eyes and nodded. "Most of them are freely given. Sometimes, I must... compel the spirits to reveal the truths they hide." He studied her for a moment longer before his small smirk returned. "Most prefer not to discuss the work of a death witch, even my own people. You do not seem to mind."

Lily shrugged. "Death is only scary because we make it that way, either by trying to avoid it or trying to command it. As long as you're not planning to raise bodies from the ground or send the dead after anyone because you like the way it makes you feel, I have nothing against a death witch."

The man's chuckle started out small and hoarse, then grew into a surprisingly warm laugh. "Are you certain you have never dealt with death magic?" She grinned and nodded. "Then I admire you for understanding what most people never allow themselves to accept. You are correct, Lily. Death itself is nothing to fear. My people embrace me because what I do is necessary to balance what magic brings to them. But I am always left to do these things in solitude. At least I now know a stranger who does not shy away so easily."

"Well, there are many worse things than death. Like children stolen from their families for who knows what." She nodded toward the grouping of homes.

"Yes." Neron sighed and the brief moment of light-heartedness faded. "This is why I do not agree with the journey to Ichacál. It does not feel like a good decision to go. It does not feel truly safe, and I have tried to understand why since the day the healing temple was suggested. But...I cannot see the reasons. I cannot hear the warning itself, only the echo of it."

"Can the dead really give you answers like that?"

He sagged a little as if the question had touched a nerve. "Possibly, but as yet, they have not. If I had some answer—some proof—to show my people, they would listen. If I could show them why this feels like a danger to all of us who wish to leave, they would find some other way to protect what children have not met with tragedy in a strange place. May the spirits provide them some comfort, wherever they are."

"You can't find the kids, either?"

"I still try every night. Death knows many things, but it is not omniscient. It simply is."

Okay, being slightly grumpy at a giant celebration suddenly seems like holding it together fairly well. This guy carries a huge responsibility on his shoulders. "Well, I hope you still plan to go with them." She stared at the firelight through the buildings. "Whoever's decided to pack up and head out for Ichacál will still need the kind of knowledge you can give them, right? And protection. It's always good to have someone with you who questions what everyone else believes. And hey, if something does happen, I imagine your people will be far more open to hearing it from you than from strangers like Romeo and me."

Neron stiffened and gave her a sharp glance of understanding. "You do not think the temple is safe, either, do you?"

"I hope it is." *And if it's not, I probably owe these people the truth about why I'm going anyway.* "We're not seeking shelter there. And we're not exactly going as tourists, either."

"I see."

"It's a long story, Neron, but basically, I'm looking for my mom. When I get to the next place, I find something she left for me. I don't have clear proof, either, but this was the last thing I found." Taking a chance on the man being nothing more than a witch bearing a heavy magical responsibility, she clicked the golden clasp on the box and opened the lid. After a long breath, she grasped the creepy stone head from the temple at Ichacál—according to her mom's friend Melissa Bore—and offered it to Neron. "I was told this came from the healing temple and that it's some kind of good-luck charm, and that's all I have to go on. If I'm right, I'll find something else my mom left at Ichacál and I'll be one step closer to finding her." She nodded and pushed the stone head a little closer toward him.

He shook his head. "I mean no disrespect, but I would rather not touch this, either." He looked at her with a frown of both embarrassment and concern. "I do not think keeping this with you as you travel will bring you good fortune."

"It's simply a feeling you get, huh?" The man nodded. "Yeah." She put the head in the box and closed the latch again. "It's creeped me out too since I found it." *And anything that gives a death witch a bad feeling isn't exactly the best talisman.*

EIGHTEEN

The villagers showed no signs of bringing the celebration to an end by the time Lily and Romeo were ready to turn in for the night. No one pleaded with them to stay or tried to stop them, and with a few good-nights to those they passed, they headed off to the Winnie and bed.

"So we've stumbled onto...what? Four parties now since we left Charleston?" He sat on the edge of the bed and kicked his shoes off. "It's totally different when one is actually thrown for us. Honestly, it kinda makes me a little antsy."

She laughed and hauled the bulky sweatshirt over her head before she shoved it back into the bottom drawer. "Well, at least you looked like you were having a good time."

"I was. But it...it feels weird to be thanked so much like that for doing something any good person with a sliver of a moral compass would do."

That made her pause and she turned to look at him. "I don't know if most good people would've been able to find those kids in the back of a broken-down van. Stopping to help someone with car trouble's one thing." She frowned. "Getting physically involved to stop a kidnapping is totally something else. Honestly, if you weren't with me on this whole treasure-hunt thing, I probably wouldn't have pulled over. And I definitely wouldn't have known there were two kid witches hiding in the back."

"I didn't know that, either." When he reached for her, she stepped toward him to stand between his legs. He wrapped his arms around her and tipped his head back to meet her gaze. "I only smelled the magic. And you were there to back me up."

"That's what I mean, though. I wouldn't have picked up on the magic part. You did." She ran her fingers through his hair. "Not every magical with good intentions has a werewolf with them who digs deeper into a sketchy situation." She chuckled. "You're always telling me not to be so hard on myself and not to take all the credit for whatever might go wrong. I think this time you should give yourself more credit. Seriously, you even brought props with you."

He wrinkled his nose with a wary laugh. "What?"

"Your bag of tools." Closing his eyes, he shook his head. "Don't start telling yourself now that you don't deserve a party being thrown for you. Even if it makes you feel a little antsy."

With a sigh, he slid his hands onto her hips and pulled her into his lap. "Okay, I definitely didn't expect you to throw my own pep-talk style back at me."

Lily laughed and draped her arms around his neck. "I've had more than enough time to learn how. Plus, I think it's important to take the pep talks and the optimism where we can get them right now."

His smile faded a little as he studied her. "Now would be the part where you tell me what's bothering you."

"I guess it is, huh?" She slid away from him and onto the bed and crossed her legs in front of her. Romeo's eyes widened, and he stretched beside her and propped his head in his hand. "When I came back to get my sweater earlier, the man we saw on the stairs was out here at the Winnie."

"Yeah, I thought you were gone a little long for only a sweater. What happened?"

"We talked for a while. His name's Neron. Apparently, these people have always had a necromancer around. To balance the rest of their magic, he said."

"And Neron is their necromancer, huh?"

She took a deep breath. "Yep."

"So, all I know about necromancers is that they talk to the dead. I think."

"That's close enough." She smirked. "He called himself a death witch, though, and said there's definitely a difference between the two. I'm not sure how much of that is true, seeing as I don't know any necromancers and he's never really left the village. But his magic comes directly from death."

"Woah." Romeo raised his eyebrows and his face grew serious. "So he has to kill people to cast spells or something?"

"Well, that would work. I don't think he's taken it as far as people. Technically, his magic comes from any kind of death, I think. Plants. Animals."

"He couldn't have done a little magic and put meat in that stew?"

She scoffed and shoved his shoulder playfully. "Cut it out about the meat, already."

He chuckled. "Okay, okay. Sorry. Bad joke. I wouldn't really wanna eat magical sacrifices anyway."

Lily rolled her eyes and shook her head but she smiled a little. "No, you probably wouldn't."

"So this guy needs death to use his magic. And... everyone else has a problem with it?"

"Not really. He said his people listen to him and respect what he does. They simply don't want anything to do with it. But he thinks heading out to Ichacál tomorrow is a bad idea."

"Huh. Any particular reason?"

She tilted her head uncertainly from side to side. "Basically, he has a bad feeling about the whole thing. And the fact that he can't find anything to prove or disprove his intuition. He talks to spirits too." She shrugged. "I think it's actually freaking him out a lot. He reminded me of Amal in New Mexico, right? She got a little nervous too when she couldn't see my 'path.'"

"And this Neron guy isn't used to not finding his answers when he talks to the dead, huh."

"Yep. That's basically the gist of it."

Romeo puffed out a sigh. "Okay, if I had all that going

on, I probably wouldn't be in much of a party mood, either."

"Right. He's concerned for his people and thinks the healing temple that's supposed to be safe is much more dangerous than staying here, even when their kids are being taken."

"So what sage advice did you give him?"

She laughed and leaned away. "Hey, I can solve riddles and put all kinds of pieces together and whip up a few decent spells." He snorted. "But I'm not exactly a fountain of wisdom."

"You're being modest, huh?"

"No. I'm merely sure that handing out sage advice is one of your superpowers."

A smile spread slowly over his lips, and he reached ran his hand over her shoulder and down her arm. She uncrossed her legs and lay sideways next to him on the bed. "So what did you tell him?"

"That he should still go with the families heading out tomorrow and they need him to protect them however he can. So if we do find anything that proves the healing temple isn't such an awesome plan, they can hear the news from someone they know and trust far more than two strangers from the US who happened to save a few kids."

"Hmm." He studied her face before he shifted his head away from her a little. "And?"

"And I told him why we're actually going to Guatemala. I showed him the creepy stone head too." She nodded toward the shelf, where she'd returned the box and the temple carving. "He didn't even wanna touch it."

"Which is probably not a good sign."

"Right. One more to add to the list."

Romeo pursed his lips, still not convinced that she'd told him everything. "A few not good signs never stopped you before, Lil. They didn't stop either of us. So what's actually on your mind?"

"You're relentless, aren't you?"

"You're deflecting, aren't you?" He smirked.

"Okay. You win." She took a deep breath. "I keep thinking about my mom's last note. The one in four-fifty-two and that box, right? She said..." She closed her eyes to pull up the image of her mother's handwriting, even though she still had the note. "'Sometimes, the places that seem the safest turn out to be far more dangerous than we ever imagined. You know how to tell the difference.' After all that other stuff about friendship and loyalty and rooting ourselves in people we can trust, I thought she was simply trying to be clever. Think about it. She wrote that note years ago, right? When she left everything with Melissa in the first place. But she was weirdly right on target talking about chains and forging our own."

"Yeah, that felt like a little jibe at me, honestly."

Lily raised her eyebrows. "I know. And now we're... what? Halfway to Ichacál, and I think I'm starting to discover what that line about safe places is supposed to mean."

"You don't think it's actually safe."

"No. I don't. That stone head in a box gave me a weird feeling from the very beginning. I thought it merely looked creepy. But now, Neron wouldn't touch it. And he really doesn't want his people going to this temple."

"Nope. That's not very encouraging at all."

She held his gaze and narrowed her eyes. "So that means my mom left this clue knowing full well that I'd follow it to a place that gives necromancers goosebumps."

He smirked. "I didn't think that would make you wanna turn back."

"It doesn't. It makes me think that we're getting really close. And I don't wanna let myself get too excited if she's not there. Or if something awful happens at that temple and we have to leave all over again because we can't stop to fix everyone else's problems."

"Oh..." Romeo tucked her hair behind her ears and cupped her cheek tenderly. "My whole 'people make their own decisions' speech really got to you, didn't it?"

Although she rolled her eyes, she had to smile when she nodded against his hand. "I guess it did. You were totally right, though. It's only that...if we have no idea what we're gonna find there, I don't know how to prepare my head for eventually leaving these people and going wherever my mom's next clue says. If there even is another one."

"You think your mom would set this all up only to leave everything hanging on a dead end?"

She snorted. "Not even a little."

"Right. And she wouldn't tell you to go somewhere if she didn't think you could handle it. Even if she knew it was dangerous."

"Except she didn't tell me anything."

He chuckled. "You are the most literal person I know."

"Literally?"

"Totally." Chuckling, he wrapped his arm around her waist and pulled her closer. "So it sounds like you think we should go with these people to the temple."

"Kinda. If we can't stay to protect them there, we might as well hang around to help them out as long as we can, right?"

"Lily, from here to Guatemala and what I'm guessing is some other jungle in the mountains is like two weeks on foot. Probably longer if all the kids are coming and these people like to take their time. Which I kinda think they do." It wasn't loud or distracting, but they could definitely still hear the music and the voices of the villagers who hadn't yet felt the need to call it a night.

"Two weeks?" She uttered a little groan.

"Yeah, I didn't think you'd wanna roll through the rest of Mexico at that pace."

"I don't. Maybe we'll start out with them tomorrow, then make sure nothing happens while they leave here. No more kidnappings or whatever."

Romeo smiled and hugged. "That sounds like a good middle ground. You know, I saw Rosalía practicing a little illusion earlier tonight."

"In front of everyone?"

"Yeah. She found her own little corner when you were having your chat with Neron. At the very least, Lil, she could learn a few things from you in the next few days. And I bet you anything she'll be able to teach her people after that."

She took a deep breath. "That kinda puts a ton of responsibility on both of us."

"Hey, that's great. Isn't too much responsibility the thing that always drives you to keep going?"

"Okay, now you're pushin' it." Lily pressed against his chest but he held her so close and so tightly, she didn't have much room to get in a good shove.

"Actually, you're pushing me." Romeo chuckled.

"Do you want me to use magic? I can push a lot harder that way"

"Oh, I know you can." He grinned. "But you won't."

"Oh, yeah? Why not?"

" 'Cause you like being this close."

"To you?"

"Yeah."

She bit her lip. "I don't know if I'd go that far—" He cut her off with a kiss and this time, they didn't have any kid witches sneaking into the bedroom to interrupt them.

NINETEEN

Some loud, talkative, and no doubt tropical bird squawked repeatedly in a tree somewhere beside the Winnebago. *I'm gonna kill that bird.* Lily rolled over and tried to block it out with a pillow but the screeching was so loud and so repetitive, there was no way to drown it out. "You gotta be kidding me."

Romeo chuckled in the bedroom doorway and she tossed the pillows off her head. "The monkeys were actually worse."

"Monkeys?" She sat up, scowled, and dragged the mess of bedhead away from her face.

"I think they were fighting. Maybe. A whole troop of them swung through the trees and chased after something. I'm honestly surprised that didn't wake you up."

"Me too." She took a deep breath, then yawned. "What's everybody else up to?"

"Eating. Packing, I think. I made coffee."

She rubbed her face. "For everyone."

"No way. Only you."

"Oh, my God. I'm so in love with—" She blinked, stared at the comforter in her lap, and looked at him. "The way you make coffee."

His eyes widened and his brows raised all the way as he chuckled. "Oh, yeah? You fell hard for the way I make coffee, huh?"

She tilted her head back and tried not to look embarrassed. *That was a close one. This is not exactly the best scenario to spill all that on him. If I was ever going to say that—cut it out, Lily.* "Yep. I'm confessing my love for your coffee."

"Should I bring you some and leave you two alone?"

"Don't be ridiculous." She snorted. "I don't take coffee to bed."

"Oh, good." He chuckled and shook his head. "I'm glad there's still room for me somewhere." He turned and stepped into the kitchen.

Real smooth, Lily. He has to know that Lily in the morning is the worst version of me, right? She puffed out a sigh, tossed the covers off, and slipped out of the bed in her pajama shorts and tank top.

He waited for her with a hot cup of coffee when she stepped out. "Thank you." She took the cup from him and headed to the bathroom.

"No problem. I definitely don't wanna keep you two apart."

"Ha, ha."

When she came back out of the bathroom, he was seated at the tiny table with his own cup of coffee. She came to sit with him and slid into the booth far more easily than he ever did with his long legs. They stared at each other and smiled over the rims of their cups as they drank and didn't say another word. *He's gonna ask me what I almost actually said.*

Romeo swallowed and took a breath. "So I have a—" A soft knock came at the Winnie's side door. He raised an eyebrow at her, then laughed. "I'll get it." His knees thumped against the underside of the table as he scooted out of the booth. Lily tried not to laugh as he rolled his eyes and stood to head for the side door. When he opened it, they were both surprised to see Neron standing outside.

"Good morning."

"Oh. Morning." Romeo smiled and studied the man's dark clothes and firmly set jaw.

"I am called Neron." He nodded. "And I know you are Romeo."

He smirked. "Well, I guess that's it for the introductions, then."

The corners of the visitor's mouth twitched up a little. "It is still good to make them. I brought you both some food. It was cooked last night but it is also good heated again for breakfast." He lifted a wooden plate with a stack of the same sugar-encrusted corn cakes from the night before.

"That actually looks excellent. Thanks." He took the plate and held himself back from eating it all at once when the steam curled up toward his face.

Neron cleared his throat. "I also wonder if both of you have decided what you will do after today. After most of my people leave." He peered past Romeo into the RV, and Lily stood from the table.

"We talked about it last night," she said. Romeo turned to glance at her, then nodded. "I think we'll come with you. At least for part of it."

"Good." Neron inclined his head and looked relieved. "I was hoping this would be your answer."

"We might have to move on ahead of you, though." He stepped aside and gestured for the man to join them. The man merely raised a hand in polite refusal and shook his head. "We don't really have two weeks to spare while everyone else walks to Guatemala."

His gaze cut quickly toward the werewolf again. "Two weeks?" He chuckled, then barked out a laugh. "You think we will take two weeks to go to Ichacál?"

"Maybe more, right? I know it's a long way to walk."

Neron laughed again, shook his head, and grinned at the couple as Lily came to stand at the top step inside the door. "We are walking—mostly. But it will only take us a few days. Not weeks."

Romeo turned back to glance at her. "I feel like I missed the punchline."

"Yeah, me too." She smiled at their visitor. "How will you walk four hundred and twenty miles in a few days?"

"Oh, you have not seen this done." He nodded, and his smile settled into a tiny flicker at the corners of his mouth. "I do not wish to spoil the surprise of it for you. I know you will find it amusing. When we bring the wagons here beside you, it will be time to leave."

"Um...okay." She smiled at him. "Thanks for breakfast."

"Of course." Neron nodded again and turned stiffly away from the door before he strode toward the huts.

"He has a weird sense of humor, doesn't he?" Romeo watched the man disappear between two wooden buildings before he closed the Winnie's side door.

She shrugged. "Maybe that's what happens when you can only use magic through death."

"That makes sense." He turned and walked up the steps with the steaming sweet-corn cakes in his hand. "Hungry?"

"We might as well eat now, right?" She laughed and snatched the top cake. "Before we find out whatever kinda super-speed or totally unexpected magic these people use to get to the temple."

"I guess. I thought the same thing at Carowinds when I was...I dunno. Seven? Eating a whole elephant ear so I wouldn't have to stop riding rides for lunch was not an excellent idea. As evidenced by me puking the whole thing up anyway after the Tilt-O-Whirl."

Lily snorted. "Was that your idea or your dad's?"

He took a cake from the plate before he set it on the counter and shrugged. "I think we came to a mutual understanding. He didn't like it any better than I did."

"Gross. To be clear, you mean the funnel-cake thing, right? Not an actual elephant ear?"

"Seriously?"

She grinned. "Hey, with you, that could've been an actual possibility."

"Oh, yeah. There are so many real elephants walking around in Charleston." He paused and squinted at the ceiling. "That's one thing I can say with a hundred percent certainty that I've never eaten."

"Yeah, that would be a really weird thing to check off the list."

"Okay..." Romeo nodded and his expression suggested he wasn't quite sure how to respond. Lily laughed again. "You know what? Eat your corn cake."

She took another bite and squealed a protest when he quickly shoved more of it into her mouth.

HALF AN HOUR LATER, the first wagon appeared between the huts, pulled by a man in a bright blue shirt. He grinned at them as they stepped out of the Winnie, dressed and full from breakfast. "So they're gonna pull all the carts like this?" Romeo muttered but smiled in response as he closed the side door behind him. "On foot over four hundred miles to Guatemala?"

"Well, they are witches." Lily shrugged. "I'm actually really curious to see exactly how they pull this off."

"You coulda fooled me, though." He raised an eyebrow and glanced at the next two carts emerging from the village. "Except for Rosalía, I haven't seen or smelled a hint of magic since we got here."

She smirked at him. "You sound disappointed."

"Not disappointed. Merely a little confused. I don't

know any witches who don't actively use magic on a regular basis, especially at a party."

"Romeo, you don't know very many witches at all."

"Well, I've met any number of them since we left Charleston. And they were all kinds of"—he wiggled his fingers in front of his face—"magic-y."

"That's the technical term for it, right?" She bit back a laugh.

"Yeah. I only now made it official." He grinned at her and took a few steps away from the vehicle. "Okay. We have two witch-drawn wagons and a—what the hell is that?"

She turned to follow his gaze and her mouth dropped open. "Uh...I'm tempted to say that's another wagon. But beyond that, I literally have no clue."

The contraption could easily have been one of the village huts on wheels, although it looked more like two or three wagons cobbled haphazardly together. It was both lopsided and crooked and rumbled slowly over the packed dirt as the only wagon pulled by not one of the oxen but two.

"I can't imagine anything but magic holding that thing together," Romeo muttered.

"You're probably right."

One more regular-sized wagon joined the procession for a total of four, plus the monstrous, oxen-drawn contrivance. More villagers crowded around them, all of them smiling and embracing those who'd decided to stay behind. The few families among them lucky enough to still have their children had all agreed to make this pilgrimage. Their home—their village—would soon only consist of the younger adults without families and those who were too old to make the trek.

The six children, Rosalía and Filipe among them, darted through the gathering of their people beside the Winnie, laughing and shouting at each other, fueled by the excitement and the trepidation of stepping farther beyond their village and this mountain than Plan de Ayutla.

Aluino and Chalina stepped toward the young couple. The man nodded and thrust his hand toward Romeo for another handshake. His wife embraced Lily quickly and released her. "We begin our journey now," he said with a wide smile. "We have heard you wish to accompany us."

"Only for a little while," she said. "We might move on ahead of you to the temple, but to start, yes. We'll come with you."

"You think we will slow you down, don't you?" Chalina asked.

They glanced at one another and neither of them could come up with anything to say that wouldn't sound ridiculously or even possibly rude.

"This is fine." The woman nodded.

Her husband smirked at them. "Perhaps you will change your mind when you see how things are done."

I doubt it. Lily glanced at the villagers saying their goodbyes and located Neron. The man carried a tall, thick walking stick, the bark whittled away to reveal the hard, glistening wood beneath. A few feathers and stones dangled from brightly colored woven thongs tied to the tip of the staff but beyond this, the death witch carried nothing else with him. He met her gaze with the ghost of a smile and nodded.

"Are we prepared?" another villager shouted. Those leaving the only home they'd ever known raised their fists and voices together in a cheer of readiness. The children still chased each other about. One woman took hold of the oxen harness between the two beasts towing the large, ramshackle wagon and led them forward across the dirt. Four men took up the smaller wagons, holding the harness shafts in each hand like picking up a wheelbarrow before they followed the oxen team.

Aluino watched the procession move off with a proud grin, then turned to the young couple again. "You may follow us in your... This is your home, correct?" He nodded at the Winnie.

They exchanged glances again. "Uh...for now. Yeah." She nodded.

"The adventuremobile's growing on us." Romeo grinned.

"Good. You may follow us in your adventuremobile." He winked, took his wife's hand, and followed the wagon procession on foot.

The young witch and her werewolf friend turned to the RV. He shook his head. "I really thought he would've picked up on the fact that it's a nickname."

"What do you mean?" She opened the side door and climbed the short flight of stairs.

"I mean I didn't translate *adventuremobile*."

She laughed. "Are you gonna tell him that's not actually what it's called?"

He smirked and headed to the driver's seat. "I know it's not doing them any favors, but I kinda like the idea of letting the name stick. After all, isn't every RV an adventuremobile anyway?"

Sliding quickly into the passenger seat, Lily turned toward him and smirked. "Not like ours."

TWENTY

"Okay, I don't know how much longer I can handle this." Romeo dropped his head back against the driver seat's headrest and sighed.

"It's only been an hour."

"That's what I mean. We've literally moved at five miles an hour for an hour. Do you think we could maybe hook all those wagons together and tow them? I wouldn't mind cramming all these people into the Winnie, either, if it means we can move faster." He jerked on the steering wheel as the vehicle bumped and jarred along the uneven, barely existent dirt path from the village.

"We've sat in traffic before."

"This isn't traffic, Lil. This is old-school travel from before cars even existed. This is like the Winnie took us back in time to the beginning of America to try crossing the Rocky Mountains with the pioneers."

She laughed. "That would make a good story, though. Right? Winnebago Time Machine?"

He flashed her a narrow-eyed, sideways glance. "That's not funny."

"It's totally funny."

"Okay. He snorted. "A little. Maybe I'd enjoy it more if we weren't a bunch of oversized snails right now."

"Hey, we said we'd join them for a little while, right? If you really can't handle it, we'll simply let them know we have to keep going."

"I can handle it. I merely don't want to." He ran a hand irritably through his curls and shook his head. "And I honestly don't know if I'd be able to get us back to the highway from here."

"You mean you don't have everything mapped out on your GPS again?"

He turned his head slowly to meet her gaze. "I mean there's literally zero reception or Internet. I could try it with a map. Do you have one of those?"

Lily pressed her lips together and looked out at the large parade of slow-moving villagers in front of them. "Nope."

ONLY HALF AN HOUR LATER, the wagons came to a full stop. "You gotta be kidding me!" He squeezed the steering wheel, his eyes wide and his jaw clenched in an exaggerated grimace.

She shook her head. "Whatever it is, I'm sure there's a reason for it."

"You actually want to keep moving like this?"

"Of course not. But everyone we talked to about heading to Guatemala looked like they were trying really hard not to explode and spill the big secret."

He grunted. "Yeah. The big secret is that they don't know how to go anywhere at a decent pace."

"All right. We can ask why they stopped, and then we'll—"

Someone knocked briskly on the driver-side window. They both looked out to see Aluino standing there with another wide grin. Romeo rolled the window down. "Is everything okay?"

"Of course." The man nodded. "We have stopped to perform the first passage. I wanted you to know that you may stay in your adventuremobile"—Lily fought really hard not to laugh—"or you may step outside to join us. As long as you do not break our circle, yes?"

"Oh. Uh...sure." Romeo glanced at Lily.

"Yeah, I don't think we'll have a problem with that," she said.

"Good." Aluino's excitement lit up his entire face and he nodded briskly before he almost literally skipped away to join his people.

The werewolf rolled the window up again and frowned.

"I told you they were planning something besides walking." She smirked at him.

"What passage?"

"I have no idea. But I'm fairly sure we're about to find out."

When they looked out the windshield again, all the

villagers began to form a large circle around their traveling group—the Winnie, the five wagons, and the children. Once every space was filled and the circle complete, the adults joined hands and bowed their heads.

"Please don't start singing," he muttered.

She snorted, dismissed the comment, and focused on the witches gathered around them.

The villagers' lips moved together in a silent chant, which quickly rose into a low hum. In under a minute, the sound of their combined voices—still low and droning in the cadence of practiced incantations—grew so loud, they could hear it inside the vehicle.

"Do you have any idea what they're saying?" he asked.

"No. It's kinda weird that—"

The ground trembled beneath them and rocked both the RV and the wagons outside. *That's not an earthquake. Nothing's moving.* She tried to get a better view of what was happening but couldn't move. Everything around her trembled, oscillating like the first time she'd used an electric toothbrush and held it between her teeth to free both her hands. Her skull vibrated, making it impossible to see anything clearly. At the moment when she wanted to shout for somebody to explain what was going on, the non-earthquake stopped and everything fell still again.

She shook her head and glanced at the villagers she could see through the windshield. All of them still had their eyes closed but a few smiled. When they opened them, they released each other's hands and most of them broke out into huge, excited grins. Then she realized where they were and her jaw dropped.

The traveling procession had stopped on the top of a slow rise only a few minutes before, most of the light blocked by the thick jungle stretching far overhead. Now, they were somewhere else entirely—an open clearing within the jungle, where the sun beat down on short, green grass beside the rocky bank of a wide river to their right. Everything was damp-looking and dark, covered in moss, and sprouted thick foliage, but this was not the same place as the small hilltop where the village witches had stopped to perform their spell.

"Oh, my God," she whispered. "They cast a massive transportation spell. You can see this too, right?" She turned toward Romeo, but he had slumped in the driver's seat, his arms limp at his sides and his head hanging loosely toward his shoulder. "Crap. Romeo?" She gave his shoulder a gentle shake. "Hey, are you okay?"

He groaned something unintelligible and tried to raise his head. It bobbed precariously before he managed to turn it mostly toward her, his eyes glazed over and wildly unfocused.

"Jeeze. I knew it was intense—" Lily scrabbled in the center console and located the Ziplock bag that held what little wolfsbane flowers he had left. She retrieved two of them, closed the bag and replaced it, and climbed over the center console to reach his face. "Hey. Okay, come on. Open up." She patted his cheek as his eyes rolled mindlessly in their sockets. He looked he'd be sneezing right now if he hadn't been too drunk on the villagers' insanely powerful spell. She squeezed his cheeks enough to get his mouth open and chuckled a little as she shoved the purple flowers between his lips. "Eat up."

His lips smacked over and over as he slowly and lethargically moved the wolfsbane around in his mouth. After a few seconds, the flower worked enough to make him aware of what was happening, and he started to chew. Finally, he swallowed awkwardly, rested his head back against the headrest, and exhaled a long, slow breath. "What the hell was that?"

She grinned and clambered into the passenger seat. "That was probably the most powerful group spell I've ever seen."

"No kidding." He rubbed both hands through his hair, drew them down his cheeks, and shook his head. "That was like all the magic in that nightclub in Montreal, but... all at once."

"Yep." She sighed and stared out the window again. "Do you notice anything different?"

The village witches had all left the circle now and moved around the wagons to unload various items and while they chatted happily with each other.

"Wait a minute." Romeo blinked. "Are they unpacking?"

"Oh." She tilted her head, a little surprised by the question. "That's not what I was talking about, but yeah. I think they are."

"Why? We've covered, what? Maybe five miles. It's not even noon yet, and they—" His mouth fell open when he realized what she had been tried to point out from the beginning. "Where are we?"

"Well…" She pressed her lips together and shrugged. "We're definitely not where we stopped. I know that."

"No, we're not…" He froze and warily eyed the cloth and food and hollowed gourds of water the villagers removed from the carts. "This looks very much like setting up camp."

"Maybe we should get out and make sure?"

"I'm already on it." He opened the driver's door and almost fell out. Lily stepped back through the Winnie to open the side door and step out into the humidity and warmth of wherever the witches had transported them.

As soon as she joined him again in front of the RV, Aluino approached them, grinning widely and spreading his arms. "I will say by your faces that neither of you expected this."

The werewolf chuckled and scratched the back of his head. "That's one way to put it."

"Your people were expecting this, weren't they?" Lily asked.

"Of course. Our ancestors moved through these mountains and across these lands in this very same way. We have not needed to use these old ways until now." The man's smile faded only a little. "Did I not say the land would do the rest of the work for us?"

"You did." She narrowed her eyes. "What does that mean, exactly? We watched you cast the spell—"

"Ah." Aluino nodded. "This is only our part to play in the passage. The earth has special…sites. Of energy, perhaps you would say. My people's magic opens these doors and the earth allows us to step through."

"To another site." She grinned.

"Not quite. The next is some kilometers from here. We will travel that way tomorrow and we will step through the second passage." The man turned toward Romeo and nudged his shoulder with a fist. "Now you know this does not take us weeks, eh?"

He chuckled and shook his head. "Now I know. How far did we...travel?"

Aluino shrugged. "Something like one hundred and seventy kilometers. So, you see? Only a few days' journey to Ichacál."

"Oh, yeah. I get it now." He glanced down at Lily with wide eyes and laughed. "I gotta admit, Aluino, this was the last thing on my list of what to expect. You guys are impressive."

"Oh, no." The man laughed and dismissed him with a wave. "It is not anything we do. All our magic—what we do here and at home in our village—comes from the earth. Let her impress you, eh?" Another chuckle escaped him. "Come. The river is a little swift after the rains, but it feels the best right now while the sun smiles down on us. We stop now to rest, bring joy to our families, and try not to worry so much. Not as much as I think you do, Romeo."

"I'm not really—"

The villager cut him off with another sharp laugh as he walked away, shaking his head.

Romeo never got to finish, but he turned to Lily with a half frown and a skeptical twist to his lips. "I'm not worried."

She laughed and slipped her arm through his. "Of course not. I wouldn't mind seeing the river, though."

"Yeah. The river. That wasn't here five minutes ago."

"No, we weren't here five minutes ago. And now, we are." She grinned at him and he grimaced and mumbled under his breath, still trying to wrap his mind around the idea.

TWENTY-ONE

They reached the riverbank and removed their shoes to step into the fine, dark sand beside the water. The children they hadn't met yet had beaten them there and already splashed, fully clothed, in the cool water and the deep swimming hole on this side of the river closest to the traveling caravan. Lily caught sight of Rosalía seated on the bank farther downstream, her legs crossed beneath her on a large, flat rock as she pressed her palms together and slowly drew them apart again. That faint pink glow of the illusions spell stretched between her hands, exactly as she had been taught. Not even the sound of the other children at play—and Romeo laughing with them as they turned the splashes onto him—distracted the girl from her magical practice.

She's gonna nail that spell in the next few days. And then, she's gonna ask me for more. She took a deep breath and tried not to think about it too much.

Carefully, she stepped across the slick, moss-covered

rocks and deeper into the water. The kids and Romeo stopped splashing a little as she approached and all of them grinned. "What?"

"Nothing." He shrugged, slapped at the water, and sent a spray of it across her face and the front of her shirt.

She gasped and froze while the excess water dripped into the river. The other children exploded into laughter again, and she saw Filipe among them, doubled over and holding his stomach. "Okay..."

"You can't say it doesn't feel amazing." He smirked at her and spread his arms.

"True." She puffed a spray of water off her lips. "There's only one problem."

"Oh, yeah?"

"You're still completely dry." She took a chance on the slippery rocks to kick and send a huge splash over him. It almost tumbled her into the water, and before she righted herself and caught her balance again, he'd sloshed quickly through the river toward her.

He caught her and hauled her back to the swimming hole. "So are you!" Despite her shriek of protest, he lifted her and tossed her into the much deeper water, which was fortunately much calmer than the swift current in the middle of the river.

Lily pushed herself up to the surface and swiped the wet hair back from her forehead. She glared at Romeo, who laughed a little longer until he saw she wasn't laughing with him and the other kids. "Hey, you can't be mad at me for that." She didn't say anything, so he waded toward her. "Lil, don't tell me you forgot how to play in the—"

A stream of river water arced from her pursed lips into his face. The children erupted into laughter and splashed and screamed again, and this time, she laughed with them.

"Oh, it's on." He shoved both hands through the water until the wave broke almost over her head.

She turned her head to avoid getting most of the water in her face and blew more of it out of her mouth. "You really wanna turn this into a competition? Because we both know I'll win."

He grinned and wiggled his eyebrows. "Bring it." He pushed through the water again, but she flicked the oncoming wave with a finger and redirected the whole thing back at him. A sheet of river water burst against his face and chest and knocked him into the pool. One of the kids screamed for the sake of screaming, and they were all back at it again.

THERE WAS NEVER any call made for the kids to leave the river for lunch, but they slowly filtered out of the water anyway to head back to their families' encampment. None of them seemed to care about their soaking wet clothes as they climbed the shallow bank toward the clearing and their bare feet left wet, dripping trails in the earth behind them.

"I wish I could still be that comfortable in soaked

clothes." Lily sloshed out of the river and waited for Romeo to join her.

"If it wasn't so ridiculously humid, I probably wouldn't mind, either." He shook his head like a wet dog and sprayed water everywhere before he ruffled his damp curls.

She rolled her eyes. "We have towels, you know."

"But that's no fun." He grinned as they stepped up the rocky bank and paused when he saw Rosalía still seated on the rock downriver, her palms upturned on her knees and her eyes closed. "She's been at that the whole time, huh?"

"Yeah." She wrung her hair out over the rocks and flipped it over her shoulder. "I think she's really close to getting it under her belt."

"Did you choose something else to teach her yet?"

"What?" *I swear he can read my mind.*

"You know. When she comes back to her teacher saying, 'I did it. Now show me how to do something bigger.'" His impression of the girl fairly accurate but it sounded ridiculous in his deep voice.

"She's definitely gonna come ask me soon." She shook her head and navigated her way off the rocks and back onto the short grass of the clearing. "I'll hafta come up with something before she does."

"Americans!" The shout came from one of the gathered circles of villagers. They looked up and to where Chalina waved her arm straight in the air. Aluino shouted again, "Eat with us!"

"Well, at least we're not running low on food in the Winnie." Romeo chuckled, stopped abruptly, and frowned. "Is there any of that beef jerky left?"

Lily laughed. "Nope. You killed that a few days ago."

"Perfect. I get to eat nothing but vegetables. Again."

When they reached the circle where Aluino and Chalina sat with a few of their own people, they found two open places saved for them on the grass. They sat and thanked their hosts again for the plates of food passed around the circle toward them. This meal was served cold and tasted more like the four-bean salad her grandmother used to make. Before her first mouthful even reached her lips, she looked around the villagers seated with them and froze.

"Hey, Rosalía."

The girl looked up from her wooden plate with wide eyes.

"How'd you get here so fast?"

Her only response was a wide, flashing grin.

"What?" Romeo glanced at Lily, then saw the child seated a few places down from her parents, her plate already half-eaten. "Wait a minute..." The young couple both leaned back and glanced over their shoulders at the wide, flat rock downriver. Another Rosalía sat there on the rock, her eyes closed, legs crossed, and palms upturned.

Lily barked out a laugh, pulled herself together, and tried to sound a little stern when she spoke to the girl. "You were waiting for me to catch on, weren't you?"

Rosalía merely grinned, although a small giggle escaped her before she returned her attention to her food.

"What is this?" Aluino squinted at his daughter and glanced at Lily.

"Well, it looks like she's done it again." She shrugged,

but the confusion on both of Rosalía's parent's faces made her pause. "You didn't tell them?"

The girl shoveled more food into her mouth and stared at her plate, although she smiled as she chewed. After a long moment, she shook her head.

"Rosalía." Chalina leaned forward over her plate and shot a warning glance the likes of which only mothers were capable of. But the girl avoided it completely by not looking at anyone. "What did you do?"

Aluino's voice dropped to dangerously low levels. "I don't know how many times we have to—"

"No, it's okay." Everyone looked at Lily, including Rosalía. *I can't let them rail on her for no reason, right?* "It's okay. We're talking about a new spell I think your daughter mastered on her own."

The grin reappeared on the child's face and she stared earnestly at Lily.

"What spell?" Aluino glanced from his daughter to the older witch.

"It's for summoning illusions. When we...met"—Lily nodded toward the girl—"your daughter asked me to teach her some of the magic I know. I realize it's different than what your people do, but I agreed to teach her a few things—"

"Show me." Aluino didn't necessarily look upset, but his smile hadn't returned. Still, there was no mistaking the light of curiosity behind his eyes.

She nodded at Rosalía. "Go ahead."

The girl almost threw her wooden plate onto the ground and leapt to her feet. "Come on, Papa. You won't believe it." She took her father's hand before he had the chance to stand and tugged him down the gentle slope and out of the clearing toward the river. "See?" Her skinny arm pointed directly ahead at the image of her herself seated on the flat rock.

Aluino blinked quickly, looked at his daughter holding his own hand, and stared at the illusion once more. "By my own eyes..."

"I did that, Papa. I can do that!"

"Yes. I see that." The man laughed, knelt in the grass in front of his daughter, and said something to her in a voice low enough that no one else could hear. Rosalía nodded, beaming, before her father stood again and led her back toward the clearing.

By now, all the villagers eating in the few other circles around their caravan had noticed what was going on, even if they still had no idea *how*. Some of them stared from the illusion of Rosalía on the rock to the real girl who stepped toward the camp with her father. Others spoke quietly to their neighbors. Even the two oxen tied to a few trees upriver—which they could have snapped into if they weren't so docile—raised their heads from where they grazed to watch the scene. The atmosphere of excitement and fascination was almost a physical rush of electric antic-ipation.

Before her husband and daughter reached the circle, Chalina leaned toward Lily and asked in a voice barely above a whisper, "Is it safe for her?"

She nodded. "That one is. Yes."

The woman nodded in appreciation, held the other

witch's gaze, and finally straightened again when Aluino and Rosalía sat in their places in the circle. "How is this done?" he asked.

Lily glanced at the girl again and smiled. "I think she's ready to show you."

She looked at her father and whispered, "I can."

"You are my daughter's teacher, then?"

"For the last few days. Maybe for a few more." She felt Romeo's gaze flicker quickly toward her. *Yeah, I know. We haven't talked about staying with these people that long. I said maybe.*

"And you can teach her more of your magic? Stronger magic for our people?"

"Husband..." Chalina sent him a small frown, her lips pressed together in warning. But he ignored her completely and held Lily's gaze in a firm mixture of pleading and determination.

It looks like we're both having this conversation for the first time. She licked her lips and nodded slowly. "I can teach whoever is ready to learn. But I think Rosalía might be the best witch to teach the rest of your people. She's a fast learner and she knows how to use this magic responsibly." That last part wasn't quite true, but she hoped it would serve as one more warning for the girl. *She has to understand how much bigger this is than merely wanting to be a powerful witch. If she can't handle it now, she shouldn't train with me anyway.*

Aluino nodded and glanced at his wife. Chalina still didn't look entirely happy about the whole thing but she read his determination and focused her warning gaze on him now too. "Lily, what may my people offer you in return for this?"

She startled. "I'm sorry?"

"Your magic is very strong. It will be a new weapon my people can use to protect themselves and it is more valuable than I think you understand."

"Oh." She raised her eyebrows. "Don't underestimate what you can do." She gestured at the clearing around them. "I've never seen anything like what you did today."

"It is not always enough for us so we will give you anything you ask in exchange for your teachings." The man pressed his lips together and steeled himself to hear the worst of what the American witch among them thought her knowledge was worth.

Her brows drew together quickly and she shook her head. "Nothing, Aluino."

He looked like he'd been slapped in the face. "You cannot mean this."

"I do. Absolutely." She glanced at every village witch's eyes now centered on her and the man speaking for all of them. "I didn't teach your daughter how to perform this type of magic because I wanted anything in return. Exactly like...like Romeo and I didn't bring your children home expecting anything. I knew she was ready. And I'm very sure that if I wasn't willing to start her on a few basic fundamentals, knowing she was learning them correctly from me, Rosalía would very likely have made some dangerous attempts to use this kind of magic all on her own —without anyone's guidance."

Oh, my God. I sound exactly like Mom.

And as was always the case with Greta Antony, her little speech had also caught every single person's attention and held them rapt and eager for more despite the fact that she hadn't raised her voice or caused anything remotely close to a scene. "Helping your people protect themselves and teaching your daughter how to handle these spells correctly is all I need. She's incredibly powerful too, you know."

Aluino held her gaze the whole time and barely blinked under the early-afternoon sun's growing intensity. Finally, he nodded. "We know this. Yes. And I think she has chosen the perfect teacher."

She tried to hide her surprise and simply returned the nod before she looked slowly at Romeo. He smirked at her, having not expected her to give an answer like that but also not surprised by anything she'd said. "I guess that's it, then, huh?"

Lily snorted and rolled her eyes. "I guess." The regular sounds of the traveling villagers striking up their own conversations again and finishing their meal filled the clearing once more. *And all these witches are gonna cling to every last thing I show them.* She didn't try to meet anyone's gaze when she looked around the circles of villagers. Still, she unexpectedly shared a glance with Neron the necromancer, who swallowed his last mouthful, allowed the tiniest smile to twitch at the corners of his mouth, and nodded. *I got myself into this, didn't I?*

TWENTY-TWO

The rest of that day felt remarkably like another celebration, and the only difference was that they were out in the middle of Nowhere, Chiapas, in a tele-porting caravan of wagons instead of a settled village on the mountainside. The villagers passed the time weaving more blankets and rugs with materials from the wagons, braiding the girls' hair, patching clothes, cooking over another quickly made fire, and playing in the river. A few of them ventured into the jungle and returned in less than twenty minutes with overflowing baskets of fruit, greens, and nuts Lily couldn't begin to name.

"So they're really good at foraging." Romeo scratched the side of his head. "The more I watch these people, the more I think we're really not prepared to be out here without them. Like...I don't know how to find any of that stuff. They simply went out there"—he gestured vaguely toward the thick jungle around the clearing—"like we take a short drive to the Harris Teeter or something."

Lily laughed and readjusted the braided crown of flowers one of the other boys had brought her, his cheeks pink with both excitement and embarrassment. "I wouldn't call it grocery shopping. I think they use their magic for that, honestly." She nodded at the full baskets of brightly colored fruits.

"Seriously? And they have to go all the way out into the forest to do that?"

"Well, I think perhaps they did that part for you, actually."

"Oh." He continued to study the villagers around them curiously. Some of them gave him wide smiles and nods and others merely went about their easygoing business as if the Americans with the giant RV in their midst had been part of their community all along. "That was really considerate of them."

"Nobody wants a sneezy werewolf stumbling around." She winked at him and made herself laugh.

"True, I guess." He chuckled with a little shrug. "It's probably a good idea anyway. I'm startin' to run out of the wolfsbane Melissa gave me."

"Yeah, I noticed."

"I can help with that." They both twisted where they sat in the grass to see Rosalía standing behind Romeo. The girl folded her arms and smirked at him. "You eat a lot of that poison medicine, don't you?"

He laughed and glanced at Lily. "Only when I'm around witches and considerable magic."

"So all the time?"

Lily barked out a laugh and gestured at the girl who

could send their sarcasm right back in spades. "Look who's throwin' down."

"Yeah, yeah." He grinned at Rosalía. "If you can get me more wolfsbane, kid, I'll let that one slide."

"I don't have to get you anything. Where is it?"

"The wolfsbane?"

"Yes."

"In the center console." Lily pointed at the Winnie. "You have to squeeze the handle underneath to open it."

She grinned at her, spun on her heel, and ran to the RV.

"She doesn't have to get me anything, huh?" He snorted. "Okay, I know she had attitude when we found her, but—"

She shook her head. "I think she meant she won't have to go looking for any." She nodded toward the Winnie's passenger window, where they could see Rosalía's dark hair and most of her profile as the girl closed the center console again and climbed onto it. A deep green glow illuminated her face and most of the RV, then faded again. She looked a little surprised for a moment but stood and returned through the Winnie without delay.

When Rosalía stepped through the side door, she walked toward them again with her arms held behind her back. Her eyes were wide, and she stopped a few feet away from Romeo with her head tilted a little dubiously. "Maybe I was too excited...but I don't think you'll be angry."

He smiled at her but kept the mild concern he felt out

of his face. "Well, that's one way to soften the blow. Let's see it, then."

The girl slowly removed her hands from behind her back. One held the empty Ziplock bag, and the other clutched what was essentially an entire wolfsbane plant—roots, stem, leaves, flowers, and all. "It's not bad..."

He snorted and couldn't hold back the bellow of laughter. "No. It's definitely not bad."

Rosalía glanced at Lily with a sheepish smile and a shrug. "I can find a pot and then maybe he won't run out."

"That's a great idea." She nodded, and the girl dumped the fully grown plant unceremoniously into his lap before she sprinted toward one of the wagons.

"What"—he laughed again and gestured at the huge plant in his lap without touching it—"am I supposed to do with this?"

"Most of the time, it's fairly simple. Put it in some dirt, pour water on it sometimes, maybe stick it in the sun for an hour a day..." She shrugged.

"Okay, when you say it like that, it sounds like the easiest thing in the world."

Lily smirked. "Well, it's one of them, at least."

"No, it's not. I can't even keep bamboo alive. That's like one of the easiest plants to grow, right?"

It was hard to keep a straight face at all when Lily shrugged. "You know what got me to start keeping plants alive?"

"You're gonna tell me it was a spell, aren't you? Again, what am I supposed to do with this?"

She shook her head. "No, I didn't use magic...well, okay. It was magic-related."

"Uh-huh."

"My mom left me a clue once inside an actual flower."

Romeo leaned toward her and widened his eyes. "What?"

"Yeah. I think it was an orchid. I got through this entire mini scavenger hunt she did right after graduation. The very last thing was a key code to get into this hotel room she booked for me, blah, blah, blah. But I had to get the orchid to bloom first 'cause she obviously messed with the seeds or something."

"Your mom made a flower with numbers on it?"

She chuckled. "Yep. It was definitely the best way to keep that plant from shriveling up, even with all the stuff I was busy—no." Shaking her head, she laughed again. "I was actually busy wasting my time. I'm starting to realize now that it's probably why she left a clue inside an actual flower."

"Man, if anyone can do it..."

Rosalía skipped back to them with a medium-sized clay pot painted bright red with a yellow rim. She struggled a little to set it down gently rather than drop it on the ground beside him, but then she stood, dusted her hands off, and gestured toward the wolfsbane plant's new home. "Mama said it can be a gift for you." She put both hands on her hips.

"It's a...great gift. Thank you." Romeo peered over the rim of the pot and gave the girl an uncertain smile. "Do you have any pointers for how to put the thing in here the right way?"

She frowned and stared at him for a moment, then giggled. "You're really smart and strong but you need a ton of help still, huh?"

Lily burst out laughing and immediately clamped her hands over her mouth. He leaned toward Rosalía and whispered, "Well, now that you've discovered my secret, yeah. I could really use your help. Again."

The girl grinned, rolled her eyes, and pointed to the pot. "Bring that. I'll show you the best dirt to put in it."

He nodded solemnly and once she turned away, he looked at Lily and mouthed, "Smart and strong." She suppressed another laugh as he stood with the giant wolfsbane plant in one hand and the rim of the red pot in the other.

ALTHOUGH THE MUSICIANS from the village celebration hadn't joined the travel party to Ichacál, someone had still thought to bring a flute and a drum. One woman had filled an empty gourd with sand and a few small pebbles, which she used as a maraca that night while they played. Chalina and Aluino approached Lily and Romeo after everyone had eaten their fill of dinner. The woman bent to grab Lily's hands and grinned at her. "Come with me. I will show you a dance you will not forget." She tugged on her hands until the younger witch had no choice but to stand.

"Um...okay." She laughed as Aluino thrust his hand out to haul Romeo to his feet too.

"You too," the man said.

"Oh, no." Although he let the villager help him to his feet, he stood his ground and shook his head. "I'm not...I don't dance, really."

"This dance is important. Not for looking pretty." Aluino nodded at the two women. "Well, maybe for them. And you are not too old to learn new things." He clapped a hand on his shoulder and led him away from the women.

"Um..." He turned toward Lily and shrugged.

"It is not dangerous for him." Aluino shot her a wink, then laughed and prodded his unwilling companion forward again.

"It is not dangerous for anybody," Chalina muttered and stared after her husband with her hands on her hips. "Men and their danger, eh? They like to call it with their words"—the woman opened and closed her hand like a moving mouth—"and when it finally finds them, they are mute." She snapped the mocking mouth shut with her fingers and shook her head, chuckling.

Lily smiled and let the woman lead her away from where she'd eaten dinner with Romeo on the soft grass. "I have a feeling you balance that for your husband very well." The villager flashed her a sharp glance. "Not that you talk too much. Only that you're a little more...subtle about the danger part."

She tossed her head back and laughed freely, her long, straight black hair dangling below her hips. "That is a woman's calling, yes? To handle all the danger a man cannot without needing to constantly boast about it." She winked at the other woman, and they both laughed. "Of course, I know some women who like to talk as much as their men. They talk at each other all the time, bidi, bidi, bidi." Chalina flapped her hand again and wiggled her head. "Then the danger has already found them and they are too busy talking to see it there." She nodded with wide eyes as if reminding the younger woman to take notes on this for the future.

Why does it sound like she's trying to give me relation-ship advice? For a relationship I'm not even sure I actually have. She smirked as they joined a group of other women who'd separated themselves a few yards away from the cookfire at sunset and the musicians playing beside it. All of them grinned and beckoned Lily forward, grasped her arms, and brushed their fingers against her blonde, sundried ponytail. One of them adjusted the flower crown on her head and chuckled. "I looked exactly like that once."

"When was this, Pila, hmm?" Another woman wearing a white blouse with bright, embroidered flowers folded her arms with a smirk. "I want to know when your skin and your hair were this white. And oh. You had blue eyes once?"

The woman laughed and jostled Pila playfully, who rolled her eyes and grinned. "I meant her face. No, not how thin it is." They all laughed again, and she lifted Lily's chin a little with a gentle handle. "This look in her eyes, yes? This look we all know." The gathered women hummed in agreement, nodded and smiled, and gazing at her with more admiration than when she and Romeo had arrived in the Winnie with two kidnapped children.

This is totally real-life Twilight Zone. Whatever they're about to do, roll with it.

Chalina clapped her hands as the song ended and nodded at the musicians. The woman with the sand-filled gourd nodded in response, grinned, and a new song began. The villagers who hadn't joined either the woman or the men uttered a few whoops of excitement and turned to watch the groups.

"Okay, now you're putting me on the spot," Lily said with an uncertain laugh, "and I have no idea what I'm doing."

"That is why we are here." Chalina nodded and took her shoulders to position the younger witch a particular way in the grass before she came to stand beside her. "We will teach you this dance and you will use it, yes?"

She took a deep breath and nodded warily. "Okay..."

"Okay! Do you know the Latin dancing?"

"Yeah, actually."

"Well, throw all that out. It is useless now."

That made her laugh again, and she shrugged. "I'll try."

"No, no, no. You will watch me and you will do it." Chalina nodded brusquely and started a dance step that was vaguely like salsa dancing but with far more stamping involved. The music carried over all the conversation in the clearing, and she did her best to repeat after all the women who tried at the same time to show her what came next. "You are all fish flopping around like this," Chalina snapped. The others laughed and made faces when they almost fell over each other. "I told her to watch me." The woman smirked and nodded at her again. "One more time."

Across the clearing, one of the kids shrieked in a fit of giggles before the explosion of men's laughter. When Chalina stopped her dance steps to turn, Lily did the same and found a good number of the men gathered around Romeo rolling around on the floor in hysterics. He must have tripped over his own feet and was quickly caught under the arms by a surprised Aluino, who shoved the werewolf upright and pounded his back. Whatever they said to each other, she couldn't hear a word of it, but his face looked a little redder than what a day in the sun had given him. He spread his arms and shrugged, and another round of laughter issued from the men.

Chalina clicked her tongue and rolled her eyes before she turned to face the woman. "That is their danger, huh? While we are dancing." That brought a few more chuckles before Lily was pulled back into learning a dance she'd never heard of and trying to ignore how weird this felt. *They're all acting like this is the most important thing I'll ever do and I don't even know what it's called.*

ALMOST TWO HOURS LATER, Lily had pretty much gotten the dance down from start to finish. It was ridiculously complicated.

"Right arm out."

"Do this with your hand."

"You step forward only when the other dancer moves to your left."

And Mom did such a great job teaching me how to memorize. I guess spell signals and choreography aren't that different. The thought made her laugh as she wandered toward the Winnie. Romeo shuffled closer and shook his lowered head.

"Woah. It looks like they were pretty rough on you."

He scowled at her and snorted. "I keep telling everyone I can't dance and no one wants to believe me."

She gave him a sympathetic grimace and slipped her arm through his beside the vehicle. "If your teachers were half as dedicated as mine, I'm sure you learned something."

In response, he simply rolled his eyes, turned to face her, and put his hands on her hips. "I'm tellin' you, Lil. It's torture." She laughed and a few hoots and joking shouts came from around the cookfire, which now blazed in the darkness. They both turned to see a few of the men stumbling around, their arms flailing as they fell on top of each other while their friends caught them and pushed them upright again. "See? They're laughing at me and they still think I'm gonna be able to do any of that stuff."

Lily pressed her lips together and tried not to laugh herself. "Try to think of it as laughing with you."

He raised a skeptical eyebrow. "I feel like that's something our third-grade teacher used to say."

"I think it is."

Chuckling, he turned and raised a hand to wave briefly at the men. "Goodnight, dancin' fools!" They doubled over in laughter and waved them both away as they returned to enjoying the rest of their night with their wives and what few children still remained among them. "Yeah, I don't think they get the reference."

"Um...I don't think I do, either."

"What?" He opened the side door and waited for her to step inside first. "Really? 'Dancin' Fool,' the song?" She turned and stared at him expectantly. He shook his head. "Frank Zappa? None of this rings a bell for you?"

She fought back another laugh. "Sorry."

He threw his hands in the air and let them drop back to his thighs with a muffled smack. "Now I really feel alone, Lil."

"Come on. When it comes to your ridiculously broad taste in music, I think you might be." The laughter escaped her anyway when he hung his head in mock hopelessness.

"That was a low blow," he protested but peered at her from below his lowered brow and smirked.

"I had to." She shrugged. "But hey, I bet I could make it up to you."

"I dunno...my pride's all wounded and everything. You're probably gonna have to try really hard."

"Oh, whatever. Come on." She took his hand and pulled him toward the bedroom, grinning at him over her shoulder.

Romeo didn't even put up a fight, and when they stepped through the doorway, he jerked her toward him and slid his arms around her waist. "Okay, you win. This might make me feel better." He kissed her and she laughed and pushed him away gently.

"It might?"

He shrugged. "I guess we'll just hafta find out."

"Hmm." She smirked and studied his green eyes. "Did they even tell you what that whole ridiculous dancing thing is about?"

"Lily"—he shook his head and walked forward, easing her gently back toward the bed—"I really don't care."

TWENTY-THREE

Their second day of this oddly appealing journey on foot—and, of course, through the passages—passed almost exactly like the first. They woke, ate breakfast together, loaded up their belongings from the temporary camp, and took a final dip in the river for good measure. Lily spent a little time walking with the half-dozen villagers who showed interest in the process of summoning the glowing ball of light, and Rosalía eventually took over for her without being asked. While her people practiced with the light, the girl practiced the illusion spell. The next time Lily walked past to see how everyone was doing, the child jumped to her feet and ran toward her.

"I'm ready for something else."

"I had a feeling you'd say that soon." She nodded and squinted up at the treetops. "I'm still thinking about the best next step."

"What about that pulling?" Rosalía balled her hand into a fist and pulled it toward her side. "When you held that woman back and she couldn't do anything to stop you."

Well, yeah. That's exactly what I was thinking about. I guess I shouldn't be surprised that she brought it up first. She smirked at the girl and tilted her head. "Maybe."

"Maybe. Okay." Rosalía nodded, spun away, and dropped onto the ground to keep practicing with the others.

Shortly after that, they moved on, the oxen once more hitched to the massive, unruly wagon-like structure while new villagers took up the duty of pulling the smaller carts along behind them. This time, they walked for two hours through the thickening jungle. The children spent most of that time piled into the largest wagon, and Romeo fell asleep in the passenger seat for at least the last third of it. Lily had no problem driving at the speed of a leaky faucet behind the procession.

When the villagers stopped again at mid-morning and dispersed to form a circle around their odd caravan, she parked the Winnie, turned the engine off and crawled halfway onto the center console and shook his shoulder. "Hey." He snorted and rolled head his toward the window. "They're gettin' ready to...jump. Or whatever. *Romeo.*"

He jerked awake and winced when his shins cracked against the underside of the dash. "Okay, we need to move this seat way back or shave, like, six inches off this thing." Scowling, he glanced at her and rubbed the sleep from his eyes. "What's going on?"

"They're circling."

"Oh, jeez. Okay." He had to try twice to push himself

out of the passenger seat, but then he moved quickly enough toward the kitchen table and the carefully potted wolfsbane plant that sat snugly in the corner of the booth.

Lily turned in her seat to watch him. "You really gotta find a better place to put that."

"Yes, I'm aware of the...precarious situation." He smirked and she rolled her eyes. "Seriously, Lil. The second-best option was to put it in the shower. The pot's about the same size. And this thing definitely won't fit under the table. But if you want me to strap it down somewhere—"

"You should probably hurry." She gestured toward the other villagers, her eyes wide, and faked a grimace.

"Right." He turned to delicately pick two fully opened purple blossoms from the plant, popped them into his mouth, and joined her at the front again. "Do you think Rosalía's magic gave me my own never-ending supply?"

"I couldn't tell ya."

"Who knows what the side effects are of super-growth-hormone spells, right?" He stopped chewing and frowned. "Are there any side effects?"

She snorted. "Probably not. Obviously, magic always does something. But if you haven't noticed a difference with those flowers yet, I'd say they're normal—for being an extremely poisonous plant that helps you deal with highly concentrated magic, of course."

"Right." He slipped into the passenger seat. "I'll probably ask Rosalía about—"

That humming drone from the circling villagers, all connected by their clasped hands, filled the Winnebago again.

She had expected it this time, but it didn't stop her from leaning back against the seat and gripping the armrests tightly. He muttered something, but she couldn't hear it over the low chanting that now seemed incredibly loud while the rest of the world vibrated and shook like an earthquake on fast-forward.

In a moment, it was over and Romeo whistled. "Okay, it's totally different when I'm...hey, what do we even call that? Magically sober?"

Lily snorted, tucked her hair behind her ears, and grimaced at the odd sensation of all her bones settling again after the passage. "Sure. We can go with that."

He chuckled and sucked a tiny piece of purple flower from between his teeth. "Still. This is really, really cool."

The only thing that had really changed about their surroundings was that they seemed to be on top of another hill in the mountains, and the three trees toppled beside the RV—all of them covered in thick moss and strung together with thick, twisting vines—had clearly been there for quite some time. But their traveling party obviously hadn't.

"I guess it's time to explore the new campsite, huh?" He pushed out of the seat again and headed to the side door.

"Hey, it sounds like you're happy with the idea of sticking with these people all the way to the temple." She stood and followed him.

"Well, maybe. Yeah, it would've taken us another eighteen hours or so once we brought the kids home. Driving on the highway, right? But this is...better?"

"Yeah. I wasn't sure if turning two days of driving into four days of walking-slash-teleporting sounded like a good idea, either."

He opened the side door, stepped outside, and held it for her. "It kinda feels right, though. Doesn't it?"

"What? You mean even with all the vegetables?"

"Ha, ha." He let the door close behind her. "You know what I mean, though, right?"

"About trying to do a good thing for a couple of kids and ending up feeling morally responsible for and connected to basically a whole coven of witches who have no idea how powerful they are? Like that?"

His expression suddenly blank, he studied her for a minute before he raised an eyebrow. "Is that a trick question?"

She snorted. "No. I'm feeling flippant, apparently. We can ignore that and I'll simply say I totally agree with you. It does feel right in a way I don't quite understand." Lily took his hand, and the acrid scent of thick smoke over-whelmed her. Her nostrils flared, and she licked her lips, trying to make the taste of it disappear. "Did they get started on the fire already?"

"What do you mean?"

"I mean what's burning? You really don't smell—"

"What is it?" someone shouted. A few gasps rose from the villagers in front of them and Lily looked at the huge, dark wingspan of the black bird made of smoke. The apparition was equally as massive as the last time she'd see it—at least six feet from wingtip to wingtip, and it swooped through the jungle canopy, rushed like water over rocks, and left twin trails of black smoke behind it.

Her eyes widened. "Mom?"

"What?" Romeo jerked his head toward her.

Why did I say that? She didn't have the time to answer her own question. The black shadow-bird hurtled toward her faster than she could even think about a deflection spell. The werewolf growled and ducked into a crouch, and the shadow-bird pounded into her body. A cold wave of something dark and dangerous filled her from the inside out, the taste of ash exploded in her mouth, and she whirled instinctively. The bird was gone, but the warning remained.

"Something's wrong."

"Yeah, you were pummeled by that bird that's been chasing us since—"

"No." She turned again and looked at Romeo with wide eyes. "Something's—"

A streak of red, crackling light careened from within the jungle. Fortunately, it missed the villagers and the wagons but the attack spell seemed focused on the Winnie. At a grating metallic screech and a dull thud, she twisted and grimaced at another charred dent in the RV's side. A few birds erupted from the tree branches behind them and squawked in surprise and irritation.

"Come on. Like I didn't get enough of those in Charleston?"

Another flashing, crackling line of red darted toward one of the wagons now, and she raised her hand to throw up a deflecting shield over it. The attack sparked violently against her spell and ricocheted into the trees behind the Winnie.

"Everyone, get back here!" Romeo waved the villagers away from the tree line and toward their vehicle. Surprisingly, none of the other witches screamed or panicked but they all obeyed instantly, abandoned their provisions, and ran toward the werewolf with the silver-flashing eyes and the witch who kept them all protected. The children were ushered forward first, and as soon as they reached the RV, they were pushed back behind the adults.

Lily studied the trees, waiting for the next attack, and looked for signs of movement. "Is there any way whoever that is came here for the kids too?" she asked and leaned back a little to glance quickly at Neron.

"It is possible," the necromancer said behind her. "I do not know if those who took our children used magic."

"Okay." She stepped forward while Romeo told everyone one more time to remain near the RV. He moved beside her and took a deep breath through his nose. "Did you see where that came from?"

"Only from the trees."

"So who—"

The jungle lit up again with that crackling red light, this time with a massive ball that would have probably blown a hole through Lily and the Winnebago. She raised both hands barely in time and deflected the attack. Her aim was almost perfect too. The sizzling red orb of energy boomeranged toward its source and hissed malevolently until it disappeared in the darkness of the thick jungle undergrowth.

"Do you think you got 'em?" Romeo asked softly.

"No...that looked more like fusion."

"What?"

"Whoever it is...sucked the spell back in to—wait."

There was definitely movement now between the trees. A dark form almost floated through the jungle, lacking the rise and fall of regular footsteps. It made absolutely no sound as it approached, nothing to distinguish it from the constant buzz of insects and the slowly retreating screech of whatever bird or monkey thought it was the right time to make noise. The figure stopped a few paces before it would have entered the muted light streaming through the jungle canopy and onto the collection of wagons.

"With as much magic as we felt here, we expected you to put up more of a fight." The male voice was low and a little nasally.

It'd kinda be nice right now to know if I'm hearing English or something else my little translation spell's picking up. Lily tilted her head and waited a few more seconds before she responded.

"That wasn't a fight," she called into the jungle. "That was me being cautious."

A tense silence followed before another streak of flaming red erupted from between the trees.

Her teeth gritted, she deflected that one immediately before another came from her right. That one, she hurled toward the ground in a spray of damp earth and lush greenery but the attacks didn't slow. *Come on.* Both her hands jerked up at her sides, and she activated a warded shield around the wagons, the villagers, and the Winnie behind them. The red attacks struck her shield and vanished, leaving jagged cracks of glowing silver in her spell before they faded and reappeared wherever the next red streak made contact.

"This looks familiar," Romeo muttered.

"Probably." She grunted and kept the shield up as long as she had to until the attacks fizzled out and finally stopped. The silence seemed ominous and threatening. She waited a little longer to make sure their surprise visitors didn't try anything stupid. Apparently, they were thinking the same thing about her.

"Why are you here?" the voice demanded from the darkness.

"We're literally passing through."

"Lies." A deep rumble echoed through the jungle, and she was jerked forward across the ground.

The werewolf snarled behind her and prepared to shift if he had to, but she didn't let anyone get that far. Even as she was dragged against her will across the jungle floor, she flicked her hand toward the shadowed figure in the trees. The same blue flames she'd used on the club owner in Canada flared to life on his clothes. The attacker's compulsion spell was instantly severed and she regained her footing to take a few large steps backward again.

Someone shouted behind the trees, and the figure that now flailed in growing blue flames staggered back before he tripped over something and landed with a hard thump. A bright light flared behind the fallen newcomer, and the flames were extinguished.

No one said a word as the person who hadn't yet fallen under Lily's almost unquenchable flames sat slowly. The dark hood that had covered his face—and she only knew it was a man after hearing his voice—had fallen back to reveal short dark hair, a surreally pale complexion, and the red eyes of a warlock. He stared at her and his red eyes narrowed. "Is this still your caution?"

She tilted her head in a challenge. "Do you still wanna find out?"

The warlock bowed slightly but held her gaze the whole time. "No." He spread his arms, and at least half a dozen more cloaked figures appeared from within the trees, all of them with skin equally as pale and eyes that glowed the same dark blood-red. "We want to know why you have trespassed on our lands. Why you have brought so much power with you if you do not mean to fight us with it."

"This power is not ours." Aluino stepped forward from the villagers gathered in front of the Winnebago.

With a flick of his wrist, the warlock summoned another crackling sphere of red energy in his palm and held it there, the same color reflecting in his eyes. Lily raised her hand and silently warned their adversary to wait before she turned briefly toward Aluino. The tall man moved cautiously toward them and passed Romeo with his silver-glowing eyes to stand only a foot behind Lily.

"This man speaks for his people," she said and gestured toward the villager. "If you quit throwing attacks for a few minutes, I bet you'll get your answers."

The warlock's gaze flickered from one to the other before he slowly nodded his agreement.

"We are traveling," Aluino began, "to protect what children still remain to us. Our destination is the healing temple in Guatemala. Ichacál. Our home is in Chiapas, and we left it for the safety of the temple and perhaps some answers. All this power you sense is not ours to command. It comes from the earth and it belongs to her still."

"Refugees." The warlock looked unimpressed. "We felt your arrival. It interrupted one of our"—he clasped his hands together and rubbed them—"ceremonies. Is this your magic, witch?"

It's not like we had time for introduction, but I'm gonna assume he's talking to me. She shook her head. "No. These people accessed it." She glanced at Aluino, who could manage to describe the whole process without sounding like he had no idea what he was talking about. *I'm not sure I understand it enough myself.*

The man pressed his hands together as if in prayer and nodded at the warlocks. "My people know how to access the passages within the earth. That is all. Ten minutes ago, we were almost two hundred kilometers northwest beside the river. Now we are here, yes? We opened the passage together and the earth allowed our crossing."

"Then open another and leave." None of the opposing men moved but the coiled tension filtered through the air again.

"We cannot manage two in one day." Aluino shook his head and lowered his gaze toward the jungle floor in deference. "And not from this place."

The leader looked thoughtful. "You mean to reach the portal on the next ridge over."

"If this portal and our closest passage are the same, yes."

"We will wait for you to move your...people there." The warlock's red eyes narrowed again. "Now. Our ceremonies cannot wait much longer before they are broken completely." He scanned the villagers in front of the RV and his gaze settled on the death witch. "We think some of you recognize how crucial this is."

Neron blinked and the slow nod of his head was barely visible.

"Yes." Aluino spread his arms and bowed again before he took a few steps backward. "We will continue to the next. We did not mean to disturb what you do here."

"When you are gone, the disturbance will be ended."

He didn't exactly accept an apology but at least he didn't say we're all gonna pay for crashing their warlock party. "We understand," Lily said.

The villager retreated toward his people and spoke in low tones with words she couldn't hear. The lead warlock stepped toward her. Immediately, a low growl rose from Romeo's throat behind her, and he moved toward her in response. The other warlocks spread throughout the jungle shifted, their faces still shrouded within the hoods of their cloaks.

She paused and waited for the tension to die down a little before she took a few more steps toward the warlock. It seemed obvious he meant to speak more directly to her than anyone else who'd apparently trespassed on ceremonial lands. She held his red gaze and pressed her lips together, waiting for whatever it was he still had to say.

"There is much you do not understand. We have seen this. Soon, you will see it too." He clasped his pale, long-fingered hands in front of his chest slowly as if he were gesturing in thanks for trying to retain whatever patience he hadn't lost when attacking first and asking questions later.

Great. It sounds like everyone else seems to know something about me that I don't. "What else did you see?"

His eye twitched as his gaze flickered back and forth across her face, studying her. Something like a cold, feathery hand brushed over her skin and she fought back a shudder. "Someone is watching you. Good tidings and bad come on dark wings."

Yeah, that's nothing new.

They stared at each other a few moments longer before she simply nodded curtly. "Will you allow these people the time to gather their things and leave this place?"

"Yes."

"Thank you."

The warlock bowed, his hands still clasped in front of his chest, and floated backward across the jungle floor in the same eerie movement without the natural rhythm of real footsteps. In seconds, his cloaked form disappeared into the darkness of the thicker jungle around them. The other warlocks followed suit, leaving the caravan alone in a beautiful part of the mountainside that now simply felt dirty.

Finally, she turned and met Romeo's gaze as she walked toward him. "What was all that about?" he muttered, leaning closer so no one else would hear.

"Only more misunderstandings and riddles." She looked up at him. "But I'm totally convinced now that these people traveling with us have no idea what they're capable of. It's enough to bring an order of warlocks out of the woodwork. If they don't learn how to protect themselves, they might not even make it to the temple."

"So we're definitely sticking around."

"Yeah. And I think I'm gonna have to start teaching much more advanced magic."

Romeo smirked, but it felt tight on his face. "Rosalía's gonna love that."

She glanced at Aluino and Chalina, nodded, and waving them forward so their people could collect the wagons and move off for another few hours of the journey they'd planned to travel tomorrow. Rosalía followed her parents, looking cautious but completely without fear, and she made it a point not to meet the girl's gaze. "That's what I'm afraid of."

TWENTY-FOUR

No one complained about having to walk the extra ten kilometers through thick jungle and muggy, wet terrain. Romeo drove the Winnie behind them, and Lily had to get out three times to blast away a large stone or solidify a particularly sticky mud puddle to get the RV through. A few times, she did the same for the wagons. Though Aluino's people were generally joyful and easygoing, their run-in with the warlocks had left everyone somber.

When she got out again to help mend one of the large wagon's fractured wheels—the villagers in awe of the fact that she could fix something like that so quickly—she didn't immediately return to the Winnie. Instead, she found Chalina and took her arm gently. "How's everyone doing?"

The woman responded with a subdued smile and a resigned shrug. "Tired, mostly. And a little confused, I think. Personally, I do not understand why those sorcerers think our magic is so much a threat."

"I understand that." She nodded. "I think people are generally threatened by things they don't understand."

"Then it was mutual, yes?" The woman's eyes were wide and unblinking.

Why does everyone think I have the answers? "I guess so."

"Were you threatened by them?"

She took a breath before she offered the woman a tiny, conspiratorial smile. "Only enough to hold back."

Chalina chuckled. "We are fortunate again and again to have you with us, Lily." She put a hand on the younger witch's shoulder and nodded.

"Well, by the time we get to Ichacál, I think your people will have a better understanding of how to be fortunate all on your own."

"Without you."

Lily nodded. "Yes."

"After today, I think this is a better decision." The woman chuckled. "Maybe do not tell Aluino I have said this."

She laughed with her. "I won't say a word."

When she returned to the Winnie, Romeo watched the children climb up into the massive wagon. "It's the first time since we left Sierras de Órganos that the smoke-bird thing showed up."

"I know." She sat in the passenger seat and sighed. "This time, I swear, it felt like a message. Like I could almost hear the words whispered in my head but they were still too far away."

"And you said 'Mom.'"

Lily turned to look at him, studied his green eyes flecked with gold, and took a deep breath. "I have no idea why I said that."

"But you did dream about her being carried by that bird, right?"

"Yeah, but I wasn't even thinking about the dream. Obviously, I know my mom's not a giant bird made of black smoke. But it felt like her for a split second before it was a shadow-bird hurtling toward me."

"And through you." He frowned and narrowed his eyes. "Do you still think it's trying to help you?"

She nodded. "I think so. It warned me. At least I think it did. Honestly, the warning could've come from anywhere else, but the fact that the bird went right through me and didn't hurt me at all means something, right? I still won't rule it out as a threat, though. I dunno if it's actually a friendly shadow-bird."

He chuckled and took her hand. "You'll find the answers."

"Hopefully before it has to blast through me to warn me about any other attacks, from warlocks or otherwise."

He squeezed her hand and brought it to his lips for a quick kiss. "Whenever it is, it'll be the right time." The villagers began to move again at the painfully slow pace the wagons and the mountainous terrain demanded. He slowly eased them forward behind the procession.

THEY REACHED the next passage by midday, all of them weary, exhausted, and still a little shaken by that morning's surprise warlock visit. Romeo and Lily had offered to drive anyone who didn't want to walk—or couldn't—the whole way, but everyone refused. The first half-hour in their new temporary camp was spent seated on fallen logs and beds of moss and drinking from the gourds they'd filled at the river that morning, now kilometers away.

"We will not need to walk anywhere tomorrow," one man commented. That brought a few laughs from those sitting closest to him and the mood shifted. Eventually, the villagers rose from their seats to unload the wagons, unhitch the oxen, spread blankets, and raise something as shelters.

Lily pressed her lips together. "If we get rain, though, the only real shelter anyone will have is the Winnie."

"Yep. And something tells me they still wouldn't take us up on the offer."

They were beckoned toward the small gathering circles for another meal and soon, the food brought a new wave of optimism to everyone. Conversation started, laughter appeared, and the villagers smiled at each other again. When they finished, Lily drew Rosalía aside from the others to have the serious conversation the girl had been waiting for.

"Do you think you can cast that illusion charm at a moment's notice?"

Rosalía grinned and clapped her hands. Immediately, the pink glow stretched between her palms until she'd enveloped herself in a glowing pink bubble. The light faded, and the girl merely stood there, grinning at her and staring with unblinking eyes. About a foot beside the girl, another head of dark hair appeared, seemingly from thin air. Rosalía jumped beside her small illusion and folded her arms with a brisk nod.

Lily blinked. "Okay." A laugh escaped her, and she swallowed it quickly. "I want you to practice making that bigger and bigger, right? At least big enough for you to hide all of us, the wagons, and—"

"The adventuremobile." The girl nodded sagely. "I know."

Okay, I gotta nip that one in the bud. "That's what Romeo calls it. Like a nickname." Rosalía frowned. "It's called an RV. Or a Winnebago. That's the make. Not adventuremobile."

"Do I have to tell Papa?"

She laughed fully at that and the child joined in with a giggle. "I'll leave that up to you. Right now, I want to start working on that restraint spell you talked about yesterday."

"The one you used?" Her eyes lit up.

"Yeah, that one. And the shielded wards I used this morning."

"Those are good."

Lily nodded. "They are. Powerful spells, right? And no one gets hurt." The girl opened her mouth but Lily stopped her. "And no, I'm not gonna teach you the blue fire. That was a last resort."

Rosalía lowered her gaze and slid one bare foot around on the damp jungle floor. "Okay."

"Okay. Ready to start?"

"I'm always ready, Lily." She put her hands on her hips and nodded.

"I know you are, kid."

They chose a secluded area for themselves a few yards beyond the new camp. The tree branches hung low and snaked across the ground before they curved up again toward the canopy. There was so much moss and so many vines, Lily was sure that going any farther than this from the others would get anyone instantly lost—herself included.

Rosalía was as quick a study with the restraint spell as she had been with her first two lessons, if not quicker. "That was good," Lily said and tried not to fight against the hold on her wrist. "Release it." The child opened her clenched fist and she was finally able to lower her wrist into her lap, although the spell didn't feel anything like someone's hand clamped around her wrist. *It's so weird to have these spells used on me again. Last time that happened was when Mom was teaching me.* "So, you've gotten past my whole hand and up to my wrist. Try again."

The girl squinted, glanced quickly at Lily, and clenched her fist again as her teacher's hand swung in slow-motion. The force of that restraint spell stopped her arm in mid-swing. "Great. What happens now when the rest of me can still move?" She summoned a ball of light in her other hand as an example of a hypothetical opponent about to cast another attack.

The minute the white light burst in her palm, Rosalía jerked her fist down and raised her other hand. Lily was yanked to the ground by her wrist as her other palm with the light orb whipped back, spun her onto her back, and pinned her to the jungle floor by both her arms. She grunted and gaped at this tiny, skinny young witch who'd disabled her in two seconds.

The minute her student realized this, her eyes grew incredibly wide and she jerked both open hands toward her face in surrender. "Are you okay?"

She snorted. "Oh, yeah. You'd be surprised how many times I landed on my back when I was training."

"Someone threw you around like that?"

"Threw me around?" Smirking, she held the girl's gaze before she cast the restraint spell again. This time, though, she added a little levitation. With a flick of her fingers and two clenched fists, she'd toppled Rosalía off her feet, lifted her high, and held her suspended there, lying flat like she'd raised the girl out of bed. She expected her eager apprentice to struggle a little or at least look frustrated by the fact that she couldn't move an inch. Instead, she burst into sharp, pealing laughter. She chuckled and slowly lowered her protégé to her feet.

"I didn't think you would use it on me."

"That's part of learning how things work."

"Who taught you?"

Lily raised an eyebrow. "My mom."

Rosalía 's mouth popped open. "And you listened to her?"

Careful with this one, Lily. "Well, not always." She

caught the girl's quick glance at her own mother and added quickly, "But I should have. Mothers and teachers are the two most important people to listen to, okay?"

"I'm glad you aren't my mother." The child grinned. "And I'm really glad she's not my teacher."

She laughed and shook her head. "Good. You're lucky to have one of each. I want you to practice that restraint spell until you think you can pin someone down every single time. Or hold their whole body back. Then go talk to the others who wanted to learn."

"I will." She nodded vigorously and with a wide smile. Lily turned to rejoin the other villagers mending clothes, telling stories, and stoking the temporary cookfire.

Before she reached the main group, Neron seemed to appear out of nowhere. "Lily. May I speak to you?"

She paused, caught Romeo's gaze, and turned her attention to the death witch. "Sure. Is everything okay?"

"Yes. I think." He stared at the jungle floor and took a deep breath. "I want to ask you how much you know about the sorcerers."

"The warlocks?"

"Yes."

"Well, other than what they look like, I know most people have a hard time telling the difference between warlocks and necromancers."

The man nodded slowly. "I also know this. I think when we arrived in that place this morning, they were practicing a type of death magic."

She raised her eyebrows. "Really?"

"And they knew me."

"You've seen them before?"

He shook his head briefly and squinted at her. "What I am. The one who spoke saw it in me and recognized it. I do not think they meant harm within their ceremony—or toward us beyond protecting what is rightfully theirs."

"I know."

"Yes. That is why you chose to speak with them before fighting."

"Which thankfully didn't have to happen." She nodded.

"They are like me in some ways, yes? Misunderstood."

"Yeah, I know what you mean. I've seen so much of that in the last few weeks." *Werewolves, warlocks, death witches, witches born without magic. And whoever tried to kill me in Charleston obviously misunderstood me.*

"There was also a warning there." Neron's brows drew together into a small frown of concern. "I feel the need to... ask deeper about this warning, yes? To use what I was given."

"Sure." *He's gonna be working up some death magic, then.*

"In our village, I have a shrine for this, yes? A place everyone knows is meant for my magic only."

She nodded. *Why does he look so embarrassed?*

"Will you speak to Romeo for me? Tell him that—"

"Tell me what?" Neither Lily nor Neron had noticed his approach until he'd almost joined them. Smiling, he glanced from one to the other. "I can handle it, Neron. I promise."

The necromancer cocked his head and squinted at

Romeo. "Yes. I will...perform one of my own ceremonies tonight, Romeo. It will require certain elements that may be difficult for a wolf-man to resist. Do you understand?"

"I think so."

Neron sighed. "Please do not eat the beasts I have sacrificed. It will hinder my sight and my communion, and I do not think it will sit well within you."

"Within—" The werewolf lifted his chin and studied the man over his nose. "Oh. You mean literally."

"That too."

"Yeah, no problem."

"Thank you." He started to turn around.

"Neron?"

"Yes."

Lily offered him a small smile. "Would you look at something for me tonight too?"

His eyes widened as if no one had ever asked this of him. "What would you like to see?"

"Anything you can tell me about that black bird this morning." She shrugged. "The one that found us before the warlocks."

"Ah. Your wings of smoke."

"What? No, that bird thing isn't mine." She shared a glance with her friend. "Definitely not mine."

"But it recognizes you, yes? It knows you enough to find you." The man's head tilted slowly like he was trying to study her from slightly different angles all at once.

She nodded. "That's part of what I'd like to know."

"I see. Yes, Lily. I will ask for you."

"Thanks."

Finally, Neron left them and headed across their makeshift camp to whatever place he'd carved out for himself behind the wagons.

Romeo cleared his throat. "You know, I'm not so into the literal translation of werewolf in Spanish."

She smirked up at him. "I heard wolf-man."

He wrinkled his nose. "Yeah, see, that sounds so *American Werewolf in*...well, Mexico, obviously."

"Well, you heard the man, right? Don't eat his sacrifices." She poked him gently in the chest.

"I wanna say I wouldn't even dream of it, but I'm honestly really curious now."

She laughed. "I choose to believe you're joking."

"Mostly, yeah."

TWENTY-FIVE

When some of the villagers began to prepare the final meal of the day, Lily was drawn aside by a few of the other women. "Come." Chalina grabbed Lily's wrist and pulled her farther into the jungle until they could barely hear the others' voices beyond the drone of all the insects and the squawking birds and whatever other creatures rustled in the lush vegetation during the day.

"What's going on?" She smiled and watched the women who gathered around her much like they had the night before, giggling and grinning at her.

"You will dance again. Practice. Practice." Chalina waved her forward.

"But...there isn't even any music."

"That does not matter if you know how to move." The woman stamped her foot, and the others echoed it with a few laughing shouts.

"Okay, okay." Feeling ridiculous, she obliged them and went through the motions and the steps she'd essentially mastered the night before. When she finished, the women clapped and grinned at her and touched her shoulders, her hair, and her bare arms. "Does anyone wanna tell me what this is for?"

"Oh, you will know when you need to know." The woman named Pila nodded with wide eyes.

"Every woman does," Chalina added. She laughed and headed toward the camp and the cookfire. The others followed and beckoned Lily to join them, but she gave herself a moment simply to stand there and think.

"I'm missing something really important."

———

APPARENTLY, that night after dinner was when she needed to know. With the food eaten, the cookfire stoked into larger flames, and the sun all but completely set, Lily looked at Romeo and frowned. "What's wrong?"

"Something feels off." He squinted and gazed around the fire. "They're waiting for something."

"Who?"

"All these people..." His eyes shifted over the gathered villagers, then he chuckled. "I'm not trying to freak you out, by the way."

She snorted and playfully smacked his arm. "Then maybe don't start a conversation with 'Something feels off.'"

"Hey, I'm merely being honest." He laughed. "I get it. Find a better opener."

"Yes, please." Without any warning, the drummer

struck up a beat, followed quickly by the lilting flute and the woman's sand-filled gourd. She nudged him with her elbow. "Oh, so they were all simply waiting for the music."

"Maybe."

About a dozen villagers gathered behind them and began to raise them to their feet. They giggled and shouted things Lily couldn't make out over her own surprised laughter and the fact that she could only focus on trying not to fall over or onto any of them. Finally, when both she and Romeo were standing, the countless hands released her and a cheer rose from all the villagers together.

"What is going on?" She looked up at him, and his eyes were as wide as hers felt.

"I have no clue. Hey, this isn't what Neron was talking about earlier, right? You don't think we're—"

"We are not sacrifices," she muttered and slapped his arm. "That's awful." They both began to laugh, catching the contagious good humor all around them.

"Now, you dance," Chalina shouted.

"What?" Romeo shook his head.

"Both of you." Aluino folded his arms and nodded.

"Okay, I don't know how many times I have to tell people. I don't—"

"Do the dance!" Rosalía shouted.

He pointed at her with a mock frown. "You are not helping."

"Dance! Dance!" The other children joined in, then the adults, and it basically became a chant for the two American magicals within a traveling group of indigenous witches to simply do the dance.

Filipe walked slowly toward them and scowled at Romeo. The kid stopped and folded his arms. "I thought you were brave until now." His people cracked up at that, but the kid didn't even blink.

"You know, kid, I get the feeling you actually mean that."

The boy simply shrugged and raised his eyebrows before he walked away.

Romeo sighed so heavily through his nose, it almost sounded like a growl. "I can't back away from that challenge, can I? Okay, fine!" He spread his arms and stepped away from Lily. The villagers broke out into even louder cheering. "Fine. We'll do the dance."

"We?" She laughed and Chalina prodded her forward into the ring of open earth beside the fire.

"I believe the man said both of us." He wiggled his eyebrows and she rolled her eyes but they turned to face each other.

The music changed abruptly, the drumbeat much slower now while the flute uttered fast, twirling notes, high and low and high again. Chalina leaned forward to nod at Lily. "Now."

"I don't even know what this is." Still, she performed the first series of steps. At the end, she raised her arm and held it in the right position, waiting exactly as she'd been taught. Another round of loud encouragement bombarded her from all the villagers watching, and it made her laugh.

Romeo moved through a few shuffling, awkward movements. The men had a good chuckle at that and didn't even try to hide it, but someone else shouted, "You dance much better tonight!" He clenched his eyes shut and laughed with them, and the music changed enough to bring a whole different feeling to the scene.

"Keep going!"

When Lily stepped forward, so did Romeo. They laughed to see their own movements mirror each other, sometimes as a reflection and sometimes in opposition. He stumbled a few times but managed to release all the awkwardness and simply dance with Lily around the fire. "It looks like you know what you're doing," she whispered when the motions brought their faces inches apart.

"Honestly, I'm only copying you."

She laughed, spun in a tight circle, and threw her head back to catch a glimpse of him doing something like a bow. By the time they both stamped their feet into the damp earth beneath them, he had stopped thinking about where to put his feet and how ridiculous he felt. She had stopped feeling dozens of eyes watching her perform something she didn't understand. They didn't touch each other until the very end, when she spread her arms and he clapped his over his head before he pulled his fists toward his chest. Neither of them expected him to catch her around the waist and dip her so low to the ground that her hair brushed the dead leaves on the jungle floor. She shouted in surprise and grinned. When she looked at him, his chest heaved and he stared at her like he'd just discovered he could fly.

The flute stopped on a high, fluttering note. They hadn't realized how completely silent the camp had fallen around them until the villagers burst into raucous applause, whistling and hooting, while they stamped their feet. A few cheers followed, and the music picked up again at a much faster pace. Laughing, Romeo lifted Lily fully onto her feet again and the villagers around them began to dance as well. Aluino pulled Chalina into a quick, whirling spin, and when they passed the young couple, the woman caught Lily's gaze and raised her eyebrows. "Now you know." She disappeared with her husband into the flickering firelight and the jumping shadows and the moving bodies of her people.

"Know what?" Romeo asked, still breathing a little heavier than normal.

"That's the thing." She laughed. "I still don't know."

"That was one of the weirdest things I've ever done." He ran a hand through his hair. "They cheered but I think they were only trying not to hurt my feelings."

She slid her arms around his waist and looked at him. "Actually, that was some good dancing. Whatever it's called. Nice dip at the end."

"Yeah, well, I only did what felt right in the moment, I guess."

"I'm sure that's what dancing is."

He chuckled and hugged her closer while they watched the villagers celebrating a little more vigorously than they had since leaving their home. With her ear pressed against his chest, she heard and felt his racing heartbeat.

THE CAMP BUSTLED with activity the next morning when Romeo and Lily opened the Winnie's side door and stepped out into the jungle. A second later, the villagers cheered at them again, pumped their fists, and whooped like the two had done something unfathomably heroic. They only had enough time to exchange a confused glance before Aluino approached and placed a hand on each of their shoulders. "You should stay out here with us through the passage." He grinned and shook them a little.

"Is this one different than the others?" Lily asked.

"For you, yes!" The man laughed. "The earth takes great joy in blessing new unions. You will feel it if you stand within our circle."

"Wait, what?" Romeo leaned toward him. "What new unions?"

The man merely laughed and turned away from them to take his place in the growing circle of villagers.

Romeo looked at Lily with wide eyes. "That sounded a lot like—"

"Yeah. I think he meant us." She tried not to laugh. "What did we actually do last night?"

"It's how our people join their lives together." Rosalía approached them with confident steps and stopped in front of them to study them from head to toe. "Mama said it always feels different as husband and wife. Maybe that's why you're so confused."

Lily blinked furiously. "As what, now?"

"Husband and—"

"Yeah, okay. We heard you the first time." He chucked the girl gently under her chin.

Rosalía jerked her head away and laughed. "You really don't know how things work here, do you?"

"Shouldn't you be practicing something super-important?" Lily raised an eyebrow and the girl straightened out of her playful posture.

"After we pass through, I will. I promise."

"Good. Do you have a place in the circle right now?"

"Yes!" The child danced away toward the ring of villagers now starting to hold hands, paused once to grin at them, and added, "Take your shoes off."

They stood in silence for a minute, and Romeo glanced at his sneakers. "That's simple enough, right?"

"Sure." They slipped out of their shoes and stood barefoot in the damp soil. Lily took a deep breath.

"Okay, so..."

"It was the dance, right?" Turning toward each other, they froze and burst out laughing. "I knew it was the dance."

"These people are sneaky." He shook his head.

"Would you have done it if they'd told you what it meant?"

He shrugged. "Not if you didn't know too. Would you?"

Her mouth opened and closed a few times before she could think of an answer. "That's one of those big things that kinda needs to be talked about first, right?"

"That's what I thought. And we were peer-pressured into..." He cleared his throat. "Uh..."

"Getting married by an indigenous tribe in the jungle." She barked out a laugh.

He sighed dramatically. "That kinda sounds cool, but only a little." His eyes widened and he leaned away from her. "You're not...are you taking this seriously? Or—"

"Are you kidding?" She slipped her arm through his and grinned at him. "Again, that's something that needs a conversation first. I'm not...we're not married."

"Okay. So what happens in Mexico stays in Mexico." He swallowed and looked at the now empty camp and the circle of villagers preparing for the next massive teleportation.

Lily watched him closely. *I can't tell if he's relieved or disappointed.* "Hey." He looked at her. "Nothing changed, okay?"

He smiled. "Good. I mean...I know that. But still. Good." He leaned down to kiss her, and they might have talked about it more if the villagers hadn't already begun their chanting.

Their voices were a lot clearer outside the Winnie, although Lily still didn't understand a word of the incantation. The low, droning buzz was a lot more intense too, and she clutched his arm with both hands even before the world vibrated around them. Through her shaky vision, she saw the huge trees around them blink in and out of focus, then she couldn't see anything for a fraction of a second. The earth grew warm beneath her feet and hummed like some kind of soft, purring engine springing to life. Her legs tingled as the energy moved up through her body, and by the time it reached her head, they'd already passed through.

Romeo stumbled beside her. Trying to steady his

weight, she lowered him awkwardly onto the ground so he wouldn't fall and maybe crush her too. The Winnie's side door banged shut, and she turned to see Rosalía race across the ground toward them.

The girl skidded to a halt and opened her hand to reveal two of the purple wolfsbane flowers. "Is he always so forgetful?"

Lily chuckled and took them. "All this takes a little getting used to, I think. Thanks." She knelt beside him and worked the flowers into his mouth again. *This is not as bad as force-feeding him a poisonous tincture to save his life, but it still feels weird.*

In less than a minute, the wolfsbane had done its work and Romeo gradually focused on the girl who stood in front of him. "You had already planned to do that, hadn't you?"

She fixed him with a challenging look very reminiscent of her mother. "Only if you didn't. I waited to see first. I think maybe that pot would fit better in the shower."

He turned toward Lily. "See? That was the next best place."

"I won't take showers with a whole poisonous plant." She pressed her lips together and caught his hand for a little squeeze before she released it. "So where did we end up this time?"

Nodding, Rosalía stepped aside to reveal the full view of the next mountain peak before them. "We are almost at the temple." She pointed at the few white spires and most of a white arch that protruded above the jungle canopy. "Papa said we'll be there tonight."

This time, Romeo squeezed Lily's hand. "That's some seriously impressive traveling." He pushed himself to his feet and offered her a hand up too. "Are we going right now?"

"After eating, I think. Are you hungry?"

"I...think I'll wait for a while." He ran a hand through his curls and smirked. With a shrug and a careless tilt of her head, she skipped away to rejoin her parents and the other villagers setting out food and water for everyone. He shoved his hands into his pockets and stared at the white stone of Ichacál in the distance. "Okay. This is the final stretch."

"Yeah." She studied what little she could see of the healing temple. "Now we get to see what kinda place it really is."

INSIDE THE WINNEBAGO and the wooden box on the shelf behind Lily's bed, the carved stone head with black-hole eyes and a perpetually open mouth stirred. It rattled a few times within the box before the carving's eyes and mouth illuminated with a sickly green glow. The light pulsed in a quick series of rhythmic bursts, alerting those who awaited its return. More and more people traveled to Ichacál every day for safety and the promise of renewed hope, but the stone carvings answered only to their masters.

TWENTY-SIX

I t took them almost eight hours to navigate the wagons and the RV through the mountainous terrain—one steep decline before an even steeper ascent toward Ichacál. At one point, Romeo got out to help push a few of the wagons through the worst of it, and when he returned to the Winnie, it was only to usher the completely exhausted kids inside so they could sit and not add any extra weight to the wagons.

The sun hadn't quite set when they pushed over the final rise and found the dirt road leading directly to the temple. The surrounding jungle, though, blocked almost all of the remaining daylight. When the wagons finally began to roll more easily over a better-maintained road than anything they'd traveled thus far, a few haggard cheers rose from the villagers who weren't pulling said wagons. But even those subsided under exhaustion. Still, the relief of having finally made it to their destination brought a wave of excited whispers that drifted through the travelers.

After another kilometer, they found the path illuminated by glowing white stones lining the dirt. The intricate arches, spires, gateways, and windows of Ichacál's healing temple emerged from the trees. With a renewed burst of energy, the wagons were pulled and pushed much faster now toward the temple itself. The whispers grew to exclamations of awe and gratitude, and Lily had to really step on the gas pedal for the first time in five days.

At the small courtyard outside the temple—which was really nothing more than a rounded circle of packed earth and a few flowers sprouting around its edges—the travelers were welcomed by the Wisemen of Ichacál.

That was the first thing that caught her attention when she turned off the Winnie and stood. "We made it."

The kids curled on the couch, in the armchair, and even stuffed into the booths at the small kitchen table all scrambled from their seats toward the side door. Filipe reached it first and shoved it open, followed by the others. "The Wisemen," one of them whispered, her eyes wide as she paused on the stairs.

"Get out so we can see." Another boy pushed her from behind, and the rest of them tumbled out into the courtyard.

Lily stepped cautiously out of the RV and looked around. The place was definitely well-lit, both with those glowing stones along the pathways and with tiny versions of the light orbs she'd first taught Rosalía. Romeo stood outside and she stopped beside him. "Who are the Wisemen?"

"If I had to guess, I'd say all the dudes in blue robes."

She finally saw them—about a dozen witches, all of them male, streaming in two lines from the temple's main entrance toward the weary travelers in their midst. The men's sleeves fell far past their hands and their robes trailed behind them on the ground. It had the same visual effect as the floating warlocks the day before, but these witches still moved with a graceful rise and fall to their steps.

"Welcome to Ichacál," they said and opened their arms in greeting to shake hands and offer quick hugs. The courtyard filled with subdued conversations. "Come share our shelter and our food."

"We also seek advice," Aluino said. "Maybe your help, but only if you are willing to offer it."

The Wiseman standing in front of him closed his eyes and nodded. "Yes. We may speak of all these things in the morning. Tonight, what your people need is to rest in the comfort of knowing you are all finally in a safe place."

"Yes. Thank you." The villager nodded and placed his arm around Chalina's shoulders. Filipe and Rosalía followed closely behind their parents. A few villagers went through the wagons to gather what they wished to take with them into the temple before they too joined the others and the Wisemen ushered them all inside.

The young couple hung back for a moment. "So far, it feels like a safe place." Romeo folded his arms. "That's a decent welcome, right?"

"Yeah. But it feels a little weird that those Wiseman didn't seem surprised at all to find dozens of displaced people from a different country showing up on their doorstep. It's almost like they were expecting us."

"Maybe they were." Neron stopped on the other side of Romeo and stared at the temple entrance. "I did not have the time to tell you sooner. I could not see any deeper into the warning."

Her eyes widened. "Really?"

The death witch shook his head. "The spirits' voices are silent. The visions..." He sighed. "Only a blur I cannot understand."

"Even the shadow-bird?"

"Yes."

She nodded. "Okay. Well, that simply means we're gonna have to keep our eyes open for absolutely anything that might feel off."

"It shouldn't be any harder than it normally is," Romeo added.

One of the Wisemen turned from the temple entrance and beckoned to the trio with a broad, sweeping wave. His blue sleeves fluttered through the air.

"Maybe." Neron stepped forward and nodded at the Wiseman, although his next words were only for his companions. "But I feel very strongly that there is someone who wishes us to not see at all." With that parting remark, he made his way toward the temple.

They exchanged a glance. "That's good to know," the werewolf said.

She sighed as they set off after the necromancer. "Only

if we can find out who that someone is and what we're not supposed to see."

———

THE HEALING TEMPLE of Ichacál revealed no surprises that night, though. The Wisemen brought baskets of food—thick, doughy rolls and crocks of butter, baked fish, vegetables cooked and spiced, rice, and a thick brown sauce that smelled like chocolate. The villagers politely declined the fish but Romeo attacked it like he hadn't eaten since they set out for Guatemala. There was no music, little conversation, and fewer words that could capture how grateful these people were to be there.

"We have more than enough space for all of you." The Wiseman who spoke gestured toward the travelers seated on the floor and in one of the large anterooms beyond the entrance. "When you are ready to lay your heads down, we will show you."

No one stood immediately and everyone apparently still needed a little more time to let the reality of their circumstances fully settle. Soon, however, couples and families stood slowly from the white stone floors, thanked the Wisemen for the food and for shelter within the stone walls that offered so much more protection than even the wooden huts of their abandoned homes.

One of the men in blue robes stopped beside Romeo and Lily when they stood from their empty plates as well. "Would you also like a room for yourselves?" His thick, draping sleeves came together in front of his waist, completely hiding his hands within them.

"Oh. No, thank you." She smiled and shook her head. "We brought our own place to stay." The man frowned in confusion, and she added, "We drove here in our RV."

"Through the jungle?"

How does he know that? "I'm sorry?"

"You arrived with these people, did you not?" The Wiseman gestured toward the villagers who wandered out of the anteroom to be shown their beds for at least tonight.

"Yeah. We thought we'd take the scenic route, you know." Romeo shrugged. "It turns out that was through the jungle with our new friends. It makes the trip more authentic-feeling, you know?"

The man blinked and bowed his head. "I understand. We do not see many tourists, though. The temple does not provide the type of excitement most tourists seek. This is a peaceful place of healing."

"We know." She glanced at him and smiled. *Way to take the lead on spinning the lie, Romeo.* "The trip is a little more personal for us. My aunt came here years ago. She had cancer." Her friend tried to keep the range of reactions to that one from seeping out into any expression whatso-ever. "The cancer went into remission three weeks after she came home, and she's been cancer-free for at least five years now. The woman swears it was Ichacál and the healing in this place that cured her."

A thin smile graced the Wiseman's lips. "Yes. We hear these stories from time to time, although we cannot take credit for every miracle within these walls. Have you come to us seeking healing?"

She swallowed. "Kind of. It's a...difficult story."

"Of course. Perhaps tomorrow, once you have rested, you may feel comfortable enough to speak of these things aloud. We always try to make ourselves available for those in need of advice." The man glanced at the werewolf. "Or even merely a willing ear. I hope you will choose to find us when you are ready."

"Thank you," she whispered.

"We're glad to be here," Romeo added.

"Good. I trust you can find your way to your RV."

"Yeah. Thanks."

"Then I'll take my leave for the night." The Wiseman bowed a little from the waist and closed his eyes briefly. He straightened and turned away from them, his smooth, graceful steps taking him toward some of the villagers who straggled down the hallways of white stone.

"Nice work with the cover story," Romeo muttered. "Why'd you go with cancer?"

"It was the first thing that popped into my head." She offered him an empathetic smile. "Sorry."

The corners of his mouth turned down as he shrugged. "Don't be."

As they turned in the main hall to make their way out to the courtyard, Neron emerged from the anteroom with the last of his people. A Wiseman brought up the rear to usher their guests out for the night. The death witch met Lily's gaze and raised his eyebrows briefly. His slight nod of acknowledgment, reminding them to be careful, was barely visible. They both nodded in response. While she wanted to turn and see which hallway the Wiseman would lead him down, she didn't want to risk the chance of it looking like she didn't want him to be separated from them. Because that, at least, was the truth.

The sun had set completely when they stepped out of the temple and into the courtyard. The brilliant splash of stars they'd grown used to over the last week had faded now with all the white-glowing stones. Most of the jungle canopy around Ichacál blocked them out anyway. The night was silent, much cooler but still insulated within so many trees.

Romeo took a deep breath and stared at the canopy. "I can totally see why people come here to find peace."

"It's definitely beautiful." Lily opened the Winnie's side door and he held it for her as she climbed up the steps. "And the Wisemen seem to genuinely care about what happens to people when they get here."

The side door closed with a soft snap as he let it fall against his hand. "And you still don't completely trust it, do you?"

"No." She shrugged. "It's only... I have what Neron told us in my head, plus my mom's last note. She said the places that seem the safest are sometimes the most dangerous, and a necromancer can't even see that danger beyond a gut feeling. I can't simply let it go. And my mom left that creepy head for me, so now we made it and I have to find out what's going on."

"They kinda keep getting harder, huh?" He stepped toward her and pulled her into a warm embrace.

She pressed her cheek against his chest and hugged him in return. "Yep. Maybe we should actually talk to one of these Wisemen tomorrow. Bring them the stone head and ask what they're for. That might give us something."

"Yeah, sure. You should probably come up with that difficult story first to explain why we're here for healing."

She snorted into his shirt. "I'll think of something."

TWENTY-SEVEN

L ight, repetitive tapping on the Winnie's side door dragged Lily from sleep and she rolled in bed. When it stopped, she thought maybe she'd been dreaming it but it started again with even more urgency, and she sat quickly, tossed the covers aside, and stood in almost the same motion.

She summoned a ball of fierce orange flames in her hand, just in case, and stepped slowly down the first stair to unlock and open the side door. "Neron?"

The man's eyes flickered wildly in the light of her spell, but even when she extinguished the flames, the earnestness in his face remained. "I am glad to see you lock your doors, Lily, but it makes it difficult to get your attention."

"What time is it?" She squinted at him and pushed the door fully open.

"The darkest hours of the night. Please, may I come inside?"

"Oh. Sure."

He nodded briskly, held the door open for himself, and brushed hastily past her in the narrow space of the two steps.

"What's going on?" She licked her lips, her brain still trying to fully surface from sleep.

"One very important thing first." He spun in the living area and searched the darkness in which she could barely see. "Where is it?"

"Where's what?"

"The totem. The symbol of good fortune." He wiped his hand along the back of the couch and peered over the driver's seat.

"Sorry. I'm still..." Lily shook her head. "What totem?"

The death witch stopped and stared at her. "The stone head. You said it came from Ichacál. Where did you put it?"

"Oh, it's in the bedroom—" She didn't even get to fully extend her arm and point before Neron hurried across the Winnie and down the short hall to the back. "Hey, I can get it. Romeo's still sleeping."

That clearly didn't matter, so she tried to give the werewolf at least a little warning by flipping on the hallway light. In the sudden illumination, she noticed the black bag clutched in the man's hand. *Weird. Wake up, Lily.* Romeo groaned and rolled toward her side of the bed, where the necromancer now kneeled on the mattress and stretched toward the wooden box on the shelf.

"Uh, Romeo?" she called.

"Why'd you turn the—shit!" He jerked in the bed,

snatched a pillow with both hands, and held it out in front of him like a shield. "What are you—Neron?"

"I apologize for waking you both. One moment, please." The death witch stepped off the bed and held the box out to her. "Please take this and open it."

"Okay..." She took the heavy box, undid the golden latch, and pulled the lid open. He shoved his hand in the black bag, grasped the stone head, and turned the cloth inside-out to envelop the artifact with the thick material. With a deft gesture, he twisted the bag shut at the top and nodded as he raced past Lily and out the Winnie's side door again. She barely managed to keep up with him and poked her head through the door in time to see the black bag and the stone inside it hurtled into the darkness. It disappeared down the steep mountainside, and she never heard it land.

Well, now I'm awake. "So...uh, I was kinda planning on using that—"

"And now you will not." Neron stepped into the RV without being invited this time and began to pace in the area that was really too small for his level of intensity. "That thing has been watching you. Both of you. All of us." He shook his head and didn't look up when Romeo appeared in the hallway. "It does not represent good fortune but bad tidings."

"Okay, can you slow down a minute?" She sat in the spinning armchair and he finally stopped pacing.

"I did not see the answers when I asked for them last night." His eyes were wide when he looked at her. "Sometimes, they do this. They come to me days or weeks later instead, when I am sleeping or awake. Earlier, the answers woke me." He spun and looked at Romeo too. "This place is not what it seems at all. Something dark is buried here. I want—I hope—you will both come with me to find it before it spreads."

The werewolf stepped quickly out of the hallway, and Lily stood again. "Are you sure?" The forceful determination in the man's eyes when he returned his gaze to her almost made her stagger backward.

"As certain as I am that my magic requires death first."

"That's good enough for me." Romeo slipped quickly into the bedroom to pull a shirt over his head and jam his feet into his sneakers. He returned and clapped a hand on Neron's shoulder. "Let's go check it out." He looked at Lily and she nodded.

"Yeah. Of course we'll come with you." She snatched a zip-up hoodie off the back of the kitchen booth table and slipped her flats on. Quietly, they exited the RV and headed swiftly across the courtyard toward the temple.

"So what exactly did you see?" Romeo whispered.

Ahead of them, Neron shook his head. "The clearest was only dark wings and something hidden in the walls. I cannot...I cannot find the words. But I will know it when I see it."

"Okay..." Lily took a deep breath. "And we're trying not to wake anyone up while we're looking through the place, right?"

The necromancer stopped, turned, and fixed her with a warning stare. "I believe this is best, yes." He swung away again and approached the temple's entrance. The couple exchanged another glance, but neither of them spoke before they stepped cautiously across the threshold and moved as quietly as they could across the white stone floors.

Neron reached the end of the main hallway, which branched both to the left and the right. He beckoned them with an urgently wave of his hand and turned left. They picked up the pace, which posed something of a challenge. It was difficult not to make a sound within stone walls where even a loud breath echoed.

The hallway they were in was also lined with the glowing white stones, although these were smaller and rested in sconces along the white walls. Their guide led them down a series of passageways, one of which was a long hallway without a northern wall. It didn't echo quite so much in there, but the twisting, grasping tree branches of the jungle canopy stretching out as far as she could see made her feel like something was about to snatch her by the ankle.

At the end of this open-air hall, the death witch stopped again and pointed to two white clay pots on either side of the entryway into another passage. It was almost impossible to see the flowers' coloring in the darkness, but even if she hadn't caught a dull tone of purple in the low light, she recognized the shape of the wolfsbane blossoms. She pointed at them and looked at her friend. "So they either keep poisonous flowers on hand merely for fun," she whispered, "or they're harboring werewolves here too." He raised his eyebrows and shrugged.

"I think harboring is perhaps not the right word,"

Neron whispered and ducked his head low as if that would keep his words from traveling farther. "I do not know if anyone is truly harbored here. Come."

"Well, that's very reassuring," Romeo muttered, but he plucked a few of the purple flowers. He popped two into his mouth and shoved the others in his back pocket as they followed the other man down another left turn and a new hallway.

After the next turn within what was clearly Ichacál the labyrinth, there were no more glowing stones within sconces on the walls. Lily gave her eyesight a few seconds to adjust but when her vision didn't improve, she summoned a smaller sphere of light and raised it toward the stone ceiling. Neron spun quickly toward her, realized what she'd done, and nodded his thanks. She nodded in silence.

They moved far more slowly now because the death witch paused to examine the wall on their right every few feet. "Did you come through here before you came to get us?" she whispered.

He shook his head and pointed at his temple while he bent his knees and brushed his fingers down the wall to search and probe the stone. "The dreams stay until I no longer need them."

"You dreamed about how to get here through the temple?" Romeo asked.

"Yes. So far, it is all exactly the same. Come." He waved them forward again, and they followed at a much quicker pace down the incredibly long hallway. Abruptly, he stopped and forced himself not to shout. "Lily. The light."

She moved the floating orb of white light from the ceiling to the wall beside the necromancer and grimaced as the shadows stretched and changed shapes around them.

Neron's eyes flickered from one stone to the next and his palm hovered over each one until he froze. "This is it. I do not know what it means, but I was told to find it." He stepped aside and gestured for his companions to look.

Lily stepped cautiously toward the wall and lowered the light slowly toward where he still pointed. "What are we looking at? I'm not sure I—" She drew in a sharp breath. "Oh, my God."

"What is it?" Romeo leaned forward to peer at the wall but he couldn't see a thing.

"Do you see this?" She brought her finger toward the single stone but didn't dare to touch it yet because she still tried to process what she saw.

"Uh...yeah. Looks like symbols."

"My mom's symbols."

The death witch leaned forward between them. "You can read their meaning?"

She gave him a hasty sideways glance before she returned her attention to an extremely well-hidden message without any use of magic whatsoever. "Oh, yeah. I was taught by the same woman who created their meaning in the first place."

Neron drew in a hissing breath through his teeth. "What does it say?"

Lily squinted. "'Press farther only if you're ready for the truth.'"

They all paused for a moment before the necromancer straightened. "So we continue and find the truth. Come." He gestured down the hallway and strode forward.

"Wait." The man paused at her command and glanced at her over his shoulder. Romeo gestured for him to return to where they stood and his nod was convincing enough that he did as he was told. Lily fixed them both with a calm, determined expression. "If my mom was here, she might've left these. Even if she didn't, anyone who knows her symbols—anyone who would actually use them here—has to think the same way she does. She wouldn't share this with simply anybody."

"How is this helpful?" Neron sniffed in irritation but that was his only tell.

"Because I think this was meant literally." Finally, she let her fingertip touch the white stone carved with her mom's secret language. After a moment, she added the weight of her entire hand and with a muffled crunch, the stone slid into the wall like a giant button. A series of metallic clicks sounded behind the wall, and the trio stood upright and stepped away a scant second before the fierce roar of stone sliding over stone filled the hallway. A narrow panel of stone wall dropped a few inches and slowly sank lower and lower into the ground. When it stopped level with the floor, a loud boom echoed down both sides of the hallway.

"Press farther," Romeo muttered.

Neron nodded and stared at the gaping black hole in the wall. "Quite literally."

With a flick of her wrist, Lily lifted the small orb of glowing light away from the wall and sent it through the darkness ahead. A narrow, winding staircase descended before them, and when the orb's light disappeared and left everything in darkness again, she drew it back up so it would light their way.

"You said something dark was buried here," she whispered.

The death witch looked at her. "Very, very deep, I think."

"It seems like a good reason to keep going." Romeo tilted his head to listen intently and stepped through the wall first. The others followed but it was easy enough for all three of them to walk side by side down the twisting staircase. Her light glowed ahead of them beneath the low ceiling, illuminating the way to whatever truth they were about to find buried beneath Ichacál.

TWENTY-EIGHT

O kay, I feel like we've been walking down these stairs forever.

Their footsteps were silent enough on the steps, helpfully muffled by the thick layers of dust coating every stone. Lily didn't miss the other footprints in that dust and the toes facing both up and down the stairs, but it didn't seem like the best time to say anything.

"Hey." Romeo's whisper was still loud enough to catch their attention in the almost complete silence. He raised a hand and stopped, so his companions stopped too. "Do you hear that?"

She tried to listen but all she heard was the three of them breathing in the stairwell. Irritated with herself, she shook her head.

"You will soon." He raised his eyebrows. "Voices."

They descended even farther on the winding stairs until those in front of them look like they were straightening. At that point, she did hear the voices—soft whispers and shuffling bodies, a few coughs, and someone sniffling after a barely restrained sob. In the moment when her orb rounded the last curve in the wall before them and spilled its light into the room beyond, all the voices ceased. It left a quivering silence in the air for the few seconds it took the three investigators to reach the bottom of the stairs.

Lily lifted her sphere higher and directed it out into the cavern. Her gut reaction was to draw it back toward her and away from what it revealed—something she knew she wasn't supposed to see. But she steeled herself and let her light drift past the rows and rows of iron bars that stretched from the cavern's ceiling to the stone floor beneath, fashioned in narrow rectangles like full-length cages.

It took a full minute of incredulity before her mind processed exactly what they were—cages full of people.

The first two shrank away from the ball of light and their fingers slipped off the iron bars as they retreated toward the stone wall behind them. In the next cage, a woman clutched two bars with dirt-caked hands, her fingernails black around the edges, and pressed her face as close to the light as she could. Everywhere the orb moved, there was another cage and one, two, three or more people inside it. From where she and her friends still stood at the bottom of the stairs, she floated her light around the cavern, which was nothing more than a large oval lined with cages. She didn't see any other exit but the way they'd come down the stairs.

A man with copper-colored hair cleared his throat on her right. "Greta?"

At the sound of her mom's name, she moved swiftly across the cavern toward the man's cage.

"Lily..."

She ignored Romeo's whispered warning. *This man knows my mom.* Her glowing sphere followed closely until she stopped in front of the man. In the bright white light, his copper hair could have been flickering flames on his head, matched by a long, scraggly beard of the same color. Although his eyes were red-rimmed and glassy, she knew he was completely lucid and aware of her standing in front of him.

"No," she said. "I'm her daughter."

He blinked rapidly and leaned away from the bars of his cage. A lazy smile spread across his lips like he'd forgotten there were both metal and freedom between them. "Yes, you are. You're Lily, right?"

She swallowed, knowing she had to tread carefully with this even though she wanted to beg the man to tell her anything he could about her mom. *Not until I know exactly what this is down here.* "Who gave you that name?"

"Your mother."

"You knew her?"

The prisoner nodded quickly and studied her face and her hair. "Only for a few months, but it was enough to know what kind of witch she really is."

"Tell me where you met her." Her heart pounded, the sound echoed in her head, the blood rushed in her ears as she willed her body not to shake in excitement and something else she couldn't name.

"A group of us took a guided trek through the mountains. It wasn't quite the Yucatán, but we all wanted to see the famous Ichacál." He glanced at the stone ceiling and walls around them and his nostrils flared. "We made it here in record time. We were welcomed—exactly like I'm sure you were—fed and given somewhere to sleep. Greta stayed here for two days, and when she left, she begged me to come with her."

Lily squinted. "Why?"

The man closed his eyes, then nodded. "She said she'd found something she'd been looking for, for a long time and she had to keep following the clues. This was two years ago...maybe more. I can't really..."

"It's okay." She nodded for him to continue.

"I stayed another two days and left. But I couldn't stop thinking about coming back here so I planned another trip on my own. March, I think. Or April. I should've listened to that woman when she said it was too dangerous here."

"She knew it was dangerous?"

The man coughed and nodded again. "She wouldn't tell me why. But yeah, she knew. It didn't stop her from coming back either, I guess."

"Wait, what?"

He licked his lips, tilted his head, and pressed his forehead against one of the bars. Slowly, he nodded against the metal. "She was here. I saw her again but only for a few months after those bastards threw me down here too. Then they took her away. She told me not to come back, but I truly thought this was a healing temple. A safe place."

Lily didn't know how long she stood there, staring at this wrongly imprisoned man while her chest heaved with every breath and her jaw clenched way too tightly against her will.

"Hey." Romeo's gentle hand settled on her shoulder to shatter whatever rabbit hole she'd spiraling down for the last few seconds.

"You saw my mother here," she said. "Greta Antony. You saw her down here in one of these—" She glanced around and couldn't bring herself to call them cages out loud. "Only a few months ago?"

"Yeah, but she was here until...it's hard to tell in here, but maybe only a couple of days ago." The man nodded again. "In there." He pointed to her right and she sent the orb to drift in that direction.

One much smaller cage existed at the far end of the oval cavern, separated from the others enough to make it feel like a punishment. At the front of the cage inside the bars was a poorly built, rotting wooden table with a candle burned all the way down into a puddle of wax. Two chains were bolted to the far stone wall, each of which ended in iron manacles that now lay open on the floor. Against the far wall, as if someone had spray-painted it through a stencil with soot and ash, was the huge black silhouette of a bird in full flight, its wings outstretched at six or seven feet across. The shadow-bird that had followed Lily since she and Romeo left Charleston, South Carolina was now plastered across the last place anyone—as far as she knew—had seen her mother alive.

"What's your name?" Romeo asked the man.

"Joseph."

She turned away from the cage that had once held her

mom, feeling stiff and not really there with the rest of them.

"What are all these people doing down here, Joseph?"

The prisoner looked away from her companion and swept his gaze over the other cages beside him. "We're all magicals. Witches. Two werewolves down at the end. They're fairies." He nodded toward the cage on his right, where two thin, young-looking faces peered out at them from between the bars. Their purple eyes and seaweed-green hair glowed, illuminated by Lily's light.

"The Wisemen," one of them said in a lilting voice. The ringing quality of it didn't hide how weak the fairy had become. "They're not here to help anyone. This temple is a shrine, and they—" She sucked in a heavy, wheezing breath, and the other fairy with her wound thin, emaciated arms around her companion's shoulders.

"They're siphoning our magic." The gruff voice rose closer to the stairwell.

"We don't have any magic," another man growled.

"Well, whatever makes you a werewolf, Reggie. They're takin' it from you, aren't they?"

Romeo took a deep breath, and Lily managed to finally force her rampant thoughts into some vestige of order. "Does anyone know why?"

"They're probably making a goddamn cake, for all we know." That was either Reggie or the other guy who'd named him.

Joseph shook his head. "We don't know anything. It's hard to...to know what's really happening down here." He frowned. "But some of these people have been down here for a really long time. Others stay for only a week or two. That one witch..." He coughed into a fist and turned toward the fairies again. "What was her name?"

"Bethany."

"Bethany. She was only here for two days. No one knows where they go or why they're taken. Why the rest of us are left here to be...sucked dry, I guess."

"Like magical fuckin' blood bags."

"Shut up, Reggie."

Joseph cleared his throat and offered Lily an apologetic shrug.

"No, it's okay. I'd probably say the same thing." *If I were unlucky enough to be down here. Still, it doesn't feel right to say it out loud.* "So the not-so-Wisemen are siphoning your magic. Is that why you haven't been able to get each other out of here?"

"You have no idea how many times we've tried," one of the fairies whispered.

"Two of them come down every night. It's the only way to tell time in this place." Joseph nodded toward the stairwell. "They put up some of the most complicated wards I've ever seen. But I think that's why nothing we try ever works."

"Yeah." A wry chuckle came from down the line of cages. "So complicated, they have to put it up all over again 'cause it blows all its power out every twenty-four hours."

"Okay, stand back." Lily nodded at Joseph, who staggered away from the iron bars as she raised her hand toward his cage.

"It's not gonna work—"

She delivered a sharp, slicing attack at the bars—sharp enough to cut through a steel door the last time she saw her mom cast this spell. The iron bars sparked with a squeal of grating metal but absolutely nothing else happened. "Yeah. Those are seriously powerful wards. And they do this every night to keep it from failing?"

He nodded. "Unless you know of another reason to stack something like that as regular as clockwork."

"No." She stepped beside Romeo and looked at him. "I think I know how to unstack it, though."

"You really are stupid, arntcha?"

"Reggie."

"You come down here with your floating light and your weird-ass friends. Yeah, I smell you, too, wolf. I dunno what this other asshole is."

She brought her fingers up to the tiny, silver-framed mirror on the chain around her neck—the first clue her mom had left in the invisible cabin on a Canadian lake.

"Seriously, Reggie." The stronger fairy looked over her shoulder and glared into the darkness. "Cut it out."

Moving slowly, Lily turned to face the solitary cage at the far side of the cavern and stared at the charred imprint of the shadow-bird on the stone.

"And you think you can simply undo those robed bastards' wards that are more powerful than anything all of us have put together?" Reggie sniggered. "You walked right into the biggest trap of your life, girlie."

Looking backward. Her fingers tightened on the mirror. *Unravel the most powerful setback. That's what her note said. Come on, Lily. You've already done it once. A* disgruntled Reggie continued to mouth off, but all the noise fell away while she concentrated on what this would mean.

In the next second, a bright flash of silver light erupted from the mirror and spread in a single shock wave from her to every wall of the cavern. The belligerent complaints cut off abruptly, and the silence was thicker now than when Lily, Romeo, and Neron had reached the foot of the stairs.

With a challenging smile, she turned to face the prisoners. "Try it now."

Reggie cackled. "You've lost your damn mind. If anyone in this hellhole is stupid enough to believe this—"

A red glow flared beneath Joseph's palms as he tightened both hands around the iron bars in front of him. Something snapped, and the man with the massive red beard and fiery hair jerked both pieces of metal out of place before hurled them aside and they clattered on the stone.

"Well, shit—" Reggie chuckled.

"I'm convinced." Joseph stepped through the hole he'd made and thrust a hand toward Lily. As the other magicals in all the other cages took the opportunity to cast the spells that would set them free, she took the man's hand and he held her there with both of his. "Thank you."

"Of course."

"You look exactly like your mom, doing all this."

She swallowed. "How well did you—"

A loud bang echoed above the cavern, muffled through so many miles of stone but still loud enough to make everyone glance automatically at the ceiling. A squeal of bending, tearing metal filled the cavern as Reggie pried the bars apart way farther than he had to in order to step out of the cage.

"Well," he said and spread his arms in an expansive gesture. "It looks like we're in time for a fight." The short, intensely muscular werewolf—his sleeves ripped off at the shoulders and his mohawk now grown out so long it flopped over his forehead and into his eyes—snarled at the stairwell. His eyes flashed silver, and the werewolf behind him stepped through.

The woman's long, curly brown hair almost looked like she'd been electrocuted, and the bruise around her eye that had most likely been black at some point was now yellow and dirty-green. When she turned to look at Lily, the bruise faded quickly. "Reggie's a dick," she said. "But if you can forget all the crap he spews, we'll fight with you."

She nodded briskly in acknowledgment. "What crap?"

"Cool." The woman snarled too and her eyes flared into silver rings.

Lily glanced at Romeo, and they both fought to keep from shrugging.

Every other magical who could still wield their magic without the wards had broken free of their cages. Those who couldn't were helped out by the others and the odd collection of prisoners and rescuers turned toward the stairwell to face the large and imminent attack.

"It sounds like some kinda stampede." She summoned the crackling red sparks of her favorite attack spell in both palms.

The werewolf whipped his shirt up over his head,

dropped it, and undid his belt. She stared at the stairwell when she heard his pants drop but she smiled when, from the corner of her eye, she saw him pull his shoulders back and tilt his head. His spine popped like cracking knuckles before his eyes flashed silver too. "Then let's go hunting," he said darkly

TWENTY-NINE

The first rippling wave of magic erupted from the bottom of the staircase before the Wisemen arrived. It thrust those closest back to stagger and stumble against the iron bars of their former cages.

Reggie and the woman snarled and shifted in place and simply shook themselves out of their already ruined clothes. The first Wiseman barreled down the stairs and the gray wolf that pounced out of the ripped shirt leapt at the man's throat with a vicious snarl. Two more in blue robes appeared in the cavern and released bright, streaking flashes of spells in all directions without really taking stock of the situation.

Romeo shifted into his huge, shaggy black wolf and darted into the fray. Lily focused her crackling attacks on the Wisemen who appeared above the entrance to the cavern on the first few stairs. If she could stop a reasonable number of them from entering, there would be that much fewer men in blue robes for the others to fight. She caught one in the arm and a shout of pain and surprise echoed from the stairwell, immediately followed by a hundred tiny shards of glass.

She raised both hands and trapped the attack in a suspension charm before she threw the whole thing into one of the empty cells with a tinkle of shattered pieces on stone. Without even a glance at her handiwork, she continued her attacks.

With a roar, Joseph ripped out the cages' iron bars from ten feet away and released them javelin-style toward the Wisemen in rapid succession. Several of the attackers fell over one another and onto the stairs when the bars connected with flesh, stone, and more metal. One of the men in blue robes directed a dark-green, snakelike tendril that darted through the brawl. It lashed out at the prisoners' ankles until Romeo snapped his massive jaws around it. The vine vanished in a puff of smoke, and the black wolf shook his head before he mauled another adversary.

At least a dozen of the temple's supposed protectors had clustered to fight them in the space, which was much too narrow and small for a battle like this. Lily couldn't take every shot she wanted with her sparking attacks. Most of them were more likely to injure one of the magicals she was trying to protect before it found its intended target. There were definitely more than a dozen prisoners, plus Lily, Romeo, and Neron, but almost half of them were too weak to fight.

The fairies huddled together in the back, having sunk to the floor as they held one another and watched. The woman who'd pressed her face against the bars of her cage had been freed, but she hadn't yet found the ability to grasp the freedom and step out from behind her captivity. Two Wisemen were definitely dead and sprawled at odd angles with a few broken bones. The brown female wolf yelped when a spell caught her in the side and singed her fur.

Lily delivered a series of blasts at the robed man who'd attacked the wolf and he actually retreated behind the curving staircase again. "Okay, this isn't going quite like I'd hoped." She threw a warded shield around the huddled fairies seconds before a conjured lightning bolt had the chance to completely annihilate them.

"Yeah, I was hopeful for a minute." Joseph grunted and raised sharpened stone spikes from the ground. One impaled a Wisemen against the ceiling and the other enemies scattered as much as they could in the confined space to avoid the missiles.

I could try the black cloud again. She clapped her hands but immediately shook her head and didn't even bother. *And that would do who knows what to everyone standing in front of me. I'd like to leave this place with more than only two weak fairies.* She set a few of the Wisemen's robes ablaze with blue fire, and they flailed for a few seconds before one of their own extinguished the flames.

A rush of green and blue sparks crackled across the walls of the cavern and rushed toward each other from every side to converge on the floor at the back. She whirled to throw another warded shield at the ground this time and block the streaking energy from coming any closer. It worked, and she was vaguely aware of Joseph redirecting an attack that was definitely meant for her before it would have struck her in the back of the head. She spun and started to thank him, but the sound of desperate chokes and gasps made her pause.

The woman who hadn't yet left her cage had been caught in the blue and green sparks. The spell must have barely brushed her hand, which was now crooked and charred. Black, peeling flesh was visible all the way up her arm and across her neck and chest. She convulsed and fell, gasping for breath where the entire side of her chest had burned completely through.

Oh, man. Lily raised her hand to at least knock the woman unconscious, but a gentle, firm hand settled on her shoulder.

"Wait." Without looking at her, Neron stepped past her across the raging battle in this small cavern and stepped into the woman's cage with her. She stared at him with wide eyes while her chest heaved and drew no air in return. The death witch knelt beside her and leaned over her. He ran a hand through her singed hair as he whispered something. She had enough strength to clasp his hand and nod intently. He nodded in return and muttered something else as he covered her eyes with his hand. With his one hand still shielding the dying woman's eyes, he jerked some kind of hunting knife from his belt and plunged the blade deeply into her charred chest.

"What the hell?" Lily shouted, ducked a wayward razor-sharp spell spiral, and firing at her attacker with a burst of intense force that pounded the Wiseman's head against the wall behind him. She stared at Neron. *He led us down here to slaughter us. Why did I let myself trust a necromancer?* She started toward him, hoping to end the betrayals now so the rest of them might have a chance, but stopped when she saw what was happening.

Thin black lines like veins spread across the burned woman's skin, snaked their way toward the knife in her chest, and slithered into his fingers and into his arm. He muttered something no one could have possibly heard over the crash of spells and the snarling werewolves and the shouts of the other freed prisoners as warnings. When the black lines reached his face, his eyes bulged before they were completely consumed by the same blackness until they were nothing but two large, lightless orbs—all black and more terrifying than she could ever have imagined.

His chanting rose above the clashing and the fighting in one long, low, continuous tone. Slowly, the death witch stood and stepped from the cage. His first attack of black, smoke-like magic struck the closest Wiseman in the chest, enveloped the man completely, and elevated with ease before it hurled him so hard against the stone that it broke his neck. More black lines flared to the surface of the dead Wiseman's skin, only to erupt and stream toward Neron's chest. The necromancer took in a quick, hissing breath through his teeth, and the volume of his chanting rose.

"Stop him!" The Wiseman who shouted was the next to go.

Neron raised his other hand toward the man, who clawed at his own throat until he drew blood but still couldn't breathe. His face turned an alarming shade of purple before he died and the black lines beneath his skin were absorbed by the death witch too.

The power of his death magic finished in a few minutes what the rest of the freed prisoners might never have accomplished. His magic stopped each Wiseman before they could cast their spells against him, and with each of their deaths, his own power grew. Lily didn't catch all the ways their attackers died. She was too busy watching the incredible power within the man who'd seemed so ashamed of what he was born to do.

Snapping bones echoed around the cavern, which was otherwise silent but for his ongoing incantation. He shouted now, his eyes nothing but all-black holes, and sweat beaded on his forehead. When the last two adversaries fell their broken bodies crumpled beneath the force of his attacks, Neron screamed. His hands shook with the force of all these men's lives having fueled his death magic, and his black eyes were fixed on the wall. The screaming didn't cease—he didn't seem able to stop, even to catch a breath—until the walls around them began to tremble. A sheet of dust and a few pebbles rained down on them, and Lily took her chance.

She stepped behind him and place a gentle, cautious hand on his shoulder. "Hey. Neron, you did it."

Whether it was her words or the fact that he'd reached his breaking point, the scream died in the necromancer's throat with a wheeze and he dropped to his knees on the cold stone. He panted, his head hanging almost completely to his chest, and swayed there for a minute before he stilled.

"Neron?"

When he looked at her, his eyes were completely clear and the whites restored to their proper place. "Did I hurt anyone?" he whispered.

She blinked. "Well..."

"Only the people who needed hurting." Romeo jerked his pants on and buckled his belt. He clapped a hand on the death witch's shoulder and shook the man gently. "That was incredible."

All the freed prisoners stared at their avenger, the cavern completely silent again. The gray wolf rose into the form of a naked man, and Reggie stepped forward toward the puddle of his clothes on the floor. "Holy shit, man." The woman shifted behind him and simply stared at Neron until her fellow werewolf bent over in front of her to collect her clothes. She stopped with a grunt of disgust, leaned away, and rolled her eyes so she wouldn't have to look at him.

"Is that all of them?" one of the fairies asked from the far corner.

"Probably." Joseph scratched his wild beard. "At least all of them in the temple right now. I bet you there are more, though. There are always more somewhere."

"They have a library." A woman with a shaved head wound a strip of cloth around a cut on her hand and nodded toward the staircase. "You might even call it a reliquary. I bet you those assholes have everything we'd need to buy ourselves more time and get everyone else safely outta here."

The still naked werewolf jerked his even further

ripped shirt over his head and smacked his hands together. "Let's get our asses to that reliquary, then."

The other magicals murmured assent and moved toward the stairs. "Hey." Romeo nodded at the two were-wolves. "Eat the purple flowers."

Reggie raised an eyebrow and decided a wolf who'd risked his ass for a group of strangers might be trustworthy enough. He nodded in response and waved everyone else up the stairs behind him.

Joseph stopped at the foot of the staircase and turned toward Lily. "Are you comin'?"

"We'll meet you up there." She glanced at Neron, still slumped on his knees, and the two fairies in the corner. "After we get them outta here."

"Okay. Be safe, huh?" He nodded at her and her friend and darted up the stairs.

By the time she looked at Neron again, he crawled on his hands and knees toward the open cage and the woman with his knife still protruding from her chest. He stopped when he could lean over her face, her legs stretched out toward the wall in front of him, and cupped her cheek upside down. "Thank you for your sacrifice," he muttered and closed her eyelids gently. When he yanked the knife free from her chest, he had to use both hands. His face expressionless, he wiped the blade on his pants a few times and returned to his belt. With one hand, he grasped one of the iron bars and pulled himself to his feet. The death witch met Lily's gaze and swallowed. "It would not have been possible without her."

"I understand that now." She glanced at the woman's

body. "What did you say to her before you..." All she had
to do was look at his knife.

Neron sniffed. "I told her that if she placed her death
in my hands, I could end this fight and keep everyone else
safe. Because she was already leaving this life, I asked her if
she wished to die faster and with a purpose."

"And she said yes." She nodded.

"I have to take a life to use my magic." He stumbled
out of the cage, righted himself, and shook his head slowly.
"And I do not take a life unless I mean to use it in a way
that serves others."

Romeo cleared his throat. "That's probably the most
powerful thing I've heard in...man, a long time."

The necromancer smirked and shrugged. "Well, I
cannot do this every day." The werewolf snorted and the
two men laughed together like they'd told a dirty joke
instead of rescuing a group of magical prisoners betrayed
by the Wisemen at Ichacál while saving their own
skins too.

Lily shook her head and turned toward the fairies. "Are
you all right?"

The stronger one nodded, but the fairy in her arms
looked like she was about to pass out. Her head rested
limply on her thin knees. "She needs help out of here,
though."

"No problem." Romeo slipped his shirt over his head
and stepped toward them. He stooped and lifted the
emaciated fairy gently from her companion's arms. The
stronger one stood and swayed a little before she nodded at

him. They moved toward the staircase, and Lily looked at Neron.

"Can you make it up there?"

"Very slowly." He smirked again.

"All right." She joined him and slung his arm over her shoulder. They were about the same height, so she could at least be a useful support.

Before they reached the stairs, he turned and looked over his shoulder at the far wall where her light still illuminated the black silhouette on the white stone. "Your wings of smoke, yes?"

"Yeah." She exhaled a long, slow breath. "Your dreams were eerily accurate. They're still not mine, though, but I'm starting to think I know who they belong to."

THIRTY

L ily and Neron caught up to Romeo and the fairies
fairly quickly, mostly because the werewolf seemed
to have a little trouble deciding how to make his way
through the labyrinthine hallways of the temple. When he
saw them, he rolled his eyes and tried to gesture around
him. It was difficult with an almost unconscious fairy in his
arms. "I have no idea how to get out of here."

"I do." The death witch removed his arm from over her
shoulder and nodded at her when she raised her eyebrows.
"I can walk now. Thank you, Lily." He led them down one
passageway after the other, and she kept her ball of white
light trailing ahead of him to light the way.

By the time they reached the temple's main entrance
hall, Neron's people had stirred from their rooms and
emerged to see what all the noise was about. None of them
had known how to find the source of the short, violent
battle below the temple itself, but they stared when the

two witches, two fairies, and the single werewolf emerged from the hallway on their left.

"What happened?" Aluino moved quickly toward them and thrust his hand toward Neron.

The necromancer clasped his kinsman's forearm with a grim nod. "We found the true nature of this place."

The villager studied his companion's face and his eyes narrowed for a second before they grew wide in realization. "Did you—"

"Yes. It was necessary."

"And totally freakin' worth it," Romeo added. "In case you were still undecided on that part." No one spoke when he moved forward toward the large anteroom where they'd been fed an excellent meal only a few hours before. He set the weak fairy on a pile of pillows against the wall, and her companion crouched beside her. "Does she need anything right now?"

"Only time." The stronger fairy's purple gaze sparkled in the semi-darkness. "Thank you."

"Absolutely." He scratched the back of his head, nodded, and turned to rejoin Lily and the gathered villagers.

"So how can we be sure we are truly safe here?" Chalina asked.

"The other witches went to the Wisemen's library first," Lily explained. "They think they can—"

"Hey! Hey...guys!" Reggie barreled around the corner from the right-hand hallway and sprinted directly toward them.

Rosalía darted forward before she could even process

what the kid was doing. With a wordless shout, the girl raised both hands and sent the same forceful spell of nothing but pressure she'd used inside the white van. The werewolf catapulted back like he'd clotheslined himself on an invisible wire, and the child clenched her hands into tiny fists. Her suspension spell was precise and essentially perfect—if she hadn't mistaken him for an enemy. His arms raised over his head, and the girl witch less than half his age stretched him horizontally in mid-air and pinned him there.

"Rosalía!" Chalina barked.

She whirled around and lost her concentration. Reggie thumped to the floor and groaned when his head cracked against the stone. "He was attacking you." Rosalía gestured toward the aching man behind her and Lily pressed her lips together as she approached her.

"He was a prisoner downstairs, kiddo. Romeo and I helped to free him, and he helped us fight our way out again." The girl's eyes grew incredibly wide as she searched Lily's face. *Please don't cry.*

"Oh." Rosalía blinked quickly, met her teacher's gaze again, and smiled. "But it was perfect, right?"

A choked laugh escaped her, and she closed her eyes to pull herself together again. "Yeah. Yeah, it was perfect. Do you know how to make it better?"

"How?"

"Make sure you're casting your spells on the right person." She raised an eyebrow, and with a flashing grin, the child darted around her and disappeared through the villagers milling around the entrance hall.

"Jesus Christ." Reggie finally managed to roll over and push himself to his feet. "I swear, this place is a goddamn—"

"You were gonna tell us something," Romeo cut in.

The other werewolf shot him a scathing glance but nodded. "Yeah. Those witches found the reliquary, I guess. They're working up this magical doohickey spell thing to protect the temple grounds and everything in it. They wanted to spread the word that everyone needs to stay here until they finish their little ritual or whatever. Ow." He pressed his hands into his lower back, leaned a little, and cracked his spine. "What's wrong with that kid?"

Lily glanced at Chalina and Aluino with a proud smile. "Absolutely nothing."

IT WAS BASICALLY impossible to go back to sleep after everything they'd been through that night, especially for those who'd fought their way through Ichacál's false Wisemen and witnessed the terrifying power of a death witch who only used his magic when all else failed. The sun had been up for less than an hour when Lily and Romeo strolled across the temple grounds, listening to the chaotic cacophony of so many jungle birds' voices greeting the dawn.

"Well, another mystery solved." She kicked at the loose earth. "Kind of."

"And it still doesn't feel like a win, huh?"

"Well, not really. I went back and searched that

cavern. There was absolutely nothing else from my mom there—no clues and definitely no hidden messages. I even searched that huge bird on the wall."

He slipped his hand into hers and squeezed it gently. "This isn't a dead end, Lil. Hey, I'll go back in there with you, okay? I can help you look. We both do better as a team, right?"

"I don't know if that's gonna do anything this time." She looked at him with a grimace of disappointment. "She was in that cage, Romeo. Right there and only a few months ago, and people saw her alive. I know that shadowbird's hers. I have no idea how or why, but I...I feel it. And there's nothing else here. I think..." She dragged in a breath. "I think she was taken away from here before she had the chance to leave me any more clues."

He tilted his head in his habitual thinking attitude. "I have a hard time believing that. Think about it. The woman carved her language into the actual stone-button that opened a hidden door in a wall. She left all that stuff with Melissa years ago. Do you really think she didn't think everything through?"

She sighed. "Not if she was taken by these people, whoever they are. Not if she was kept in a cage underground and forced to relinquish her magic to those..." She gritted her teeth and shook her head. "I don't know what to do now."

"Okay, hold on." They stopped walking. He turned to face her and took her other hand in his too. "You can't start thinking like this now. Seriously. We've come this far, and honestly, I'm not gonna let you give up."

"Let me, huh?" She uttered a wry chuckle and shook her head. "Why? Okay, I'm so glad you're here with me, but if this is it, why would you keep pushing?"

Romeo puffed out a sigh and glanced at the jungle canopy. "Yeah, I knew you were gonna ask that. Okay." He grimaced and squeezed both her hands. "There's something I haven't told you. And honestly, I have no idea how you'll react, but I can't keep not telling you."

She turned her head away from him a little. "Okay..." *What did he do?*

"Lily, I—"

"Hey! There you are." Joseph jogged across the temple grounds toward them, his hair cleanly brushed away from his forehead, although he apparently hadn't touched the beard. "I'm sorry to interrupt."

"No problem." Romeo released her hands and folded his arms.

Lily glanced at him, then looked at the other man. "Is everything okay?"

"Oh, yeah. Everything's fine. We have a few warded shields up around the place. Oh, and a couple of stacked charms and something the witch with the shaved head said would keep us silent. Whatever that is." He looked at the hardcover book in his hand and smacked it with the back of a hand. "So I'm gonna sit tight and...you know. Do some light reading." He chuckled.

"What is that?" she asked.

"It's only one of the books from the reliquary. Would you like to see it?" He held it out to her, and she almost didn't take it.

The silhouette of a heron, it's wings wide in mid-flight with the telltale, u-shaped bend in its neck, stretched across the cover of the Wisemen's grimoire.

Swallowing, she took the book and pretended she could focus on reading what was on the pages. "Is this the only book like this?"

"What do you mean?"

"With this kinda bird on the cover."

Joseph shook his head. "Nah. That image is all over everything in there. It must be some kinda order I've never heard of before. Have you?"

"No." She shook her head and handed the book back to him. "But it's an interesting picture."

"Sure, sure."

When the man didn't offer anything else, she smiled. "Did you come to find me only to say you were gonna do some reading?"

"What? Oh." He chuckled and scratched his beard. "No, actually. Sorry. I only...well, I remembered some of my conversations with Greta when she was here. Both times, you know? The first time, before things got really... dark, she kept going on and on any chance she had about this little pool on the other side of the temple. It's honestly a tiny thing and there's a little staircase to get down there, apparently. I never saw it myself, but she talked constantly about it this last time. Before she was—"

"Before they took her."

"Right. You know, for a long time, I thought I'd dreamed the whole thing after everything they put us through down here. But now, I'm not so sure." Joseph paused and licked his lips and his brows drew a little closer together. "I think your mom told me that if I ever saw you, if I ever met her daughter, I needed to tell you how much she loved that little pool."

For a second, Lily couldn't move. "What?" She glanced hastily at Romeo.

"Yeah. It sounds crazy, right? But I feel so much better without all those damn wards holding me back and this feels like a real memory so I figured I'd tell you. For whatever it's worth."

"Joseph." She took a deep breath and held his gaze. "It's not crazy. Thank you." She hurried toward the temple, intending to skirt around it to the other side, but she paused and looked back at him. "Where's the pool again?"

"Yeah, you can walk right around the building. It's—"

"Awesome. Thanks!" She flung a hand up in a vague wave and hurried in that direction. Romeo shook the other man's hand quickly and followed her, grinning to see her hope flaring up again.

THE STEPS behind the temple were incredibly steep, and Lily almost flung herself down them in her haste. *This is it. It has to be. She left me something here.*

"Hey, careful, huh?" Romeo skipped down the moss-covered stairs behind her in an effort to keep up.

When she reached the pool, she studied everything as

she paced the perimeter and searched for anything that looked even slightly off.

"Do you think it's here?" Romeo asked.

"Yeah. There's literally no other option." She stooped even lower and scrutinized the grass and the flowers until she eventually noticed a collection of stones so overgrown, she almost missed them. When she brushed aside the long grasses that shielded them, she froze. "Oh, my God." Three round, flat rocks had been stacked in a natural-looking pile, although the top stone had a crudely etched lily flower on its surface. "Yes."

She dug her fingers into the earth around the stones and yanked out handfuls of grass and whatever else was in her way. Finally, she removed all three stones, examined them carefully, and tossed them aside. The hole beneath them was barely deep enough to thrust her hand inside and find something stored in there.

"Holy crap." Romeo squatted on the other side of the hole and watched her with wide eyes.

The first thing she withdrew was another brown drawstring purse at least twice the size of the last two her mom had left her. Its contents clinked together with the all too familiar sound of so many coins held in one place. She dropped the bag in front of Romeo, who peered inside quickly and snorted. "Did she have an endless supply of gold coins, or what?"

Lily glanced up at him. "Has."

"Sorry. Yeah."

Her hand dipped into the hole again and located a plastic baggie with another note inside. She practically ripped the bag apart to get to it, and her breath caught in her throat when she read another message from her mom.

'If you're reading this, sweets, I've already been taken somewhere else. I've done everything I could to lead you down this path, to leave you the pieces of knowledge I knew you needed and could work out on your own. Now, though, I'm running out of options.

They know I'm onto them, L. I've followed this black trail for years, putting all the pieces together, and now they know I've come too far to be turned back by threats or bribes. If you're reading this now, it means you understand what's at stake. You've seen with your own eyes the foul things brewing just beneath the surface. I haven't found all the answers yet, and that's why I need your help—because I know you can.

Don't judge anyone by who they say they are, my love. You can find everything you need to know by looking into the eyes.'

She closed her eyes and released a shaky breath. "Mom's still alive. If I didn't already know it, I would now." She handed the letter to Romeo and thrust her hand into the hole one more time.

He read the note quickly, his lips moving without sound. "Wow."

Her fingers brushed against cold metal and something plastic. The object jingled in her hands when she lifted it from the cavity. Two keys hung on a simple keyring—one silver, the other gold. The plastic tag also dangling from the ring had her mom's handwriting on it too and an address that clearly wasn't anywhere in the United States—or Mexico, for that matter.

"You gotta be kidding me."

"What's wrong?" Her friend looked at her with wide eyes and she handed him the keyring. He glanced at it, frowned, and looked confused. "This...wait, what?"

"I know. She left me keys to something. And that something, apparently, is in Bucharest."

He seemed to choke on his own surprised laughter before he recovered and a little smirk appeared. "Okay. It would definitely be cool to visit Bucharest. I've never been there. But it's...you know there's only one real problem with that, right?"

"Yeah." Despite the enormity of her mom's note and the totally unexpected destination with this last clue, she grinned widely. "How the hell are we gonna get the Winnie to Romania?"

Where will the clues Lily's mom take Lily and Romeo? Find out in A Witch Apart.

Get sneak peeks, exclusive giveaways, behind the scenes content, and more.
PLUS you'll be notified of special **one day only fan pricing** on new releases.

Sign up today to get free stories.

CLICK HERE

For Hire: Teachers for special school in Virginia countryside.

Must be able to handle teenagers with special abilities.

Cannot be afraid to discipline werewolves, wizards, elves and other assorted hormonal teens.

Apply at the School of Necessary Magic.

AVAILABLE AT AMAZON RETAILERS

AUTHOR NOTES - MARTHA CARR

SEPTEMBER 4, 2019

It's two more days till I turn 60 years old. That number sounds so weird. I'm a little surprised to be here and doing so well. A little background...

At 50 I was told I had a year left to live. It was an interesting way to usher in that decade (and possibly usher it right back out again). But I went into unexplained spontaneous remission and have managed to stay there. Go figure.

And that was also the tail end of the Great Recession and I was down to a bed, a dresser, a very small TV, and two and a half chairs. I was a writer then, just like I am now, but a lot less financially successful. Plus, I was about 80 pounds overweight. Drawing quite the picture for you, aren't I?

Despite that description, I was also happy because I was surrounded by a loving crew of people that I had just met because I had only been living in Chicago for six months. People came out of every nook and cranny to help me find furniture, bring over food, give me rides to the hospital, or sit and chat with me on my back porch in Lincoln Square. One woman, Meg showed up with a dish at my back door and said a friend of hers told her to bring this to me. We're still friends.

Fast forward 10 years and there's been a great corporate job, a loss of those 80 pounds, a move to Austin and this dream house and a few more bouts with cancer (all is well right now), and collaborating with Michael Anderle and I'm still happy for the *same reason*. I still have that crew in Chicago (and I'll see all of you in November for the Hot Chocolate Run to celebrate this birthday plus there will be a FAN LUNCH on me – keep your eyes on my newsletter for the details), a new crew of authors everywhere – and now I also have this new tribe – most of them in my neighborhood, who gathered at the pool last weekend with far too much food to wish me well as the new decade starts.

In the end, it's not the things that matter, and for me it's not always even health that's at the top of the list – it's the people – including all of you – the Fans who have made these past few years such a great ride. Thank you for taking the journey with me and being so interactive and supportive and fun!

I'll be in Niagara Falls on my birthday and I'll be sure to post lots of pictures in my Facebook Fan Group – join us if you're not in there already – and you can find me every weekday at noon CT Live on Facebook reading a chapter from one of my books – new and old. Till then, thank you. I'm forever grateful for all of you. More adventures (and books) to follow.

AUTHOR NOTES - MICHAEL ANDERLE

SEPTEMBER 9, 2019

Thank you for not only reading this book, but these author notes at the end!

It is amazing what a really messed up sleep schedule can do to your mind and ability (or desire) to be creative.

Recently, I had a lot of travel that took me from time zone to time zone for five weeks straight. When I got back to 'my' time zone (Pacific), I am napping at night and sleeping during the afternoon.

I call it my 6-hour nap and 2-hour sleep. That is 8 hours of rest, right? *Right??*

That is so wrong...

I'm typing this at 2:20 AM after I slept from about 6:45 PM to 1:15 AM. (Not very well, mind you. But I think that had more to do with the Thanksgiving dinner amount of food I ate before I crashed right after dinner.)

I'm having trouble acclimating back to Pacific Time sleeping patterns, and I am going a bit bonkers. It seems I am NOT made for traveling so much and lethargy is one of the myriad issues I'm fighting.

For a creative, it is annoying to have the feeling I could dream up the rest of a story 'just on the other side of a good nap,' and when I wake up, I'm too sleepy to put a sentence together. Much less anything longer.

Or funny.

I don't drink coffee, but I do drink Coke or other caffeinated sugar-filled drinks of evil goodness, and I have used them to work through my malaise for the most part. Unfortunately, these drinks have horrible side effects like extra useless calories.

Oh, and the sugar high and then sugar crash which makes me want to sleep... *More.*

I was talking with Author Abby-Lynn Knorr, and we talked about melatonin as an option, and I'm going to look into it.

These author notes have a happy ending, sort of. When I am on a creative high (like during a talk w/ Martha today) I can be REALLY on and all sorts of thoughts come to the forefront and drop like leaves to the ground during a windy fall afternoon.

Now, If I could just capture those excess thoughts and put them away for moments like now when I'm half awake – half asleep, I would be in a better place.

If I could just get past this desire to sleep.

Zzzzzzzzzz.

OTHER BOOKS BY MARTHA CARR

Series in the Oriceran Universe:

SCHOOL OF NECESSARY MAGIC
SCHOOL OF NECESSARY MAGIC: RAINE
CAMPBELL
ALISON BROWNSTONE
THE DANIEL CODEX SERIES
THE LEIRA CHRONICLES
I FEAR NO EVIL
FEDERAL AGENTS OF MAGIC
THE UNBELIEVABLE MR. BROWNSTONE
REWRITING JUSTICE
THE KACY CHRONICLES
MIDWEST MAGIC CHRONICLES
SOUL STONE MAGE
THE FAIRHAVEN CHRONICLES

Other series:

THE LAST VAMPIRE
THE WITCH NEXT DOOR

OTHER BOOKS BY JUDITH BERENS

OTHER BOOKS BY MARTHA CARR

JOIN THE ORICERAN UNIVERSE FAN GROUP ON FACEBOOK!

BOOKS BY MICHAEL ANDERLE

For a complete list of books by Michael Anderle, please visit

www.lmbpn.com/ma-books/

All LMBPN Audiobooks are Available at Audible.com and iTunes. For a complete list of audiobooks visit:

www.lmbpn.com/audible

CONNECT WITH THE AUTHORS

Martha Carr Social

Website: http://www.marthacarr.com

Facebook: https://www.facebook.com/
groups/MarthaCarrFans/

Michael Anderle Social

Michael Anderle Social
Website:
http://www.lmbpn.com

Email List:
http://lmbpn.com/email/

Facebook Here: https://www.
facebook.com/TheKurtherianGambitBooks/